Secret Lives of the Ton

What Society doesn't know...

Meet Julian Carlisle, the Duke of Lyonsdale,
Gabriel Pearce, the Duke of Winterbourne,
and Phineas Attwood, the Earl of Hartwick.

In the eyes of the Ton, these three gentlemen
are handsome, upstanding men who—
mostly!—play by the rules. But what
Society doesn't know is that behind closed
doors these three men are living scandalous
lives and hiding scandalous secrets!

Read Julian's story in
An Unsuitable Duchess

Read Gabriel's story in
An Uncommon Duke

And read Hart's story in
An Unexpected Countess

All available now!

Author Note

Hart and Sarah weren't supposed to fall in love. When I started writing *An Unsuitable Duchess* I simply intended them to be the best friends of my hero and heroine. But as I wrote that book it became obvious to me that these two would be perfect together. They needed their own story, and that story would open with them running into each other on a rooftop in London in the middle of the night. I just needed to figure out why they were there!

Around that time I read an article about the Sancy Diamond. This diamond was once part of the pre-Commonwealth Crown Jewels of England, but was sold by James II to Cardinal Mazarin in 1657. In 1792 the Sancy, along with the rest of the French Crown Jewels, was stolen when the Royal Treasury was stormed during the French Revolution. The Sancy Diamond disappeared, and its whereabouts was unknown until Prince Demidoff, a Russian nobleman, bought it from an unnamed source in 1828. The mystery of where it had been for thirty-six years was too intriguing to pass up, and it gave me a reason to put Hart and Sarah on that roof.

I hope you enjoy reading their story. For information about my other releases visit my website at lauriebenson.net. While you're there you can also search my blog to find information about some of the other interesting historical titbits I uncovered while doing research for this book.

AN UNEXPECTED COUNTESS

Laurie Benson

MILLS &
BOON®
™

First published in Great Britain 2017
By Mills & Boon, an imprint of HarperCollins*Publishers*
1 London Bridge Street, London, SE1 9GF

Large Print edition 2017

© 2017 Laurie Benson

ISBN: 978-0-263-06790-3

Printed and bound in Great Britain
by CPI Antony Rowe, Chippenham, Wiltshire

Laurie Benson is an award-winning historical romance author and Golden Heart® finalist. She began her writing career as an advertising copywriter, where she learned more than anyone could ever want to know about hot dogs and credit score reports. When she isn't at her laptop, avoiding laundry, Laurie can be found browsing in museums or taking ridiculously long hikes with her husband and two sons. You can visit her at lauriebenson.net.

Books by Laurie Benson

Mills & Boon Historical Romance

Secret Lives of the Ton

An Unsuitable Duchess
An Uncommon Duke
An Unexpected Countess

Visit the Author Profile page
at millsandboon.co.uk.

For Lori, who crossed an ocean with me
and let me drag her around London
in search of hiding places. And for Mia, who
has been on Team Hart from the beginning.
This one is for the two of you.

A big thank-you to my editor,
Kathryn Cheshire, for helping me bring
Hart and Sarah to life. You're a gem! And
thanks to the rest of the team at Harlequin,
especially Krista Oliver, Linda Fildew,
Tilda McDonald, Miranda Indrigo and
Lucy Gough for all they've done for me.

I'm very thankful to my agent,
Courtney Miller-Callihan with
Handspun Literary Agency,
or helping me fulfil my dream of
publishing all three books in this trilogy.

To my family—thanks for your support
and encouragement while I worked on this
book. I'm sorry about the dust bunnies and the
empty refrigerator. At least we know a good
pizza place that delivers. I love you guys!

And, last but far from least, thank you to my
readers. Your enthusiasm and kind words
about my books have truly touched my heart.

Chapter One

This wasn't the first time Phineas Attwood, the Earl of Hartwick, had stepped onto a London rooftop at night in the rain—however, it was the first time he discovered he wasn't alone.

Hart had to drag himself from Theodosia's resplendent tester bed on such a dreary night. He wished he could have taken her once more, but there wasn't time. Her husband would arrive home soon and Hart had no interest in running into the man. He could have been brazen and left by the front door, but there was nothing like the thrill of finding alternative ways to escape the town houses of his female companions—even if one was forced to do so during a downpour.

Shielding his eyes from the cold raindrops pelting his face, he stepped to the very edge of the roofline. Taunting death, he leaned over. It was a straight drop to Mount Street below, four storeys with nothing to grab on to or brace his feet against to climb down. It would also be in view of any approaching carriages.

To his left, the adjacent rooflines of the next three buildings ended at an alleyway that led to Reeves Mews. That appeared to be his best option. The building at the far end might have some architectural mouldings to aid his descent. Just as he was about to have a look, movement to his right caught his eye.

A slim, dark figure about fifty feet away was walking along the roof towards the back of an adjacent house. Apparently it was time for all assignations to come to an end. This gentleman was smart enough to wear a cape and cleric's hat to shield himself from the rain, although Hart would wager he was no priest.

'Fine weather for ducks,' Hart called out.

His interruption startled the fellow so much the man lost his footing. Skidding over the slippery slate tiles, Hart caught him by the forearm the moment the man fell over the edge. It would be a long drop to the back gardens below.

Hart dug his fingers into the stranger's arm

and prayed he wouldn't be pulled off the roof by the counterweight. 'I have you,' he ground out. 'I won't let you go.'

Even through his sleeve, Hart wouldn't be surprised if the man's nails were drawing blood as he held on to Hart for dear life while he dangled precariously over the edge. He didn't have much meat on him, which made him appear more of a boy than a man. It didn't take much effort to tug him back onto the roof.

A light mist was now falling, replacing the earlier downpour. A thank you was in order, however the huddled form next to him was silent as stone, probably mute with fear or shock. Pushing his hair away from his eyes, Hart surveyed his companion—and wished the rain would have continued to obscure his view.

'Dash it, Miss Forrester, what are you doing up here?'

The daughter of the American Minister to the Court of St James sat up. The cape she wore parted just enough to reveal the open neckline of a gentleman's black shirt and the curves of her breasts. He recalled seeing her wearing those clothes about a year ago at the Finchleys' masquerade, where she'd had the nerve to dress as a highwayman, which had also been his costume of choice that night. Now her shapely legs were stretched out before her, encased in black trews and top boots. Those legs were just as enticing as he remembered.

'Do not tell me you are leaving a masquerade from up here,' he said, tearing his attention away from those legs to stop himself from imagining them wrapped around his waist.

She arched one of her finely shaped dark brows. 'I'd ask where you're coming from, but I can already guess. Is this the time your assignations typically come to an end?'

An unmarried woman should know nothing of assignations. In the few times he had been in her presence, he had noticed that Miss Sarah Forrester enjoyed unnerving people with her candour. He was not about to let her best him.

'I'm coming from seeing a business associate. More important, does Katrina know you're prowling the rooftops of London at night?' he asked to regain the advantage. Katrina was the Duchess of Lyonsdale, a dear friend of Miss Forrester.

'No.' She looked away too quickly. Apparently his friend's wife knew exactly what this chit was up to. He wondered if Katrina would have told Julian.

'How were you planning on getting down from here?' she asked, interrupting his thoughts.

'That is the beauty of leaving in such a manner as this. It forces you to consider multiple options.' The fact that he hadn't decided how he would make it off the roof was inconsequential in this discussion.

The clomping of horse hooves and the rumble of carriage wheels on the street below caught their attention and they both crawled to the edge of the roof. A black lacquered carriage rolled to a stop directly below the house next to them and a footman from Theodosia's house darted towards it, carrying a large black umbrella. Hart had left her bed just in time and smiled at his luck.

'That might have been a bit awkward, if you remained longer with Lady Helmford,' she said.

He had momentarily forgotten the pest was beside him.

She leaned closer and the faint scent of lilacs filled the damp air. Her brown eyes held amusement mixed with curiosity as she looked up at him. 'Have you ever been caught?'

He scoffed at the absurdity of her question. 'No.'

'Never?'

'Not once.' His chest puffed up at his declaration, then he realised what he had revealed. Damn!

She sat back and removed her hat. The rain had stopped and she casually brushed the droplets off the brim and crown. 'I hadn't realised Lady Helmford was a business associate of yours.'

He hated when she found ways to use his habit of bragging against him. While she might believe she had the upper hand, it hadn't escaped Hart's notice that she had avoided his question.

'And what brings you to this rooftop? You never did say.'

She shifted her gaze momentarily. 'I'm intrigued by architecture.'

'Architecture?'

'Yes, you see I came out here to study the carvings on the buildings across the way.'

'But you don't live here.'

'Of course I don't. What good would it do me to study the buildings across from my home when I already took note of them ages ago?'

'Is that really the best you could do?'

Sarah was not about to be found out by the likes of the Earl of Hartwick. No rakish buck was going to best her. She wasn't one of those empty-headed women who would throw themselves at his feet just because he was charming and handsome— very handsome. And every time she was around him, she had the strongest urge to remind him of that.

'Those houses across the way are a perfect example of Mr Kent's work,' she continued. 'I couldn't very well stand on this rooftop during daylight hours. Someone might see me.' She had no idea what Mr Kent's work looked like, but she knew he was an architect held in high regard.

'William Kent?' Hartwick shook his head and water droplets slid from his hair down his chis- elled features.

Hoping to distract him, she brushed off her sop- ping wet trews.

His gaze shot to her thighs and remained there. 'So you chose a rainy, dark night for your view- ing pleasure?'

'The opportunity presented itself and I took it. It wasn't raining when I made my way here.'

'I see. And how did you manage to sneak away from your parents for this escapade of architec- tural appreciation?'

He needed more of a distraction and rubbing her

hand slowly along her thigh proved to be a good one. But all too soon Hartwick tossed his head, sweeping away a lock of black hair from his piercing blue eyes. 'Your parents, Miss Forrester, how did you manage to elude them?'

Lud! He was like a dog with a bone. 'I don't see how it is your concern.'

'True. Your welfare is none of my concern. I was merely making conversation—one impressive night prowler to the next.'

'You can't charm an answer from me.'

'I wasn't aware I was being charming. We're merely conversing.'

'You're trying to flatter me.'

'By calling you an impressive prowler? Darling, if I intended to flatter you, I would tell you how tempting you look in those trews.'

'Thank you for the compliment, but I still have no intention of telling you anything.'

'You misunderstand. I didn't say you looked tempting. I only indicated that is what I would say if I were going to flatter you.'

Insufferable man! If only she could give him a firm push. But with her luck he would land on his back and see it as an invitation to activities he was most familiar with—or so she had heard.

Standing up, she wiped her hands. 'Well, I really must be off.'

He jumped to his feet. 'What are you really doing up here?'

'I told you. I was admiring the architecture.'

'And I'm next in line for the throne.' He narrowed his eyes and crossed his arms. 'Are you coming from a rendezvous with a man?'

The horror on his face was rich considering his philandering ways, but if it would get him to stop asking questions, there was no harm in a small lie. 'Perhaps.' Gossip was rich with tales of his escapades with women. She doubted *he* would be one to talk of a small indiscretion of *hers* or even find her significant enough to discuss at all.

'Perhaps? Perhaps? What kind of man leaves a woman to find her way out of an assignation by herself? Any man worth his salt would visit the lady, not the other way around.'

'I live with my parents,' she said, rolling her eyes. 'And you seem more appalled by my exit than at the assignation itself.'

'I'm the last person to judge anyone's moral character.' As if counting out the town houses they were standing on, his finger paused on the building under them. 'Miss Forrester, he is old enough to be your father.' He visibly shuddered. 'I always assumed you had finer taste than this.'

She pushed past him, splashing through puddles on her way to the vacant town house at the end of the row. There was no reason for him to be insulting. Lord Baxter was not as handsome as Hartwick, and about twenty years older than the Earl, but he was not an antidote by any means. He was…mature. And why did she feel the need to mentally defend a man she was barely acquainted with? Her hands curled into fists.

Hartwick went after her and grabbed her arm. 'Where do you think you're off to?'

'I'm leaving. I've been up here long enough.'

His brow wrinkled. 'How do you propose we get down?'

'*We* are not getting down. You stated you had a multitude of solutions of your own. I'm finding my own way down.'

'Don't you enjoy my company?'

'Not particularly.'

He gave her a devilish grin. 'Now I know you are lying.'

'Women can resist you, Hartwick.'

He laughed. 'There aren't many.'

'Well, I can,' she stated firmly. 'Now, do release my arm. I have places to be.'

'Very well, go your own way. I'll go mine. But you do take the pleasure out of an evening such as this.' He granted her a slow, exaggerated bow.

She *was* fun to be with. He just thought too highly of himself to appreciate her. That was the problem. She made her way to one of the back dormer windows and carefully edged along the thin strip of roofing in front of it. She was paused precariously on the edge and her hands began to tremble. One false move and she could tumble backwards off the roof, splattering on the terrace below. Would she have a better chance of living if she aimed for the shrubbery? How much blood did one body contain?

'What are you waiting for?'

She jerked back and Hartwick grabbed her, pressing her cheek into a cold, wet windowpane. Her heart almost beat out of her chest.

'Stop doing that!'

He let go of her. 'If you plan to skulk about in the future, you need to pay better attention to your surroundings.'

'I told you to find your own way down.'

'I was, then I saw you mumbling at the window and decided you needed my assistance.'

'I can do this myself.'

She went to push the bottom sash of the window up, but it wouldn't budge. He went to have a go at it and she swatted his hand away. 'I said. I. Can. Do. It. Myself!'

He held his hands up. A few leftover raindrops trickled down the brim of her hat. If he did anything to make her fall backwards off this roof, she was pulling him along with her. The pounding of her heart in her ears was so loud she didn't hear the creak of the window as she finally nudged the stubborn sash up. Letting out a breath of relief, she closed her eyes.

'You should make certain no one is about before you enter that room. Unless you would like me to use the charms you say I possess to enchant any maids that might be about.'

Did this man ever stop talking? 'Keep those charms tucked away. The house is vacant,' she bit back as she climbed inside the darkened room. Stepping further inside, she left enough space for Hartwick to climb in after her.

'How do you know this house is vacant?' he asked, closing the window.

'I made some enquiries.' He didn't need to know that Katrina had told her about it when they had been discussing the Everills. The vacant house annoyed Lady Everill, and while she was put out that a house on her street was considered undesirable, it was a godsend to Sarah. Now, if she could just make it out of the house without the Earl of Hartwick discovering why she was on Mount Street dressed in men's attire in the first place...

As she walked into the hallway, moonlight from the rooms on either side streamed onto the dusty floorboards. Hartwick walked quietly behind her until she opened the door leading to the servants' staircase.

'How did you know that door led to the staircase?' he whispered.

'The arrangement of the homes on this street is similar to mine and there is no need to whisper. We're alone.'

'I find it best to be safe, just in case,' he said, close to her ear. The deep rumble of his voice sent a ripple of awareness through her. 'There still could be someone about.'

That gave her pause. 'You're saying that to frighten me.'

'If I wanted to frighten you, I'd inform you of

the rats that are probably scurrying around this house or spiders or any number of creatures that could fall down on us from holes in the ceiling.'

'What?' she squeaked and looked up. Her heart slowed when she spotted the ceiling was intact. She stopped dead so he walked into her.

'What was that for?' he asked.

'For trying to scare me.'

'Why don't you let me go down the staircase first?'

'Why?'

'In the event there is someone else in the house, I believe I am more equipped to deal with them than you are.'

'I may surprise you.'

'Miss Forrester, tonight I'm learning you are full of surprises, but as a gentleman, I must insist.'

The light from the dirty window across the way helped them navigate the spiral staircase. Peering over the wooden banister, Sarah could see all the way to the bottom—to the very dark bottom. Was Hartwick right? Was someone living in this house unbeknownst to the neighbours? Would it be some unwashed mountain of a man who would be angry he was discovered?

'Very well,' she whispered, 'I'll let you go first.'

Down and down they went. And when they finally reached the ground floor, Sarah held him back. 'There will be a door to the back garden nearby,' she whispered. 'From there it should be easy to leave through the garden gate and into the alley leading to the mews.'

'I agree. Stand back while I open the door.' Hartwick crouched and retrieved a knife from his boot. The muted light shimmered off the silver blade.

She stepped back. 'What do you have that for?'

'One never knows who one will run into on a night like this,' he replied with an amused grin.

Her palms started sweating as he slowly turned the doorknob and peered out into the hallway. She took off her gloves and wiggled her fingers in the event she needed to scratch an attacker's eyes out.

Dear God, let us be alone.

He signalled her to follow him while keeping his attention on the silent, dark hallway. She would never admit to him how grateful she was for his self-assured presence tonight. Anticipating having to walk through these houses without being caught had upset her stomach all day. She had no experience at this.

They reached the door leading to the garden

and he placed his hand on the doorknob. 'Are you ready?'

She nodded and took a deep breath. The thought that someone might be close by watching them made the hair on the back of her neck stand up. She nudged his shoulder and got a whiff of leather and rainwater.

When they stepped out into the overgrown garden, the damp air was a welcome relief from the musty smell inside. She was finally finished with her evening of breaking and entering.

'Do you require assistance returning home?' he asked, searching her face in what appeared to be true concern.

'No, thank you. I assumed the house was empty but you're correct. One can never be too cautious.'

'Words to remember as you go forward with Lord Baxter,' he said with a friendly smile.

It took her a moment to recall his earlier assumption about why she had been on the roof. 'Yes, well, thank you again.'

They were facing each other in the moonlight and she had the strongest urge to close the distance between them. His blue eyes, framed with thick black lashes, had her transfixed. For a long moment, she looked back at him. He really did have lovely eyes—but they gave away his suspicions about her story.

She went to walk past him, but he pulled her back by her hand. He stepped closer and his gaze dropped to her lips. The heat from his body travelled to hers through the cool damp air. The rain began to fall again, but she hadn't noticed.

'You should go,' he said softly.

She nodded, but part of her was having a difficult time walking away from him.

His lips slowly curved into his familiar cocky smile. 'You never thanked me for saving your life.'

She released his hand and stepped back. 'Do not look for a kiss from me. The kiss you received from another woman tonight should keep you content.'

He crossed his arms. 'What makes you think it was one kiss?'

Sometimes he made it so easy to resist that pull she felt towards him. She turned and made her way through the overgrown brush to the small, delicate, wrought-iron gate. 'The details of your love life do not interest me, my lord,' she replied over her shoulder, grateful to be leaving the arrogant Earl.

* * *

When she climbed into the carriage waiting a few streets away, she met the eager expression of her dearest friend and closest confidant, Katrina, Duchess of Lyonsdale.

'Well, did you find it?' Katrina slid across the green velvet bench in the well-appointed carriage, making room for Sarah to sit down.

Sarah shook her head while removing her hat and cape. The danger she had put herself in by breaking into the Everill town house had all been for naught. 'I searched her room from top to bottom, and the bracelet was nowhere to be found. She must be wearing it tonight.'

'Now what will you do?'

'I'm not sure. If she continues to wear it everywhere she goes, I'll be forced to take it off her wrist.'

Katrina handed Sarah the gown she had changed out of in the carriage when they left the ball. Concern was etched on her brow. 'You were gone for a long time. I was beginning to worry.'

Sarah let out a sigh as she turned her back so Katrina could button her gown. 'I was detained by Lord Hartwick on the roof as I was trying to leave.'

'Hartwick? Does he know what you were doing tonight?'

'No, he believes I was coming from an assignation with Lord Baxter.'

Katrina's hand paused midbutton. 'Do you think that's wise?'

'It was better than telling him the truth. With all his indiscretions I doubt he would say anything.'

'Whatever was he doing on the roof?'

'Do you really need to ask?'

Katrina resumed buttoning Sarah's gown. 'Has he taken up with Everill's widowed niece?'

'No, thankfully she was not in residence tonight, from what I could tell by looking into the bedchamber. He was with Lady Helmford.'

'Why won't that man ever pursue an unmarried woman?'

'Because he might be forced to marry one! From what I've observed, he grows bored of women easily.' Sarah began to pin up her hair.

'I wish he would settle into marriage. I think it would do him good. He always appears rather restless to me.'

'I pity the woman who falls for the likes of Lord Hartwick. He thinks too highly of himself and is too much of a rake to ever be faithful.' She turned to face Katrina. 'How do I look?'

'You look like you never left the ballroom. I'm sorry this was all for naught.'

So was Sarah. That bracelet was the key to saving her parents great pain. She would not stop until she had it.

Playing cards with the Prince Regent always proved to be entertaining, especially when the man was losing. Hart leaned back in his chair in the alcove of the bow window of White's and watched as his friend and sovereign studied the cards in his hand with the intensity of one who was trying to decipher foreign words on a page.

His puffy face was scrunched up as he directed his gaze away from his cards and over to Hart. 'Do not look smug.'

'I hadn't realised I was.'

'You always do. You have not won this hand yet.'

'You're quickly running out of money to bet. I might win by forfeit.'

'Unlikely.' Prinny turned to his cards again.

Hart took a sip of brandy and checked his watch. It was close to four in the morning, but it felt much later. He would bow out after this hand and get some much-needed rest. 'I don't think the cards will change however long you stare at them.'

'Don't rush me, boy.'

Granted Hart was young enough to be the man's son, however at thirty-two, he was far from a boy. 'Very well, if I nod off, someone wake me when it's my turn.'

Prinny finally selected his card and placed it on the table. Hart won the hand and the remainder of his friend's money. Now he could escape to his bed and sleep for days.

'One more round, Hart.'

Dammit! How was it possible he was not tired of losing? 'You have nothing left to bet.'

Prinny turned towards his three companions behind him, ready to plead his case, when they quickly walked away. 'Useless, the lot of you are useless,' he called after them.

'You see,' Hart said through a yawn. 'We cannot continue.'

'One last round. How about we wager for a favour?'

It was always wise to store as many favours as one could. You never knew when you might need them. Considering the luck Prinny was having tonight, Hart was certain he would win. 'Very well, but this is the last one.'

They went back and forth till finally it was down to one hand. Prinny placed his card down, a victorious smile on his lips. 'I win.'

Hart had to rub his eyes twice to make certain he was truly awake. Dammit! Now he owed Prinny a favour. The Prince Regent guided him by the elbow to a quiet corner of the room. 'I mean to collect, you know.'

'I had no doubt. Something tells me you had a favour in mind all along.'

'I might have.'

'You could have simply asked.'

'True, but now you're bound by a debt to do this for me.'

'And there is no one else you could have asked?'

'No one that I trust to keep this quiet. You cannot tell a soul. Not even Winter.' If he was not to tell the man responsible for overseeing Prinny's secret guard, then Hart was truly interested.

'And you cannot tell Lyonsdale either. I know how close you are.'

'Very well, you have my word. I shall not tell a soul.'

Prinny lowered himself into a chair and eyed

the seat next to him, indicating Hart should sit. Unfortunately, there was a good chance that once he sat down, Hart would not get up until sunrise.

'Rumours have surfaced that indicate some of the missing French crown jewels are hidden here in London.'

Hart shifted closer to Prinny. 'I haven't heard this.' He prided himself on knowing important details before they became public knowledge and shook off his annoyance.

'Louis sent word to me through his ambassador. He asked for my help in locating them for France. He wants them back. There is specific mention of the Sancy, a pale yellow diamond that weighs approximately fifty-five carats. It once was part of the Mirror of Great Britain until James sold the stone to Cardinal Mazarin when he needed funds.'

'What has this to do with me?'

'I want you to find it.'

'Why? This seems like a task for the Home Office.'

'Castlereigh and I have met with them. We were reassured they would locate the jewels.'

'I don't understand. If they're locating them, why would you want to involve me? I do not work with them.'

'No, but you do work for Winter and I know how cunning you are. I want you to do this for me, without the knowledge of the Home Office.'

Either Hart was much too tired or Prinny was talking in circles, as he was known to do. 'So you want me to find the French crown jewels that the Home Office is already trying to locate and return them to you?'

'Just the Sancy.'

'Why?'

'Because that diamond should be ours. Just imagine me reclaiming it. It's too delicious a notion to pass up. I have no intention of returning it to France. I'll never let Louis or Castlereigh know I possess it. France believes the thief, Guillot, broke apart the crown jewels. He hid clues to the Sancy's whereabouts in a bracelet shortly after he arrived in England. This bracelet recently surfaced in Rundell & Bridge and was purchased by Everill for his wife. To find the Sancy, you need that bracelet.'

Hart tossed the lock of hair out of his eyes, getting a better look at the man sitting across from him. There was a chance Prinny had too much to drink.

'Come now, Hart. Ever since you were a small

boy, you were drawn to danger. You should be begging me to do this. Your uncle often said it would be a miracle if you reached the age of twenty with your penchant for reckless acts. It is a miracle you are still alive after tumbling down that cliff not long after your mother died.'

Hart shifted in his seat, not at all comfortable with recalling his mother or that day when he was a boy of seven—a boy who only wanted to stand in the last place his mother had stood before he lost her forever.

'So you will find it for me?' Prinny's voice broke the painful memory and, for the first time, Hart was grateful to be interrupted by the man.

He rubbed his eyes. 'Do you even know what this bracelet looks like? I imagine Lady Everill has quite a few.'

'As a matter of fact I do know what it looks like,' Prinny replied rather smugly. 'I was told there are square gold links with paintings on porcelain. The links are also engraved in a Grecian style. The thief left a note for his accomplice that the bracelet would help him locate the Sancy. Find that bracelet and you find the key to where it is. You owe me this debt.'

Chapter Two

Sarah stood at the closed door to the breakfast room of her home and tried to paste on a believable smile. It wasn't working. She needed to disguise her frustration at failing to get Lady Everill's bracelet last night before someone noticed her foul mood. There would be questions—and Sarah had no answers she cared to give.

On the other side of the door, her parents were blissfully unaware of how perilously close they were from being thrown back into a world of grief and depression, with Sarah as their only hope. She had lived through that anguish with them once. She prayed she could find the bracelet so she would not have to do it again.

She struggled again to smile. Closing her eyes, she recalled the thrill of racing her horse at full gallop along the shores of the Long Island Sound on her family's estate. A small smile crossed her lips. It was the best she could do.

When she entered the room, she was met with the faint sound of forks clinking on plates as her mother read a letter and her father browsed his newspaper while they ate breakfast. If the silence continued, she could keep trying to think of another way to secure that bracelet.

As Sarah poured herself a cup of chocolate, her mother refolded the letter she was reading and smiled at her.

'Good morning. Did you enjoy the additional time you spent with Katrina last night?'

'I did. Thank you. We hadn't spent time together like that in so long and we had so much to talk about.'

'The two of you always seem to have so much to talk about,' her mother said with a smile. 'She looks well.'

'She does, but I do think she was nervous leaving Augusta for the first time at night.'

'That's to be expected. The first time I left you after you were born, it wasn't easy.'

'She wanted to return home the minute our carriage left the drive,' her father said, not looking up from the newspaper.

Her mother took off her spectacles. 'If I recall correctly, I wasn't the only one,' she teased before turning her attention back to Sarah. 'I was just reading a letter from Mrs Colter. Robert will be arriving in Liverpool in a few weeks to settle some business here. She expects him to stay for three months and I was thinking it would be kind to invite him to come down to London for a visit while he is here.'

'You do?' Sarah was well aware of why her mother thought it was such a kind gesture.

'Yes, we can find a room for him at the Pulteney.'

'Perhaps Mr Colter does not have the funds to stay in such an establishment.'

'Of course he does. That family is very comfortably settled.'

Sarah took a sip of chocolate. It was a small reprieve.

'I think it will be wonderful to see him again. He always was my favourite of her four sons.'

'Which one is he?'

'We haven't been gone that long, Sarah,' she chided. 'You remember, he is her youngest. The one who is two years older than you. The one with the lovely manners.'

'Isn't he the one who doesn't speak?'

'He speaks. I have heard him. Why would you think he doesn't speak?'

'He doesn't speak to me.'

Her father put down his newspaper. 'Perhaps the man can't utter a single word because you never give him the opportunity.'

'That's not true. I've never given him the cut.'

'I meant you talk too much in his presence,' her father said with a smirk.

'Perhaps he thinks you're beautiful and is at a loss for words when he is in your presence.' From the look on her mother's face, it was possible she actually believed that.

'Perhaps Mr Colter and I have nothing in common and therefore we have nothing to discuss.'

'Nonsense, you are just trying to dissuade me from inviting him.'

'That is not true. I am simply trying to remind you that even if you invite Mr Colter here, he will not be proposing to me before he leaves.'

'How do you know that? You have not seen one another in two years. Things can change.'

'People do not change, Mother. If we did not fall in love two years ago, we will not be falling in love now. Love doesn't work that way.'

'How do you know it does not? One day you

may suddenly look at him and realise he is the man you cannot live without.'

'He is mute,' Sarah stated more firmly.

'No, he is not,' her mother replied with just as much conviction.

'I know you want me to find a nice American man to marry and I want to find one. I do. But Mr Colter is not that man.'

'You don't know that. Can I help it if I want to see you happy and in love? Can I help it if I want to be a grandmother some day? I am your mother, and I want what is best for you.'

She looked over at her father for help, but by the amused expression on his face, he would not be offering any.

'What other news has Mrs Colter sent? I am certain that entire letter isn't all about her son.'

Dear God, let it not be all about her son.

'Any news of our neighbours?'

'Mrs Stevens has had her second child and Mrs Anderson her fifth. Both had girls.' She arched her brow at Sarah.

Sarah drank more chocolate.

'And Susan Philpott and Jonathan Van Houten are wed.' This time both brows went up.

'Has anyone suffered an injury? Is anyone ill?'

'Sarah!'

'I am simply asking because that does happen to people, too.'

Her father laughed and turned to accept a letter from Bayles, their butler. Sarah's attention was immediately drawn to it and she let out a breath when she spotted the official government seal on the paper.

'Mr Harney passed,' her mother said, drawing Sarah's attention away from her father's concerned expression as he began reading the letter.

The shadows of grief were back in her mother's eyes. Sarah didn't believe they would ever go away. Each time they got word that someone had died, the announcement would scratch at the scabs covering the fresh wounds of grief over Alexander's death.

'How sad. He was a nice man.'

'He was. Mrs Colter says she stitched a memorial for Mrs Harney since the widow's eyes are failing. Mrs Harney is very fortunate her son lives within a few miles of her. He has taken her into his home.' She picked up her stack of letters and stood. 'I'm going to write to her now to express our condolences. Then I'll pen a letter to Mrs Colter letting her know I plan to invite Robert down to London shortly after he arrives in England.'

As her mother walked out the door, Sarah poured herself more chocolate from the Wedgwood pot. Morning chocolate was the answer to everything—or it had been at one time.

Her father put down his letter. 'I'm sure this goes without saying, but your mother and I would never force you to marry someone you do not love. She is only trying to be helpful.'

'By finding every American man in England to place in my path?'

'If that's what it takes to find you a husband, I suppose so.'

'Please convince her not to invite Mr Colter here in hopes of a match. We are unsuitable for one another and both know it. He is much too dull for my taste and I believe my exuberance frightens him.' She tilted her head and tried to see what her father was reading. 'Is it bad news?'

'It's a letter from Washington. The banking problems at home have not improved. More people are being refused lines of credit and we must decide how we will respond to our countrymen over here.'

'Should we be worried by this?'

He gave her a reassuring smile. 'We are fine and our stables at home are unaffected. Men will always need horses, although I will write to Perkins informing him to be cautious in extending credit.'

She adjusted her cup in its saucer. 'It would be easier if you were home to oversee this.' If they left Britain, perhaps her parents would never learn about what Alexander did.

'Perkins is very competent. I trust him.'

'I hope President Monroe appreciates you.'

'This is not about President Monroe. I want to give back to the nation that has allowed me to live the life I lead.'

The turn in the conversation made her uncomfortable. If Alexander's treasonous act was revealed, her father might be relieved of his position. 'Have you decided what you will do when this is over?'

He shrugged. 'We will return to New York. Perhaps I'll run for office or seek a position in Washington.' Sitting back comfortably in his chair, he took a sip of coffee. 'Have I ever told you how my father fought as a colonel alongside President Washington and was instrumental in the success of the Battle of Long Island?'

'You know you have…many times,' she replied with a grin.

'Then you understand patriotism is strong in our family. My father was a patriot, I am and your brother proved to be more of a patriot than either of us.' Talking about his love for his country brought life to her father like nothing else since her brother's death.

Four days ago she had inadvertently opened a letter addressed to her father that was mistakenly placed with her mail. She read about how this person was in possession of a letter her brother had written to an English general revealing details about Fort McHenry. This person wanted to exchange that treasonous letter for a large yellow diamond that could be located using Lady Everill's bracelet.

If her father had opened that letter, there was no telling if his heart would have survived the news. They had almost lost him from the grief he suffered over Alexander's death. The only thing she found that helped him accept her brother's death was that Alexander had supposedly died a hero protecting the people of Baltimore that night five years ago. What would happen to her parents if they found out he died a traitor?

She needed that bracelet and that diamond to spare her parents further pain. It sounded easy. But it wasn't. However, nothing was going to stop her from finding that bracelet and the diamond and protecting her beloved parents.

Gravel crunched under his boots as Hart walked towards the viewing stand at Tattersall's with Julian Carlisle, the Duke of Lyonsdale, by his side. The familiar smell of hay mixed with a tinge of manure carried in the breeze as they passed crowds of gentlemen who were there to view the fine stock of horses up for auction. Approaching a spot near the auction block, Hart gave a friendly nod to Mr Tattersall and scanned the area in anticipation of seeing the beautiful thoroughbred that would make a fine addition to his stable of racehorses.

Julian peered past his shoulder. 'Do you see it?'

Hart shook his head, still looking for the shiny black coat of the four-year-old colt.

'Are you planning on breaking your bank for this one?'

'I will not be on your doorstep any time soon because I cannot afford to keep my set at Albany if that's what you fear.'

'That's a relief,' Julian said with a smirk. 'As it is, you're beginning to consume more than your body weight in food at my home.'

'Can I help it if Katrina is gracious enough to invite me to dine with you as frequently as she does?'

'It might have something to do with the matter of you arriving close to dinnertime most nights.'

They had dined together at White's most nights before his friend got married. It was what they did. They had taken most of their evening meals together since they were at Cambridge. Now Julian wanted to stay home for dinner. Hart had given the newlyweds a month to themselves before he assumed they would grow bored of each other. He never felt as if he was imposing. Was he wrong? 'Are you saying I am not welcome in your home?' His tone was teasing, but he discovered waiting for the answer was making him uncomfortable.

'You are always welcome, as you are quite aware. I'm simply remarking that should you bid more than a reasonable amount today, I might be forced to adopt you as my son.'

'You could have said as a brother. We are both lacking those.' The moment the words left his lips he regretted saying them, knowing Julian still felt the loss of his brother who had died years before. 'Forgive me.'

Julian dug his hands into the pockets of his navy blue coat and shook his head. 'No need to apologise. I'm finally at peace with Edward's loss.'

'I'm glad, but what has changed?'

'Katrina once told me everyone has a purpose in life. When that purpose is achieved, they move on. I suppose Edward fulfilled his purpose. The notion has helped me accept his loss.'

Hart didn't believe that. People died and the people they left behind were never the same. How did that fulfil a purpose? He knew of this first-hand. Everyone who had ever meant anything to him, save Julian, was dead. 'I'm glad you have made peace with his passing.' Not certain what else to say, he relied on his diversionary tactics. 'So, I suppose if I remain at your house long enough this evening, I'll be invited to dine.' He offered up his friend a teasing grin and raised his brows, expectantly.

Julian let out a low laugh. 'You are always welcome. Just be prudent with your money. Do you need another racehorse?'

What an absurd question. 'No, I don't need another racehorse, but I want this one. He has Derby potential.'

'Do you have a number in mind?'

'I think eight hundred guineas is fair.'

Julian shook his head.

'I do not have a wife to support,' Hart continued. 'I do not have as many servants as you. If he meets his potential, this horse will bring me much more than that in winnings and I can make even more money when I put him out to stud.'

As he turned his head away from Julian's chastising glare, he finally spotted the colt being led down the sawdust path. His black coat, shiny in the afternoon light, was a sharp contrast to the pale stone walls of Tattersall's. His handler paused with him at the auction block before he was paraded past the attendees. This beast was exceptional. Hart had to have him.

Mr Tattersall gave Hart a slight nod of his head, acknowledging that this was indeed the horse Hart had inspected the day before.

'Gentlemen, here I present to you a fine, well-bred, four-year-old colt by the name of Corinthian.'

'You are going to bid on a horse named Corinthian?' Julian said through a low laugh.

'That has nothing to do with why I want him.'

'Well, whatever you do, do not change his name. It's much too appropriate.'

As Mr Tattersall ran through the horse's pedigree, the animal stood perfectly still, its muscles outlined in its smooth coat, as if waiting for the men to acknowledge how magnificent he was.

Finally, Mr Tattersall rapped his gavel. 'What shall I say for this horse? Five hundred?'

Hart nodded slightly and Mr Tattersall acknowledged him. 'Thank you, my lord. Five hundred guineas are offered for this splendid animal.'

'Ten,' came a voice from Hart's left.

'Thank you, sir. Five hundred and ten guineas.'

'Ten,' Hart said loud enough to reach the auctioneer.

'Very good. Thank you, my lord. Five hundred and twenty guineas are bid.'

'Ten,' said the man again to Hart's left.

This could take some time. Hart was about to raise the bidding by fifty guineas when a familiar strong voice from over to his right called out, 'One hundred.'

Mr Tattersall nodded his acceptance before quickly glancing at Hart. 'Thank you, my lord.

Six hundred and twenty guineas are bid. Will any gentleman advance that sum?'

Julian leaned closer to him. 'Were you aware your father would be here?'

'Eighty,' Hart shouted out before he could control the volume of his voice.

'Thank you, my lord. We have seven hundred guineas bid on this horse.'

Hart turned his attention momentarily to Julian. 'Of course I wasn't aware he would be here. It's not as if I've suddenly decided to speak with him,' he bit out, unable to remain calm and rational where his father was concerned.

'One hundred,' that familiar voice called out. This time the bid was met with murmurs in the crowd. His father was never subtle.

'Thank you, my lord. We have eight hundred guineas offered. Would any gentleman like to advance?'

Hart's offer came out before his brain registered he had said anything. 'One hundred.'

'Thank you, my lord. We have—'

'Two hundred.'

'Two hundred fifty,' Hart countered before Mr Tattersall could reply.

'Three hundred.'

Dammit! His father was such a stubborn old fool! Hart leaned over to Julian's ear. 'I've lost count.'

'Sixteen fifty. Far more than that animal is worth,' Julian gritted out through his teeth. 'Do not let him goad you. He has done it before. End this. You are better than he is.'

The problem was, Hart really did want that horse and he knew his father revelled in taking away anything he wanted. They had played this game before. And he was certain they would play it again. His brain told him to walk away, but he wouldn't give in. If he let the man win, he'd hate himself.

Mr Tattersall's voice broke his concentration. 'For the last time, gentlemen, the price is sixteen hundred and fifty guineas.'

Men around them began to lay bets as to who would win the horse—the Marquess of Blackwood or his son. Hart stuck his hand into his pocket and rubbed his lucky guinea.

Julian leaned over. 'Do not do it.'

'Fifty,' a voice that sounded very much like his own came out of Hart's mouth. He closed his eyes and cursed his impetuous nature.

Julian let out an audible groan as voices around

them grew louder. Hart was able to block out what they were saying. It was probably due to the fact he was calling his father every curse he knew in his head.

He looked at Mr Tattersall, who was trying to appear unaffected by the numbers being bid for this horse that was worth approximately half as much.

'Thank you, my lord. Seventeen hundred guineas are offered. Will anyone advance?' There was a pause. He looked at Hart's father for an indication to counter.

Nausea and a sense of stupidity assailed him. He refused to look at the man whose blood he shared—a man upon whom he had wished death many a time. It was an absolute certainty he wore a smug smile. Had he finished toying with his son? Did he even realise the potential of the colt? Hart closed his eyes and filled his lungs with the smell of manure. He laughed to himself at the appropriateness of being around so much shit.

'Seventeen hundred guineas are offered for this outstanding animal. Are there any other offers, gentlemen?'

It was the longest pause in Hart's life. He

stopped himself from squeezing his eyes shut. It was best to feign a look of quiet amusement.

The hammer fell.

What he wanted to do was let out the world's longest breath. What he actually did was tip his hat to his father and smile. Let the man think Hart had enjoyed the game. He wasn't about to show him how much it upset him. Families were worthless.

Within moments his father and Lord Palmer had disappeared into the crowd. If only that would be the last time he laid eyes on the man. Unfortunately, Hart knew he wasn't that lucky. Why couldn't his father have died instead of his mother? What further torture did that man have to inflict on him to fulfil his purpose in life? No, Katrina was wrong. Death just proved there was no sense in caring for anyone but yourself.

The gentlemen around them offered their congratulations. Did they honestly believe he was happy to spend a small fortune for that horse? The worst part was, no matter the outcome, his father would have bested him either way.

Julian pulled the collar up on his coat. 'Now, tell me you won't be residing under my roof in the near future—along with that horse of yours.'

'Residing? No. Although I could use some of that fine French brandy you have. The one locked away in your study.' He began strolling past men exchanging money over bets on the outcome of his actions.

Julian followed directly behind. 'How do you know about that bottle?'

'I found it a month ago when you left me alone in there.'

His friend pulled Hart to a stop. 'You searched my study?'

'I had no other way to occupy myself. You were gone for quite a long time.'

'You mean when Reynolds informed me my wife had delivered our child?'

'Yes, that was it.'

'I was seeing Augusta for the first time. Of course I was gone a long time.'

Why did it always seem that Julian couldn't quite grasp how absurd he was at times? Hart had seen the baby. There was nothing interesting about her, aside from the fact she was the smallest human he had even seen. He waved his hand carelessly. 'I still have no understanding why you wanted to witness the birth in the first place.'

Julian pinched his brow. 'I wanted to be certain

my wife survived. I was not happy she had me wait in my study with you.'

Did they really need to discuss childbirth? Weren't his father's actions today punishment enough? 'In any event, I could use that brandy right about now.'

'Very well, I suppose this afternoon warrants it.'

'This afternoon warrants the entire bottle.'

Chapter Three

Sitting in Katrina's carriage and hearing how desperately she needed to get home to nurse Augusta, was making Sarah wonder if a bottle of brandy was hidden close by for cold nights. As it stood, she was learning more than she wanted to know about how one nursed a baby.

Who knew if you went for too long between feedings, your breasts would become swollen and tender? Just the thought had Sarah crossing her arms over her chest to ease the imaginary pain. When had their leisurely day of shopping taken such a miserable turn? While she was happy for her friend at becoming a mother, she missed the days when their discussions had been primarily about men, fashion and American politics—and their shopping trips had lasted for hours.

'Are we almost there?' Katrina winced.

Sarah peered out of the window. They had turned off Piccadilly...that much was certain. 'I haven't any notion of the street, however we can't be far.'

'If we don't arrive home soon, they're bound to leak.'

'Leak?' Sarah did not want to know how. 'That shouldn't be possible.'

'Well, it is!'

'I realise that! I am simply stating my opinion.'

'Your opinion isn't helping. What should I do? The footmen are bound to notice.' Suddenly she let out a low groan.

Oh, lud! 'It's too late, isn't it?'

Katrina didn't need to answer. The dark stain spreading across her beautiful blue spencer said it all. 'What now?' she pleaded, her cheeks turning scarlet.

The carriage jerked to a halt. They looked at each other with wide eyes. Just as the door began to open, Sarah shoved her white cotton bag containing her new beautiful pink silk slippers against Katrina's chest.

Sarah had eyed those lovely slippers through the shop window for weeks. She really didn't need another pair—her dressing room contained more shoes than any woman should own—but this pair was so beautiful—so perfect. They were in the Grecian style, with square toes and open tops that laced together with delicate pink satin ribbons. Her favourite part was the wider deeper pink silk ribbons that tied around her ankle.

She had waited weeks for them. When she'd finally tried them on an hour ago, it had felt as though she was wrapping herself in the finest present in all of London. They had cost a pretty penny of her pin money, but they were absolutely undeniably worth it. Or they had been before she had sacrificed them for her friend. She looked out the window, unable to watch Katrina clutch those exquisite ruined shoes to her milk-soaked spencer a minute longer. Sarah wasn't certain who wanted to cry more, her or Katrina.

The moment the carriage steps were lowered, Katrina sprinted inside the house in a manner not at all befitting a duchess. 'Do come inside,' Katrina called from over her shoulder. 'There's something of great importance I need to discuss with you.'

Reynolds, Katrina's very proper butler, held the massive door to the majestic house open. It was obvious it was taking all his self-control not to stare after his mistress. He gave a respectful bow to Sarah as she entered the house. 'Good day, Miss Forrester. Would you care to wait in the Gold Drawing Room?'

From past experience, Sarah knew Katrina would be a while. She handed her bonnet and spencer to Reynolds. 'Might I wait for Her Grace in the library, Reynolds?'

'Of course, miss. Shall I show you the way?'

Walking past him, she waved him off. 'There's no need. I know where it is.'

There was no sense sitting idly in a drawing room where she was sure to begin worrying about how she was going to get Lady Everill's bracelet. It would be much better to be curled up with a book in the enormous library. Within minutes she was standing on the threshold, eyeing the floor-to-ceiling bookshelves that covered all four walls. At the far end of the room, a massive carved fireplace and two bookshelves jutted into the room. For all its grandeur, it was still cosy and Sarah understood why it was one of Katrina's favourite rooms in the house.

Floorboards creaked as she began to walk beside the shelves. There had to be books on interesting topics somewhere in the vast collection.

'Is that my tea, Reynolds?' From the far end of the room, behind a wall of books, the voice of the Duke's grandmother, the Dowager Duchess of Lyonsdale, rang out.

'Forgive me, Your Grace, but it's just me.'

A small head with grey hair visible under a fine white lace cap peaked from the edge of the book-shelf. Her diamond earrings sparkled in the sun-light. 'Do you have my tea, Miss Forrester?'

Sarah curtsied. 'No, Your Grace.'

'Than why are you here?'

Sarah bit back a smile at the woman's familiar, direct nature. 'I am waiting for Katrina. She is at-tending to Augusta. I thought I'd find a good book with which to occupy myself until she is finished.'

Lyondale's grandmother resided in Lyonsdale House during the Season and had kindly taken Katrina under her wing, becoming a grandmother to her as much as to the Duke. She was smart, di-rect and frequently appeared to be up to mischief. When Sarah's hair turned grey, she wanted to be just like the Dowager.

The woman's petite form moved from behind the shelves and she hobbled with a regal air to-wards Sarah. 'Were you shopping?'

'We were indeed.'

'Did you have success?'

An image of the perfect pair of slippers almost made Sarah sigh. 'A pair of slippers I ordered were finished and Katrina accompanied me to fetch them.'

'A woman can never have too many pairs of slippers.'

'I couldn't agree more.'

'If you're searching for novels, they're at the far end of the room, my dear. Once you find one, I suggest waiting for her in the Crimson Drawing Room. The light in there is lovely this time of day.'

Sarah knew the comment was more a direction than a suggestion. As long as she had something to occupy herself with during the wait, it didn't matter what room she was in. 'Thank you. I know it well.'

'Capital.' A smile brightened the Dowager's face and made her eyes sparkle. 'I need to see what is taking so long with my tea. I'm beginning to wonder if I must to sail to China myself to retrieve it.' She walked to the door and tugged on the tapestry bell pull.

It didn't take long for Sarah to find *Waverley*. The novel proved so engrossing it was a wonder she didn't walk into a wall on her way down the hall. Upon entering the drawing room, she took the nearest chair and turned the page.

The sound of a throat clearing from her left made her jump. At the far end of the room Hartwick stood before the windows, a glass in his hand. He was dressed in his usual black attire, save for his snowy white shirt and cravat.

Oh, lud! She should have never left the library.

He strolled towards her until his shiny black Hessians almost touched the tips of her white kidskin boots. The last time she'd seen him, he'd been standing in the moonlight with his chiselled features glistening with drops of rain.

They stared into each other's eyes, challenging the other to break the silence that stretched between them. He caved first.

'Miss Forrester.' It came out almost as a scold, as if he was annoyed she had interrupted his solitude.

'Hartwick.'

'I almost did not recognise you without your trews. Should I be concerned you're developing a habit of showing up at unexpected times?'

'No more so than my concern that you're taking far too much pleasure in startling me.'

'Touché.' He tipped his head respectfully and motioned to the chair next to her. 'May I?'

When she nodded her consent, he sat down and picked up her wrist with his ungloved hand to read the spine of her book. Tingles ran up and down her arm.

She pulled her hand away. 'I'm waiting for Katrina.'

'I gathered as much.'

'This is an odd location to find you at this time of day…alone.'

'I, too, am waiting for my friend. He's attending to matters with his secretary. I imagine he will be returning shortly.'

'Returning? I always thought you and Lyonsdale met in his study.'

'Apparently he no longer wants me in that room.' He took a sip from the amber liquid in his glass. 'I believe *banned* was the word he used.'

His nonchalant manner made her smile. 'I can't imagine why.'

He looked off into the distance, then focused back on her. 'Some nonsense about brandy.'

That was not what she'd expected to hear and she glanced pointedly at his glass.

'He accompanied me to purchase a horse today

at Tattersall's. I'm imbibing as a celebration of sorts. And you, Miss Forrester, what brings you to this stupendously decorated room today?'

'Katrina and I were shopping. She's attending to Augusta. I suppose she will not be long.'

He took another drink, eyeing her over the glass. 'I assume you were on the hunt for a new pair of slippers.'

It vexed her that, from the few times they had spoken, he knew her so well. 'Why would you assume that?'

He arched his brow and smirked. 'Is it truly necessary to ask that question?'

She snapped the book shut. 'We might have been shopping for bonnets or ribbons or gowns.'

'Very true.' He nodded sagely and took another sip of brandy. 'What did you purchase?'

'Slippers,' she replied, glancing away.

'Sorry, I didn't catch that.'

She looked directly into those aquamarine eyes that were rimmed by thick, dark lashes. It was unfair God had given a man eyes like that. 'I said I purchased slippers.'

'How surprising.'

'And how surprising of you to purchase a horse. How many of them do you own now?'

He sat up straighter. 'I don't see how that is relevant. And where are these new slippers of yours? Do not tell me you are wearing them already.'

Her mouth dropped into a defeated frown. 'They're ruined. The perfect pair of pink slippers that I have wanted forever are ruined, never to grace a ballroom or garden party,' she admitted wistfully. It was so sad.

'Ruined? But you *just* purchased them. What happened?'

'It's a long story,' she said with a sigh. 'What breed of horse did you purchase?'

'A four-year-old thoroughbred colt.'

'That sounds promising. You must be very pleased.'

'I suppose.'

'You don't sound very pleased.'

'It's a long story.' He raised his glass slowly and the crystal touched his lips. For a moment he savoured the taste before his Adam's apple slid up and down with his swallow.

Her stomach did an odd little flip. It happened now and then, whenever she witnessed him doing the most mundane things. When he was not consciously trying to charm people, he was magnificent to watch.

'Speaking of things we'd rather forget,' he continued, 'reassure me you will not be traipsing about any rooftops in the near future. If I hadn't been up there to grab you, you would have fallen to your death.'

'If you hadn't been up there, I wouldn't have been startled enough to slip. You owe me an apology.' She wished he'd forgotten about their encounter. The last thing she needed was Lord Hartwick poking into her affairs.

'An apology?' he replied indignantly. 'I saved you!'

'Which would not have been necessary if you had simply ignored me.'

'I didn't know it was you. If I had, I most certainly would have ignored you. Since you have yet to thank me for saving you, I'll accept your unspoken gratitude and say it was my pleasure.' He smirked at her and cocked his head.

There were times it was impossible not to roll her eyes at him.

'And that is the response I'm given. I see. Well, the next time I find you in need of assistance, I will ignore you. Is that to your liking, Miss Forrester?'

'That would suit my needs very well, my lord.'

* * *

The problem was, as much as Hart hated to admit it to himself, he enjoyed matching wits with Miss Forrester and had no desire to ignore her. Women fell into one of two camps. Either they would throw themselves at him or run the other way, afraid of his rakish reputation. Sarah Forrester was different. He had no idea how to charm her and he wasn't completely certain she even liked him. Not that it should matter if she did. Which it did not. It absolutely did not. But he was discovering how much fun it was to provoke a reaction from her.

He should excuse himself and return to his place across the room, from where he had been contemplating how to steal Lady Everill's bracelet. Placing that much physical distance between them was the proper thing to do, considering they were both unmarried. Instead he gave her his most charming smile, settled back into the red brocade cushions and waited.

She let out a long, exasperated sigh, which caused her breasts to rise and fall in her yellow-and-white-striped gown. He took another sip of brandy.

'Must we continue to converse?' she moaned.

He laughed at the audacity of that statement by an American to a peer of the realm. 'We don't have to. We could sit in companionable silence. I'll enjoy my brandy and you can read your book.'

Those keen brown eyes of hers, which he knew missed very little, narrowed. 'I cannot imagine you could remain silent for very long.'

As hard as he tried to prevent it, a small smile snuck out. 'I find one can learn many things about a person when neither is speaking.'

'I imagine you can. However, in this instance, the both of us are clothed.'

He almost spat his brandy back into his glass. He knew she was looking for a reaction and, dammit, he had given her one. This round went to Miss Forrester.

Katrina poked her head into the room, breaking their game. 'Sarah, I'm terribly sorry about— Oh… Good day, Hartwick.' She walked towards them and waved him off when he began to stand. 'I wasn't aware you were here today.'

'I was instructed to wait in here,' Miss Forrester blurted out.

Heaven forbid Katrina think she wanted to spend

time with him. Now it was his turn to roll his eyes. 'I doubt Katrina assumed you were spending time with me by choice…alone…in a room.'

'I am simply clarifying the situation.'

Just then, Julian stepped into the room and raised his brows at the sight of the women. Perhaps cowbells were in order in this house to keep track of everyone. Earlier, he had encountered the Dowager Duchess. Was she to walk in next?

'You're back from shopping already?' Julian asked.

Katrina glanced at Miss Forrester in an apologetic way. 'I fear my shopping trips will be brief for some time.'

Some silent communication passed between the couple, before Julian nodded in understanding. Was Julian suffering from financial difficulties? He wished his friend had come to him if he needed funds. Hart would be happy to help him.

The thought of money had him recalling the debacle at Tattersall's. He took a large gulp of brandy, finishing off the glass.

Katrina turned back to them with a bright smile. 'It's actually a happy coincidence we have the two of you together. There is something we wanted to ask you.'

Miss Forrester placed her book on the table beside her and looked as perplexed as he felt.

'It's about Augusta,' Katrina continued.

He knew absolutely nothing about children. He had been one once, of course, but he was an only child and had never even seen a baby before Augusta. What in the world could they want to ask him?

It was obvious Katrina was being polite. She must want Miss Forrester's opinion on something and didn't want him to feel slighted. That was just like her. He turned to the woman next to him who was looking at her friend like a startled deer. Apparently Miss Forrester was not at all comfortable with the turn of this conversation either.

'Go on, Katrina,' she said before licking those soft, pink, full lips of hers.

He brought his glass to his lips. Bloody hell, he needed more brandy.

Katrina looked to Julian, who stepped up to her side and slid his arm around her waist. 'Katrina and I were wondering if you would do us the honour of serving as Augusta's godparents.'

Hart's brow wrinkled in confusion. 'Exactly who are you asking?'

'Both of you,' Katrina replied, looking between them.

He turned to Miss Forrester, who had grown unusually mute. There were tears in her eyes—actual tears.

'Katrina, you do not have to… I will buy another—'

'Sarah, don't be foolish. I've wanted to ask you this since the day Augusta was born. You are like a sister to me.'

'You're certain?'

'Of course, we both are.' She looked to Julian, who gave Miss Forrester a reassuring smile.

The women hugged and now it appeared Katrina was tearing up, as well. Oh, hell, he hated to see women cry! He sat back with a sigh and looked across at a life-size portrait of one of Julian's ancient relatives. From the man's expression, it appeared he couldn't abide crying women either. Could he leave now, without causing offence?

Eager to get away from the emotional display, Hart stood and walked to his friend. 'I don't exactly understand your choice,' he said, shaking his head.

Julian leaned closer. 'Katrina insisted on Miss Forrester. They are very close. I couldn't say no.'

'That wasn't what I—'

Julian arched an amused brow, telling him he understood. 'I think she will be good for you.'

Hart almost swallowed his tongue. 'Miss Forrester? I assure you I have no designs—'

'I meant Augusta. Should anything happen to me, I'll need you to look out for her. Having that responsibility on your shoulders might do you some good.'

'She is your child. Should anything happen to you, of course I would do everything in my power to see she is taken care of. There was no need to go to this measure.' Augusta slept a great deal from what he could recall of seeing her after she was born. Katrina had told him the only time she really fussed was when she was hungry. They had similar interests.

'In any event, I am honoured you have accepted.'

Miss Forrester's voice carried to where they were standing. 'But what about when I return home? I might never see you or Augusta again.'

A heavy feeling settled in Hart's stomach. Was there something wrong with the brandy?

Katrina rubbed Miss Forrester's arms. 'We will not think about that day. And when you do, you will make certain to return for visits. We would be happy to welcome your husband and children into our home.'

Her husband? Her children? He crossed his arms, recalling their encounter on the rooftop. Was there someone in particular she planned to marry? After all, he had run into her on a rooftop in London in the middle of the night and it was hard to imagine what else she would have been doing other than fleeing an illicit liaison. Common courtesy demanded he should not bring up the subject with her—however, he was curious by nature. He was determined to find out just what Miss Sarah Forrester was about, but first he needed to fetch that damn bracelet.

Chapter Four

The moment Lyonsdale and the Earl left the drawing room, Sarah could breathe normally. She didn't appreciate the way being near Hartwick left her all fluttery inside. Now that she was alone with Katrina it was easier to concentrate.

'Again, you have my apologies, Sarah, I know how much you loved those slippers. You're a true friend to sacrifice them the way you did. I promise to buy you another pair.'

'I had to do something. You would have run inside and I would have been left to face your perplexed footman.' She really needed to stop thinking about those slippers. It wasn't improving her disposition.

'Have you given any more thought to how you will get Lady Everill's bracelet?'

'I have, usually at three in the morning when

I'm wide awake and fretting about my parents finding out what my brother did. Searching the Everills' house was terrifying. I'd prefer not to do that again. And if Lady Everill has been showing it off everywhere, then the only time I could retrieve it is when they're home asleep. That idea terrifies me even more. It's maddening to know that bracelet is only the first step in finding the diamond and yet I can't get my hands on it long enough to study it so I can discover where the stone is hidden.'

'I think you should practise removing my bracelet again.' Katrina held her arm out to Sarah. The diamond-and-sapphire bracelet sparkled in the light. 'If you become proficient, you can slip the bracelet from her wrist the next time you see her.'

'We've already tried. I'm horrid at it.' She leaned back in her seat and stared at the cherubs looking down at her from the gilt moulding around the ceiling. Why couldn't they help her figure out what to do? 'I can't allow my parents to endure additional suffering because of this vile man and his blackmail. I have a fortnight before he sends word of where the exchange will be made. If I don't find the diamond by then...'

Katrina held her hand. The warm pressure

steadied Sarah's tremors. 'Are you certain this is worth keeping from your father? Perhaps you should just tell him.'

'Katrina, I can't take that chance. His heart will never survive this. It will destroy him. It will destroy them both. I'm sure of it. I don't have a choice.'

Their conversation was interrupted when the Dowager opened the door and stepped into the room. She eyed them before scanning the surroundings.

'Are you looking for someone?' Katrina asked, removing her hand from Sarah's.

'No. No. I was…about to do some reading, but I could not find my spectacles. I might have left them somewhere in here earlier today.' Her studied gaze swept over Sarah from her half-boots to her hair. 'I say, Miss Forrester, are you still here?'

'It would appear so. Would you like us to help you find them?' Sarah asked, hoping it would distract her enough to give a brief reprieve from her troubles.

'Find what, my dear?'

'Your spectacles.'

The Dowager's brows wrinkled briefly before she seemed to recall why she had entered the room in the first place. 'Oh, yes…that's very kind of you, but not necessary. Go about your conversation. Pay no attention to me.' She walked away and scanned the surfaces of the small decorative tables.

Sarah glanced at Katrina, knowing their conversation was finished. She would go home, crawl into bed and stay under the blankets until she had devised a plan to retrieve that bracelet. It should only take a year—a year she did not have.

She stood and brushed out her skirt. 'Well, I should go.'

'I shall walk you to the door,' Katrina replied.

'Miss Forrester,' the Dowager called before they reached the door, 'I was wondering if you and your parents enjoyed science.'

'Pardon?'

'I was planning on having a small gathering in a few nights' time to show off some of the wondrous things I've been hearing about during the lectures I've been attending at the Royal Institution.'

'You were?' Katrina eyed Julian's grandmother with suspicion.

Sitting through an evening of dull lectures was not how Sarah wanted to spend her time, even if she did adore the Dowager. 'I would have to enquire with my mother. It's possible we have accepted an invitation already for that evening.'

The Dowager's eyes narrowed. 'I haven't told you which evening it will be.'

Sarah looked away, trying to find something to say.

'I have invited just a few friends,' the Dowager continued with a graceful wave of her hand. 'The Tates, the Everills and a few others.'

It was impossible to miss Katrina's pointed stare.

'It will be on Wednesday. Shall I send an invitation?'

If it took two days, Sarah was going to master removing Katrina's bracelet without her noticing. 'Yes, please. A Wednesday evening that I do not have to spend at Almack's would be lovely.'

Three days later, Sarah sat in the Crimson Drawing Room of Lyonsdale House sipping tea and trying not to stare at Lady Everill's bracelet, which was on prominent display on the woman's wrist. It had to be the bracelet described in the letter. It was comprised of square gold links and had paintings on porcelain. Sarah was waiting for the perfect opportunity to try to slip it from Lady Everill's wrist without getting caught and sending the woman into hysterics. It sounded so easy in theory.

'I must admit,' Lady Everill said, lowering her teacup to its saucer, 'I am surprised you're attending scientific lectures.'

'There is no sense in wasting away at our age, Harriet,' the Dowager said, shaking her head from beside Sarah on the crimson silk brocade sofa. 'And after tonight, you may decide to accompany me to the next one.'

Sarah's mother stirred her tea. 'And what do you have planned for us tonight? Your invitation was not very specific.'

'I would prefer to keep it a surprise.'

'You always were one for secrets,' Lady Everill said, adjusting her glove so the gold links of her bracelet sparkled in the candlelight, as was the intention of the movement.

The Dowager leaned in. 'Why, Harriet, what a lovely bracelet. I don't believe I've seen it yet.'

'Yes, you have.'

'No. No, I don't believe so.'

There was a distinct preen to Lady Everill as she held her wrist out. It was only a few feet away and Sarah had to clench her fist to resist the urge to grab it.

'It shows exceptional craftsmanship,' Lady Everill pointed out. 'Are not the paintings exquisite? I'm partial to the ancient Greek engravings myself. They have been the rage for quite some time and I do not see the design going out of fashion any time soon.' She turned to Katrina and addressed her directly. 'Wouldn't you agree?'

Katrina's gaze shifted momentarily to Sarah. 'Oh, I agree. It's very lovely.'

'And the images bring to mind such happy memories.'

'My eyesight is not what it once was,' the Dowager said. 'Harriet, do be a dear and take the bracelet off, so I can get a better look.'

Lady Everill visibly bristled at the request, which made her jonquil turban decorated with peacock feathers shift against her grey hair. 'But...surely you can see it from here.' She shoved her wrist closer to the Dowager.

'There is no need to have your hand up my nose. Simply hand me the bracelet so I can have a better look at these exquisite paintings you've been going on about.'

'You can see them from there.'

'I'm afraid, my dear, I cannot. Honestly, what do you think I will do to it? Is it so poorly made you fear it will break?'

'Lord Everill would never purchase a shoddy piece.' Lady Everill's chin shook as she spoke. 'Rundell & Bridge sold him this bracelet. They have a royal warrant.' She raised her nose a bit higher.

'Then there is nothing to fear in giving me a closer look.'

Sarah's heart beat wildly in her chest as Lady Everill released the gold pin from the hinge and handed the bracelet to the Dowager. The answer to her problems was inches away. It was excruciating. She just wanted time alone with that bracelet! Was that too much to ask?

The Dowager held the bracelet up to her eye and studied each engraved gold square linked together by individual hinges, as well as the two small paintings done on porcelain. She turned it over a number of times, looked at the back of the links and weighed it in her hand. 'What say you, Miss Forrester?'

'It's a lovely bracelet,' Sarah replied, wishing the Dowager had not brought attention her way.

The Dowager placed the bracelet on Lady

Everill's wrist and refastened the pin. As she did so, she resettled herself on the sofa and stepped on Sarah's left foot—hard! Who knew such a small woman possessed such a strong foot?

'You're fortunate, Harriet. Lord Everill has fine taste in jewellery.' The Dowager took a sip of tea from the cup that had been resting on the table at her elbow. She looked at the mantel clock across the room. 'How I wish Lord Hartwick knew how to tell time.' She sighed. 'If he does not arrive in the next ten minutes, we will be forced to proceed without him.'

The Dowager hadn't mentioned she was inviting Lord Hartwick when she told her about this evening. At least with Lord Hartwick present, the evening would not be that dull of an affair. Trying to best him in their verbal sparring matches was always entertaining. She simply had to make sure he did not distract her away from lifting Lady Everill's bracelet.

Ten minutes later, the Dowager had given up on Hartwick and asked everyone to join her in the library to begin the evening's festivities. Perhaps Lady Everill would fall asleep during the lecture and Sarah would have an easier time slipping the bracelet from her wrist. She needed to find a way to sit next to the woman.

When Lady Everill stood, the bracelet slipped from her wrist and fell to the floor. It took a moment for Sarah to believe it had really happened, but glancing at Katrina's wide-eyed stare gave her the reassurance she wasn't dreaming. In an instant Sarah stepped forward and covered it delicately with her foot. Bending down, she placed Lady Everill's bracelet into her slipper while pretending to adjust the ribbon around her ankle. She prayed the bracelet wouldn't jingle as she walked.

'Forgive me for the hour,' Hartwick called as he entered the drawing room. His finely cut black tailcoat accentuated his lean muscular frame. The crisp white cravat he wore was tied neatly and that lazy lock of shiny black hair was close to falling into his sharp blue eyes.

The Dowager surveyed him as if she, too, was assuming she'd find evidence of time spent in a woman's bed. 'We were about to begin without you. What you need, my lord, is a wife to manage you.'

'What I need is a watch. There will be no wife for me.'

'Do go to the back of the line, Hartwick,' she instructed, 'I'll chastise you later for your tardiness.'

'I look forward to it, Your Grace,' he replied, passing Julian and Katrina with a smile.

His friend gave him a slight, disapproving shake of his head.

Hartwick responded with a carefree shrug before his watchful gaze landed on Sarah as she walked carefully towards the guests.

'Do come along, Miss Forrester,' the Dowager said. 'I assure you Lord Hartwick does not bite.'

A devilish twinkle sparkled in his eyes as he tipped his head to her in greeting. 'At least, not in polite company,' he said low enough that only Sarah could hear.

'Then I count myself lucky we are among the Dowager's guests. But be advised, should you bite me, I will bite back.'

He placed his head closer to her ear. The warmth of his breath danced along her neck, sending a tingling sensation down her spine. 'If that is meant as a deterrent, you've missed your mark. I now have the unnatural desire to pull you away and find the most delicious places on your body to sink my teeth into.'

No man had ever been that forward in their

speech with her. The bold suggestion brought an odd quiver below her stomach. Thank heavens the cad would never know.

'Shall we wait a moment for you to steady yourself, or did that hesitation stem from your desire to steal away with me?'

Did he have to be so observant? 'Not every woman falls for your charms, Hartwick. There is a rare breed of us that finds it quite easy to see through your false flattery.'

'I never lie. Not to you. I'll prove it.' He looked deep into her eyes. The intense effect made her entire body still. 'Miss Forrester, I find your beauty incomparable, your intelligence stimulating. Your body tempts the very core of me—'

'Oh, do hush, Hartwick. If I could push you over right now, I would.'

The teasing grin on his face made it difficult to hold back her smile.

As they resumed walking, his attention dropped to the hem of her skirt and his brow wrinkled. 'Have you injured your foot? Has Boreham finally done permanent damage to one of his dancing partners?'

If only she could use the clumsy lord as her excuse for the way she was walking. She attempted to adjust her gait, trying not to step directly onto the bracelet lodged in her shoe. Deflection was her best option. 'What do you know of Lord Boreham's knack for harming his dance partners?'

'Since we were at Cambridge, I've witnessed many a woman leave the dance floors of England with a limp. So what is causing yours?'

'I do not have a limp.'

'Forgive me, your hobble.'

'I tied my slipper too tight.'

'Then we should stop so you can adjust it.'

'It will loosen as we walk.'

'Or it will loosen faster if we don't stop and you retie it.' He tugged her arm, bringing them to a halt.

She could retie it twenty times and it would not make one bit of difference. 'It is best not to keep the others waiting. I assure you, it's no inconvenience on my part. It will loosen on its own.'

Those sharp eyes narrowed on her, making her palms sweat.

A curious smile spread across his lips. 'You are an unusual creature, Miss Forrester.'

As they finally reached the doorway of the library, Sarah was relieved she hadn't jingled once during their short walk. However, she could not have the bracelet remain in her slipper the entire night. Eventually her hobble would give her away.

She noted Hartwick's attention was drawn to the far end of the room where Sarah's mother was speaking with Lady Everill.

'Are you acquainted with her ladyship?' Sarah asked, taking note of his furrowed brow.

'We've met once or twice.' He looked over at Sarah. 'We don't generally move in the same circles.'

'I imagine conversing with chaperons is not your preference.'

'I avoid it at all costs, if I'm honest. I don't want them assuming that I've decided to find a bride.'

The Dowager cleared her throat, bringing everyone's attention towards where she stood on the opposite end of the room near the massive fireplace. 'I have invited you all here tonight to share with you the wonders of electricity.'

Sarah glanced at Hartwick, who eyed her sideways. All Sarah knew of electricity was the experiment she heard Mr Franklin had conducted with a kite over thirty years ago and Signor Galvani's experiments on the reactions of muscles to electricity.

'I've purchased an electrifying machine,' she

continued, stepping to the side and revealing a small cylinder on legs that came up to the petite Dowager's knees. 'It is ingenious really. If we crank this handle, it will create friction, which will carry an electrical shock from the machine through this string. If someone holds the string and you touch that person, the electricity will flow through them and into you.' She looked around eagerly at her guests. 'If one person would like to crank the machine, the rest of us can hold hands and receive a spark. Doesn't that sound exciting?'

It did actually. How many people could say they knew what it was like to feel electricity move through their body?

'Is it safe?' Sarah's father asked sceptically.

'They would not sell them if they were not.'

He bobbed his head from side to side. 'I don't believe that's entirely true.'

'You may be our cranker, if you like, Mr Forrester,' she said, apparently not wanting to miss the electrical shock herself.

Sarah's father approached her side. 'Do not hold that string,' he quietly warned her.

Since Alexander died, he had become very protective of her. As a child, he had encouraged her adventurous nature. He had found it amusing. But now he feared he would lose her, too, and she was all he had left of his children. Yet how could he expect her to miss all the fun? Who knew if she would ever have the opportunity to try this again? And it was safe. The Dowager had confirmed it.

So when the stately old woman asked who would like to hold the string, Sarah couldn't stop herself from immediately stepping forward—at the exact moment Hartwick did the same. They looked at each other and surprise flickered in his eyes.

There was a distinct clearing of her father's throat behind her.

The Dowager clucked her tongue. 'Only Lord Hartwick and Miss Forrester are brave enough to have a go?'

Katrina eyed the machine near her foot. 'What does it feel like?'

'A wonderful zing moves through your body,' the Dowager replied, looking pointedly at Lord Sissinghurst.

'Perhaps it's best if a man holds the string,' Sarah's father said, still not convinced she would not spontaneously combust if she held it. 'His body is more sound,' he continued. 'It will hold the greater amount of shock.'

Hartwick bounced on his toes as if he was re-straining himself from going after the string. 'Fear not, Mr Forrester. I shall be the sacrificial lamb and spare your daughter.'

But Sarah wanted to feel the shock first! Why should men have all the excitement in life? As the daughter of a diplomat she was forced to suppress her daring nature and appear subdued—or as close to subdued as was possible for Sarah. Back home, her brother had taught her how to ride a horse sitting astride without a saddle. She had climbed trees, swam in the ocean and had allowed two different men to kiss her. She lived for new experiences—experiences like having electricity run through her body.

'The shock will be the same regardless of the size of the person holding the string, Mr Forrester,' the Dowager replied to his question.

'How long will it last?' Lord Everill enquired from where he was inspecting the device over the rim of his spectacles.

'As long as we continue to turn the crank and generate the friction.'

Lady Everill's eyes grew wide. 'How long do you intend for that to be?'

The Dowager shrugged. 'However long we

want. The residual effects can be quite fun. Electricity can make the strands of your hair raise. You can pick small pieces of paper up by merely waving your hand over them. And if you kiss someone who has been electrified, you will feel a sharp spark of fire from their lips.'

'Maybe this isn't such a good idea,' Katrina said, stepping away from the device and approaching her husband's side.

'Their lips catch fire?' Lady Everill all but shrieked.

'No, Harriet, but it feels that way.' The Dowager glanced once again at Lord Sissinghurst and they shared a smile. 'Or so I've been told.'

'Oh, dear Lord,' Lyonsdale groaned, pinching the bridge of his nose.

Sarah looked at Hartwick, who was rubbing his lips as if to wipe a grin off them. It wasn't working very well.

If Sarah didn't know any better, she would think the Dowager and Lord Sissinghurst had tried the kissing experiment themselves, but the woman had to be in her seventies. Surely people had no interest in kissing at that age. Did they?

The Dowager walked back to the machine. 'I promise you. We will start with a short spark of electricity. It will not harm you. I know you are all curious. I am not the first person in London to hold an electrical soirée. Certainly you have heard of the others. Wouldn't you love to say you have tried it, too?'

That was all it took for Lady Everill to agree. 'I'll do it,' she said much too quickly.

Then everyone seemed to be in agreement.

'Capital,' the Dowager said with excitement shining in her eyes. We will try a few experiments for fun. Be warned, you should remove any substantial metal from your person. That would include jewellery, snuff boxes and the like.'

Wonderful! Now what was Sarah to do? She should have volunteered to crank the contraption. How was she to remove the bracelet without anyone noticing? Where would she put it? How horrible would it be if she kept it in her shoe?

'My bracelet!'

All heads turned to Lady Everill and Sarah's body grew cold. She was certain everyone would know the woman's latest prized possession was in her slipper.

The Dowager's clear voice gave her a small bit of comfort. 'What is wrong, Harriet?'

'My bracelet is missing! Oh, Eleanor, someone has stolen my bracelet!'

'Nonsense! I can assure you no one here stole it. It must have fallen off. We will all help you search for it. Katrina, why don't you and Miss Forrester look in the drawing room? You remember where we were sitting. Harriet, you, Everill, Mr and Mrs Forrester and I will search the hallway, and, Julian, you remain here with Hartwick to look for it.'

'What does the bracelet look like?' Hartwick enquired, looking at the lady in question.

'It is engraved gold links and two of those links have small paintings on porcelain.'

Hartwick nodded in understanding while Sarah's heart felt like it would jump out of her chest. Once she made it to the Crimson Drawing Room, her heartbeat slowed.

'I cannot believe her bracelet just fell off her wrist like that,' Katrina said, closing the door behind her and locking it.

Neither could Sarah and now she was fairly certain the Dowager had been eavesdropping on their conversation yesterday. 'I have the woman's bracelet in my slipper,' she whispered back harshly. 'I'm amazed I did not jingle down the entire hallway.'

'As am I. I don't know how you did it.' Katrina opened the drawer of the game table and withdrew a piece of paper and a pencil. As Sarah sat to remove the bracelet, Katrina handed the drawing implements to her. 'Use these, but be quick.'

The bracelet was of substantial weight, leaving Sarah to believe the links were solid. She studied each link and hinge, and found no way to open it. She placed it on the table and began to sketch it out to size. Although the back of the bracelet was free of any etchings, she took a rubbing of each link just to be certain she was not missing anything. Then she made indications of the colours of each of the images.

She folded the drawing and shoved it inside her stays, between her breasts. She was an intelligent woman. She could do this. She would not give in to doubt.

They discovered Lady Everill sitting in the library, fanning herself and drinking wine. Lyonsdale was pacing slowly near the doorway, studying the carpet under his feet.

'We found your bracelet, Lady Everill,' Katrina called out as they entered the room.

Lady Everill rushed to them, grabbed the bracelet out of Sarah's hands and clutched it to her chest. 'Oh, thank heavens.'

A loud thud came from under a nearby table, and Sarah dropped down to find Hartwick on his hands and knees, rubbing his head.

'What are you doing under there?'

'Searching for that bracelet,' he bit out. 'What did you think I was doing under here?'

Sarah shrugged at his unusually harsh tone.

'See, Harriet,' the Dowager said from the doorway. 'No one had taken your bracelet. Wherever did you find it?'

'It was near the doorway of the drawing room. The clasp must have come loose when we were on our way to the library. You may wish to have a jeweller repair it for you,' Katrina suggested with a sympathetic smile.

'Oh, dear, I will at that,' Lady Everill said, dropping it into her reticule and securing the satin braid of the bag around her wrist. 'I'll bring it to Rundell & Bridge myself tomorrow.' A team of wild dogs would not be able to wrestle that bag from her firm grasp.

As people began to return to the library, relief that she finally had what she needed washed over Sarah, improving her mood greatly. Once she was able to use the bracelet to locate the diamond, she could rest soundly, knowing her parents' wounds from the death of Alexander would not be reopened. If they knew he died while giving over plans to the enemy, they might never find any peace in his passing. It had taken both of them over two years to find levity in life again. The only thing that helped them accept his death was the knowledge that he had died fighting for what he believed in. His death had had a purpose in the outcome of the war and they were proud of his sacrifice. She could not let anyone take that from them.

This had been a perfect night so far. Sarah took a deep breath and smiled as her father walked up to her.

Hart stared at the reticule Lady Everill clutched to her chest and wanted to kick something. Julian had mentioned Lord and Lady Everill would be in attendance tonight, along with the Forresters and Sissinghurst. He had used the earlier part of this evening to prowl through her house on Mount Street with relative ease, searching for that damn bracelet—the one that, if he had been given the drawing room to search, would be in his pocket right now.

He tried not to let his frustration show. Thankfully he possessed a keen ability to mask his emotions to the world, otherwise Lady Everill would be shocked by how badly he wanted to rip that reticule out of her hand.

As the rest of the guests filed back into the library, Mr Forrester pulled his daughter aside. From the appearance of their conversation, he was instructing her not to hold the string of the electricity machine. For her part, Miss Forrester seemed to be trying to reason with him. Hart could sense he was respecting her opinions on the matter. All the fathers he knew would have simply forbidden their daughters from participating. What an odd family the Forresters were.

'Is everyone back now?' The Dowager went up on her toes and surveyed the room. 'Capital! Now that Lady Everill has her jewellery, we can return to our evening of experiments.'

Hart approached Julian's side. 'I'm surprised she did not invite your mother this evening. I would think the Dowager would relish the idea of shooting electricity through the woman.'

'My mother would have a fit of the vapours

if she knew we were doing this. She finds her mother-in-law's interest in science and society's interest in these electrical experiments unnatural.'

'Which ignites your grandmother's interest all the more.'

'Exactly. I would not be surprised if the purchase of that machine was in response to a heated discussion between them not long ago.'

'Let's begin with the chain of electricity,' the Dowager said rather dramatically. 'You may place your metal objects on the table over there. Lord Hartwick, Miss Forrester, how shall we determine who is to hold the string?'

Miss Forrester lowered her chin and looked up at her father with her large brown eyes. She was good. He would give her that. She was skilled enough to know the effect that expression would have on the man. Hart himself would never be swayed by a look like that, but he could see how it might change the minds of other men.

Just as he expected, her father let out a sigh and gave the slightest nod of his head. Her expression immediately brightened and she turned to Hart, excitement radiating off her. Out of politeness he should have acquiesced and given her the turn. However, he really wanted to hold the string and receive his shock from the machine directly and not from a current flowing from someone else.

Although it was rather erotic to think of the electricity travelling through Miss Forrester's entire body—*her* most intimate areas—and then flowing directly into him—touching *his* most intimate areas. His trousers began to tighten and he needed to shift his stance to relieve the strain. What a ridiculous notion to get one aroused. He recalled the outline of her legs in those trews of hers. Her calves were slim and her thighs shapely. It was as if he could feel her legs wrapped around him. She was an impudent thing and Hart had often wondered if her vitality would translate into sexual play.

She was the last person he should be picturing in a bed. Or up against a wall. Or on her knees in a carriage. She was an unmarried woman from a respectable family, for goodness' sake. A breed he avoided like the plague. He had no use for any of them—except it was so much fun to tease her.

'I will leave the decision to Miss Forrester,' he said, executing an extravagant bow to the woman who stood a few feet to his left.

She narrowed her eyes. Her suspicions were warranted.

'Thank you, my lord,' she said with an apprehensive smile. 'That is very kind.'

He looked up at her from where he was still bowing as if he knew a great secret. She wavered just a bit. No one else in the room would have seen it, but he did. She was wondering what he knew about the machine that made him change his mind about holding the string. Her eyes darted to the cylinder with the crank and back to him. The indecision was there, right where he'd planted it. It was difficult not to smile.

'I appreciate your offer, Lord Hartwick, however I will let you take the string.'

'I do not mind having you take the lead.' He used his most neutral expression.

Her eyes darted once more to the machine. 'No, I insist. I shall be second in line.'

'Very well, if you insist.' He tipped his head and gave her one of his most charming smiles.

Then he saw the look in her eyes. She knew she had been bested, but it was too late to rescind her statement. He took such perverse satisfaction in knowing that she knew he had tricked her.

As they went to take their places in line, her father approached his side. 'Thank you, my lord, for what you did.'

'I assure you, sir, I did nothing but offer your daughter my place at the front of the line.'

'And yet she declined your offer. I'm not sure how you managed that, but I am grateful. Some day when you have children of your own, you will understand how a father worries about them.' He smiled and moved off to join the line.

Hart was taken aback by the intimacy of the statement. No one ever spoke to him about having children, not even his own father. Their house would die with him. He would never marry. He saw no reason to risk growing attached to someone only to have them die on him, as well. And he always made certain to wear French letters during sex, ensuring he would not have children as a result of any of the liaisons he had. Leave it to an American to have a romantic view of life.

He stepped up to the machine. The Dowager stood in front of him with the string in her hand. 'I knew you would enjoy this, Hartwick. You've been attracted to the thrill of danger since you were a small boy. Your grandmother could never understand the fascination you had with high places. Do you remember that? Do you remember how you would climb trees to the highest possible branch and how you would walk on the parapets of your home?'

He was surprised she remembered. 'I do indeed. I also remember how my grandmother would shake her fist at me and demand I climb down immediately.'

'You were all she had left after your mother died. She loved you very much and was afraid she would lose you, too. She wanted to protect you the only way she knew how.'

He tossed a lock of hair out of his eyes, uncomfortable with the mention of his mother. He always tried to keep those memories hidden away where they couldn't see the light of day. Remembering the care and affection she had showered on him was painful. He'd been a small child when she'd fallen to her death from that cliff, forcing him to fend for himself in a home where he was completely ignored by his other parent. And if his grandmother had loved him that much, she would have taken him away from the hellish home where he'd grown up.

Miss Forrester interrupted his thoughts when she took her place beside him.

'Are you all ready, my dear?' the Dowager asked her.

Miss Forrester nodded with an eager expression.

'Take her hand, Hartwick,' the Dowager instructed.

Her hand was delicate with long, graceful fingers and fine bones. It was the kind of hand you held softly so as not to crush it in your grip. He wrapped his fingers around her warm palm and his skin tingled upon contact. Thinking it must have been the Dowager's electricity machine giving off a current, he glanced at it and realised he was not yet holding the string in his other hand.

She must have felt the same odd sensation as well, because her eyes also were on the Dowager's machine. Then the delicate hand that he was afraid he would crush gripped his with a strong, firm hold.

'Are you ready, Hartwick?' she asked, eyeing the string the Dowager was holding out to him.

'I'm ready.' He grabbed it with his right hand. The fine metal thread running through the string sparkled in the candlelight.

The Dowager took her place on the other side of Miss Forrester and then everyone else began to hold hands. Mr Forrester had agreed to turn the crank and Lady Everill stood beside him, not willing to give up her bloody reticule.

He cranked the machine slowly. After about a minute, a warm buzzing feeling moved through Hart's body. Miss Forrester must have felt it, too, since she let out a low, pleasant laugh. Their eyes met. Then his eyes dropped to her soft, pink lips that were a bit too full for her delicate features.

He had heard about the reputed electric kiss from Theodosia. She had attended the Duchess of Skeffington's electrical soirée and told him that her husband had tried to kiss her after they had used the electricity machine and a spark of electrical fire had impeded him from touching her lips. He wondered if Miss Forrester's lips held a spark and found he had the strongest urge to see if it would stop him from kissing her. Deep down he didn't believe it would.

Certainly the electricity was affecting his brain if he was noticing Miss Forrester's lips. He should not be looking at her lips or noticing how nicely her hand fit inside his. Yes, they were probably under the influence of too much electricity.

He dropped the string and the warm tingly feeling stopped. There were low groans from the other guests who seemed to be enjoying the unusual sensation.

The Dowager released Miss Forrester's hand

and approached the table with small pieces of paper scattered about. She ran her hand a few inches above the paper and the small squares rose up into her palm as if by magic. Everyone wanted to try it and it wasn't until he went to move his hand over the papers that Hart realised he was still holding Miss Forrester's hand. He quickly dropped it, surprising them both with the immediacy of his action.

'I say, Hartwick,' she said, hovering her hand over the table, 'this is just what you would find if you walked through Almack's on a Wednesday. I bet if you did, women would attach themselves to you like this paper.'

'Are you volunteering, Miss Forrester? You could save me the trip.'

'To attach myself to you? Heavens, no, although it would be amusing to be a spectator at such an event.' She turned away from him without waiting for a reply.

It was no wonder the woman found herself still unmarried at whatever age she was. What man would want to manage a woman like that?

Chapter Five

As she sat by the window in her bedchamber the next morning, Sarah's vision was beginning to blur from staring at the drawing of the bracelet for so long. How could she possibly hope to spare her parents more heartbreak, if she couldn't manage to decipher the only clue she had to the diamond's whereabouts? When Katrina arrived shortly after breakfast and suggested they take a stroll through Hyde Park, Sarah was grateful for the reprieve. It was overcast and not the ideal weather to be outside, but it would give Sarah's mind a much-needed break.

'I hope you don't mind that I've called so early,' Katrina said as they strolled the deserted pathway that ran alongside the bridle path of Rotten Row.

'I was awake with the sun. You could have called then,' Sarah said with a small smile.

'I've missed our walks.'

The admission warmed Sarah because she had missed them, too, since Katrina had had Augusta. 'Are you certain there will not be any unexpected occurrences?' She looked pointedly at her friend's chest.

'No, I just fed Augusta before I called on you. I've learned my lesson and now have been taking note of the times she eats. I won't have to be back home for at least another three hours. Have you had time to look at the drawing of the bracelet? Have you determined how to use it?'

Sarah looked up through the branches at the large grey clouds, searching for a spot of sunlight. 'I was so certain I could do this, but I've studied that drawing and I'm no closer in finding the diamond now than I was before.'

'Maybe you should tell your parents. Perhaps they will take the news better than you think.'

Sarah shook her head with determination. The cinnamon-coloured ribbon of her bonnet swished behind her. 'You did not see them after we learned of Alexander's death. The only thing that finally gave them some sense of peace was their belief that he died a noble death, doing what he loved. And that he died sacrificing himself so the people of Baltimore would be safe. I cannot take that away from them. I do not know how they will react when they find out none of that is true. I cannot bear for them to go back to grieve as they did.'

Katrina nodded.

It was bewildering to Sarah how Katrina had been able to marry Julian and move away from her father and her country, especially since her father was a widower. Sarah could never do that. She was all her parents had left of their family. Granted, Katrina's father was no longer in diplomatic service and was able to visit her whenever he chose, for as long as he liked. But Sarah's father planned to resume his career in Washington when his mission in London was over. He would be tied to that position and it would be impossible for her parents to spend months away from Washington to visit her here. She could never marry an Englishman and live an ocean away from them. Some day one of them would need her to help them get through the loss of the other.

'Why don't you tell me what you've learned about the bracelet?' Katrina said. 'It may help to discuss it.'

She rubbed her aching forehead. 'There are five separate square links. The first, third and fifth links are gold squares engraved with a Greek key pattern. The second is a painting of a bridge with a pagoda. The fourth is a painting of a steeple one would see atop a church. And that is all I have to find the diamond.'

'Do you think it's a map of sorts? I mean the two paintings. You did say the first was a bridge.'

'That is my belief, but I'm not familiar enough with London to identify those images. In addition, there's no certainty those locations are even in London.' Her stomach began doing that queasy flip again.

'That is much too depressing a thought. Let's assume they are here. You mentioned the bridge had a pagoda. That should help identify it.'

'It should, however I've never seen a pagoda on any bridge I've crossed here. Have you?'

Katrina shook her head. 'Lady Everill mentioned her husband thought she would enjoy the bracelet because it brought back fond memories.'

'Perhaps she is simply fond of the oriental style.'

'No, we have to believe wherever this bridge is located, Lady Everill has seen it.'

'Do you know where their country estate is located?'

'Herefordshire, I believe.'

'Perhaps it is there?'

'Perhaps.'

Sarah searched the grey clouds looming larger and darker now. There was no sense in going farther. 'We should return home,' she said. 'I believe a storm is on its way.'

As if she had been unaware of the poor weather, Katrina raised her head to the sky. 'I suppose you're right.' She threaded her arm through Sarah's and they turned back towards the park's entrance. 'And what of the steeple? Did it look at all familiar?'

'In truth, I don't believe I've ever really taken notice of any. I've never had a reason to look up at them until now.'

'And you believe it is the steeple of a church?'

'I'm assuming,' Sarah replied with a sigh.

'Do not be discouraged. I will speak with Eleanor this evening. She might know more about Lady Everill's attachment to the bracelet.'

'Julian's grandmother is too perceptive. I cannot have her finding out why I need to know more about the bracelet.'

'I would never reveal your secret to anyone! And I am well aware how perceptive that woman is. Trust that I can make enquiries without disclosing my purpose. I can handle Eleanor. I'll have an answer for you tomorrow.'

Sarah hoped so. But as they travelled the remaining pathway in silence, the sky grew darker and darker.

That night, while Sarah was tossing and turning in her sleep, Hart kept to the shadows of a Mayfair mews with his friend Lord Andrew Pearce. He was grateful no one was about to deter him from breaking into Rundell & Bridge. It might be days before Andrew would be available to stand guard for him again outside the shop's back door. Knowing Mr Rundell lived in the apartment above, they were conscious to keep their voices low.

'I doubt my brother would approve of this if he knew what we were doing,' Andrew commented casually while he leaned his imposing frame against the brick wall of the shop, stuffing his hands into the pockets of his black coat.

Prinny had told him to keep this search for the diamond a secret, even from Andrew's brother who was responsible for the secret organisation that protected the crown.

'Winter hasn't approved of many things you and

I have done together and not all of those have been in service to the crown.'

Andrew scanned the alleyway again. 'True… I'd say you timed this perfectly. No one is about. However, be warned—if I see someone coming, I might have to draw your cork.'

'There is no need for bloodshed. We could simply pretend I'm vomiting.'

'Where is the fun in that?'

Hart tugged off his leather gloves and stuffed them into his coat pockets, preferring to work the thin, metal lock-picking tools with his fingers unencumbered. A slight breeze lifted strands of his hair as he knelt at the door. His own breathing was mixed with the sound of Andrew's tapping foot and the distant rumble of carriages on cobblestones.

The thrill of possibly getting caught raced through his body. His heart was pounding. He felt alive and it was glorious.

'How long do you think this will take?' Andrew asked, switching the foot he had propped against the wall.

'Hopefully not long.'

'Are you returning something or retrieving?'

'I think it best if I don't say.'

'Very well, but be quick about it, will you? It smells like rain.'

After a few tries with the lock pins, he heard the welcome click. The door opened without a sound and he slipped inside.

It appeared to be the shop's office, which was rather small and square. A partner's desk stood to his left with two glass oil lamps, two ornate silver inkwells and what might be ledger books sitting on top. To his right, in front of the window, was a low wooden workbench with various magnifiers and numerous other tools. Below was a worn, wooden cabinet with long, thin drawers. Ahead was a dark velvet curtain covering a narrow doorway, which Hart assumed led to the shop.

Then he spotted the safe tucked into the corner. The polished steel was glowing in the dim light, calling to him. This was where they would keep their precious stock overnight and where Hart should find Lady Everill's bracelet. It resembled an ornately carved, six-foot-tall, steel-plated wardrobe with two doors that opened in the centre. He had seen safes like this before. His own father had one and it was what Hart had practised his lock-picking skills on when he was younger.

Experience had taught him that it had a trip

mechanism, and if he pushed the pin in the wrong direction a second lock would secure itself and make it almost impossible to break into. He needed to be careful and poke gently while he listened for the sound of the spring of the second lock.

He studied the size of the keyhole and selected the appropriate size pin. Then he went to work, pausing often to listen for the unwelcome sound of the spring. When he heard the bolt shift without tripping the second lock, he congratulated himself on a job well done.

Upon opening the doors he was faced with approximately twenty long horizontal drawers. He started with the top drawer, needing to stand on a chair to see the contents. The light was dim and he was forced to squint to look for the bracelet he had seen Lady Everill hold briefly before hiding it away. After scanning several drawers, he found the bracelet, lying beside two broken necklaces and a watch. Without delay he wrapped it in a handkerchief, placed it in his pocket and closed up the safe.

As he turned to make his way to the back door, the wooden floor beneath his boots creaked. He froze as ice spread through his veins. Was that movement above? Just the idea of breathing made him sweat. He looked at the ceiling, as if he could see Mr Rundell making his way to the staircase leading to the shop. Hart had a choice. He could run for the door or hide under the desk. Running seemed like the better option.

He strained to hear any sound from above. There was silence. Before he moved again, Hart counted to four. The silence continued. He gingerly made his way out the door.

'Have you accomplished what you set out to do?' Andrew asked, pushing himself off the wall.

'I have.'

'Good, you can buy me a drink at White's.'

'Can't tonight, but I'll have a bottle of Julian's finest brandy sent up to your set.' Andrew resided at Albany, as well. He should have the brandy within the hour.

'You're planning on getting a bottle of Lyonsdale's brandy now?'

Hart gave a careless wave of his hand as they waked out of the mews. 'No, I'm already in possession of one...or two. I'll have Chomersley bring it to you.'

'Tomorrow will do. I find I'm not ready to return home quite yet.'

They parted ways at Piccadilly. Andrew turned towards St James's Street and the gentlemen's clubs as Hart headed home, eager to study the bracelet.

As he made his way along the pavement, his broad, satisfied smile would not go away. Excitement was racing through his body. He lived for moments like this—they made him feel alive.

The image of Miss Forrester flashed in his mind, her delicate hand warming his. It was gone in an instant, but it had been there—and it made him stop walking with the absurdity of it. The palm of his left hand, the one that had held hers, tingled. It was a residual effect of the electricity... nothing more.

He turned into the drive leading to the building tucked back from Piccadilly where he had been residing for the past year. A light was shining in his window on the top floor. Chomersley, his valet, had taken to leaving an oil lamp lit for him while he was out. It was an unnecessary waste of fuel, however it was nice not to have to walk into his set without stumbling around in the dark.

Making his way up the two steps into the entrance hall, Hart patted his pocket, secure in the knowledge he soon would be able to settle his debt. When he opened his door, he dismissed Chomersley with a wave of his hand and told the man to get some sleep. He got undressed, donned his black brocade banyan, brought the oil lamp to his desk and took out the bracelet.

This was the first time he had got a good look at it. The lamplight reflected off the five square gold links. Two of the links were painted porcelain. The other three were engraved with a Greek key design. All of them were made of solid gold, so nothing could be stored inside. He studied the first panel and looked at the small painting of a bridge with a pagoda. He knew he had seen that bridge before.

All the excitement that had been pulsing through his veins had left him and now he could barely keep his eyes open. According to the clock on the mantel, it was four in the morning. He would sleep on it, knowing in the morning he would recall where that bridge was located.

He extinguished the lantern, crawled beneath the blankets and stretched out in the middle of his bed. Within minutes he was asleep, knowing that within a day or two, Prinny would have the diamond and Hart would be commended for a job well done.

Chapter Six

The morning light pushed its way through the soft white curtains in the drawing room of the Forresters' town house, making the yellow walls appear even brighter. Sarah sat in the jonquil brocade chair near the window, trying to read but having no luck. Each sound from the hallway would catch her attention and she would stare at the doorway, hoping to hear news of Katrina's arrival. Minutes turned to hours. The light shifted along the Aubusson rug. She was beginning to give up hope that the Dowager knew where the mysterious bridge was located when she was informed that Katrina had arrived.

Her mother lifted her head from where her attention had been focused on the embroidery on her lap and smiled. 'Now, that should lift your spirits. You've been fidgeting in that chair all morning. If the book was not to your liking, you should have found something else to occupy your time. Perhaps you should suggest a walk in the garden to Katrina. Being out of doors might do you some good.'

Katrina entered the room and her gaze held Sarah's a bit too long as she joined Sarah's mother on the sofa. She had news! They spoke of the health of the Dowager, Augusta and Katrina's need for a good night's sleep. All the while, Sarah's blue-slippered foot tapped the floor. As far as she was concerned, no one had had as few hours of sleep as she of late.

Finally, there was a lull in the conversation, giving Sarah the opportunity to ask Katrina to join her for a walk in the garden.

'What a wonderful idea,' Katrina replied, 'but perhaps on a fine day such as this we could walk through St James's Park. I've never been, but I've been told it's rather lovely with a charming bridge spanning a lake. We can take my carriage to the entrance and then enjoy the pathways.'

Sarah almost felt light-headed. Katrina had found the bridge. It took great restraint not to run over and hug her. 'That sounds lovely.'

Katrina looked over at Sarah's mother. 'Would you care to join us?'

Why did she have to be so polite?

Thank goodness her mother shook her head with a gracious smile. 'No, thank you. I still have things that need attending here and I'm sure the two of you would like some time to visit together without me. I was young once.'

Sarah jumped from her chair. 'It shouldn't take me long to change.'

For the first time she gave no thought to footwear as she changed into her white muslin walking dress, which seemed to perplex Amelia, her maid. By the time she re-entered the drawing room fifteen minutes later, adjusting the falling collar of her green sarsenet pelisse, she wasn't certain which dress she was wearing let alone what she had on her feet. She only knew that she was one step closer to finding the diamond. She could feel it. Nothing would stop her now.

While pulling out the bracelet from the pocket of his coat, Hart surveyed the Chinese Bridge at the end of the tree-lined pathway in front of him that crossed the canal in St James's Park. There were pairs of very tall lanterns on either side of the approach and four blue-topped pavilions on either corner of the elevated expanse. The only thing that was missing was the seven-storey Chinese pagoda that had once stood on its centre, but which had burned years before during a fireworks display.

There was no mistaking the bridge painted on the bracelet was the one he was looking at now. He just needed to determine what relevance it had to the location of the Sancy diamond. He had strategically timed his visit to the pedestrian bridge so fewer people would be about. As he suspected, the milkmaids were now settled on the other side of the park near Birdcage Walk, close to the Horse Guards. The women were smart, knowing the men would often wander across the street to flirt with them and enjoy a cup of fresh milk straight from the cows. This left very little activity on his side of the canal. The small children and their nannies were far off to his left through the trees. The sounds of their laughter and playful shouts carried faintly on the pleasant breeze.

Hart suspected Guillot would not have designed this bracelet without giving specific clues to the diamond's whereabouts. If the thief was intelligent enough to use the bracelet, he would be intelligent enough to use it to its fullest. Hart closed his eyes and took a deep breath. The faint scent of nearby roses and that earthy smell that filled the air before it rained surrounded him. He opened his eyes and stared at the image in his hand for a count of ten. Then he closed them once more. This time when he opened them, he looked at the yellow bridge, taking note of any differences he saw. The pagoda was missing, which was to be expected, and a man was leaning over the balustrade, staring down at the water.

Pink! There was no pink!

In the painting there was a cluster of pink flowers to the left side of the bridge. There had never been flowers planted near the bridge as far as he could recall. That was the additional clue he was looking for.

Strolling across the bridge, he came to stop a foot away from the man who was impeding Hart's progress in his search. He tipped his hat in greeting. 'It's a lovely spot, is it not? I would often come here with my fiancée.'

The man shifted his eyes uncomfortably and nodded. He was younger than Hart had first believed, probably just out of Oxford or Cambridge.

Hart moved closer. 'She was beautiful,' Hart

began, 'hair the colour of sunlight and skin as fine as porcelain. And she had a penchant for fine gowns. She must have had fifty in her wardrobe the day I lost her. She died, you see. Right here on this bridge where you are standing. She jumped. It was tragic.' He gave a slight sniffle.

The man edged away a bit.

Hart moved closer. 'Do you have a wife?'

The man shook his head. His dark eyes widened as Hart moved until he was mere inches from him.

'I don't have a wife either.' He sniffled again. 'I would have had one, but…'

The man muttered his apologies and hurried from the bridge, leaving Hart blissfully alone.

He wasn't sure where the idea for the story had come from. The words were flowing from his lips before he had formulated what he would say to get rid of the man. A woman's face flashed in his mind. One he hadn't thought about in ages. One he wished he could forget entirely. But Caroline would always haunt him. She had never been on this bridge, and while they hadn't been engaged, he had been about to ask her. He had often wondered if they had been engaged, would she have met the same fate?

He hoisted himself up on the top of the stone

balustrade and nimbly vaulted off the bridge onto the bank, near the water where the clump of pink flowers should be.

He studied the side of the bridge, combing over it block by block. He wasn't sure what he was looking for, but he was certain he would know it when he saw it. The bridge rose from the ground to more than double his height at its centre. Row by row he scanned the blocks and found nothing unusual. He pressed against each block that he could reach. Nothing happened. At the water's edge he stared into the murky depth and combed a lock of hair out of his eyes.

As he turned back around, his attention settled on the area under the bridge. A pathway stretched along the bank, running underneath the bridge. The shadowed underpass was out of the general sight of people strolling leisurely through the park, making it an ideal place to spend time hiding a clue. The pink flowers had been placed on this side of the bridge near the water for a reason. The clue was under the bridge.

By the time he made his way under the bridge, his boots were speckled with mud from the spongy grass. Within minutes of scanning the damp earth beneath his boots and the blocks that made up the bridge, he spotted something unusual.

One of the blocks had a carving on it. It was the rough pattern of a Greek key design—the same Greek key design that was on Lady Everill's bracelet.

He took out the knife he kept in his boot and used it to pry the stone block out from where it sat in the foundation of the bridge. It came out more easily than it should have. It was too dark to see inside the hole it left, so he stuck his hand in and felt around.

At the far back corner, his fingers felt something. He removed a folded pale linen square that was tied with a thin black ribbon, but it was too flat to be the diamond itself. He untied the small knot and unfolded the linen in his palm to discover a small iron key. Now he had the key to the diamond. The final clue must tell him where the diamond was hidden.

Hart shoved the key and linen square inside his coat pocket. It was time to head to White's to celebrate with some good brandy and cards. If cracking the other clue would be this easy, Prinny would have the diamond in no time at all.

It appeared he had found the key just in time.

By the look of the clouds, a storm was approaching. Just as he stepped onto the pathway that led out of the park, the distinct sound of female voices could be heard ahead of him in the distance. He tugged the brim of his hat down, but jerked it up when he recognised Miss Forrester's voice.

The leaves rustled above them as Sarah and Katrina entered St James's Park. 'Thank you again for having your driver take us past St George's and St James's on the way here, Katrina. It was much faster than if I'd had to walk to the churches.'

Katrina smiled brightly. 'It's my pleasure to help in any way I can. Now that you know the next clue may be in St James's Church, you have one less thing to concern yourself with.'

'Are you certain this is the bridge?'

'I've already told you twice. This is the park Eleanor said had meaning to Lady Everill. Eleanor said the lady spoke of it numerous times since she was given the bracelet. Apparently the bridge looks somewhat different but this is it. There was a celebration in this park a few years ago and that night Lord Everill declared for the first time that he was rather fond of his wife.'

Sarah stopped. 'At their age, surely he would have told her something like that sooner?'

'We are speaking of Lord and Lady Everill.'

They shared a conspiratorial smile. Clouds began to roll in, obscuring the sun, and there was the scent of rain in the air.

As a particularly sharp gust of wind hit, Katrina held the back of her bonnet. 'I don't suppose you would care to turn back to the carriage and come another day when it does not appear as if we are racing against a storm?'

She must be mad.

'I didn't think so,' Katrina continued, threading her arm through Sarah's and pulling her along. 'Let's hurry.'

They stopped abruptly at the sight of Hartwick coming down the path towards them. Was Sarah destined to be cursed with the Earl's presence for the remainder of her time in London? In the past year since she had become acquainted with him, she had barely encountered him; now that she was looking for the diamond, he seemed to be everywhere.

'Good day, ladies,' he called out with a friendly smile, raising his gold-tipped walking stick. 'This is a pleasant surprise.'

It might have been for him, but Sarah would rather have ruined another pair of slippers. He was going to delay her search. She tugged up the edge of her green kid gloves. 'I wasn't aware you frequented this park... Unless you are here to see the dairymaids.'

'They do say a cup of fresh milk is good for the constitution.'

'So that's why you're here?'

'For milk?' He visibly shuddered and Sarah couldn't help but notice the curve of his broad shoulders, shown to their advantage in his well-cut black coat. 'Never touch the stuff. I'm heading back from Westminster.'

Katrina tipped her head to the side. 'But Julian complains you never attend to your Parliamentary duties.'

He gave a careless wave of his hand. 'I hadn't planned on attending. I was looking for someone.'

Both women nodded. However, Sarah could tell he had come from somewhere else... Probably from the shrubbery with one of the milkmaids, if the state of his boots was any indication.

'And what brings you ladies into the park today?' He looked up at the sky and adjusted the brim of his hat. 'It appears a storm is on the way. Not really ideal weather for a stroll.'

'We have come to see the pelicans,' Katrina replied, smiling over at Sarah. 'It would be a pity to turn back now without seeing them.'

Pelicans? What pelicans?

'I see. I would hate to deprive you of that.' He tipped his hat. 'I will not keep you. Enjoy the wildlife.'

As he walked away, Sarah felt the oddest sense of disappointment. There was no quick quip. There was no teasing manner. In fact, he barely looked at her. It annoyed her when he was provoking. Why would her spirits be dampened at this lack of interest?

Her brow wrinkled as she turned to Katrina as they continued on towards the bridge. 'Pelicans?'

'Oh, yes, Eleanor said there are pelicans in this park. I'd love to get a glimpse of one.'

Sarah took one last glance at Hartwick as he turned off the pathway and out of sight. The wind was picking up and the sky was turning a greenish grey. Anyone else who had been in the park appeared to have headed home already. Big fat raindrops began to fall. They should head back…

but then the yellow bridge came into view ahead of them. She couldn't turn back now.

It was the bridge on the bracelet. There was no mistaking it, except it was missing the giant Chinese pagoda. The rain was coming down harder and, as much as she wanted to search for the clue now, they would only get soaked.

She grabbed Katrina's hand and they ran towards the water, seeking shelter under the archway of the bridge. They laughed at how sad they looked in their droopy bonnets. Sarah took hers off and shook out the raindrops from the straw. The green satin ribbon was a soggy mess. It might not recover. She looked down for the first time to examine her footwear. Her green silk walking boots were ruined with mud. She let out a sigh. Another lovely pair of footwear destroyed.

The rain was coming down in sheets now, creating natural curtains over the entrances on either side. They were alone and the pouring rain muffled their conversation.

'The Dowager was right. There's no doubt this is the bridge,' Sarah said with a smile.

'Do you have any idea what we should be looking for?'

Recalling the image painted on porcelain, Sarah

shook her head. If it took all day she would scour the bridge for anything that looked out of place. She walked towards the entrance of the underpass and stretched her back, needing some movement to help her think. The blurry landscape through the curtain of rain was not giving her an answer. Turning around, her eyes landed on the firmly packed footprints of one person with large feet—clearly a man—scattered near the foundation of the bridge. From the sharp definition around each print, it was apparent he had been there recently.

The wall of yellow stone blocks rose up above them to a substantial height before it arched back down over the water. She raised the hem of her pelisse and walked in the footprints that were larger than her own. They stopped a third of the way into the underpass where they scattered a bit. Why would anyone go under the bridge where the ground was soft and damp? Why would he stop and spend extra time here?

The blocks of the bridge in that area were fairly smooth and uniform in size and appearance until she came to one that wasn't sitting evenly with the others. She peered closer at it—and almost dropped her reticule. She found it! This was what the bracelet had been pointing her to.

'Katrina, come quick! Look!'

Her friend's eyes widened at the Greek key design carved into the stone that Sarah pointed to. 'It looks just like the design on the bracelet.'

'This has to be what we are looking for.' She reached into her reticule and pulled out a silver letter opener.

'When have you taken to carrying one of those?'

'Since I thought I might be required to dig for the clue.'

She used it to jimmy the block out a bit. It was only four inches thick and behind it was a dark hollowed-out area.

'Can you see anything?'

Sarah hesitated before stepping closer. What if there were spiders in there? She held her breath as she reached inside to feel around.

There was nothing there.

'No! No! No!' Whatever clue this bridge held, it wasn't there now. 'It's gone. Whatever was hidden here is gone.'

'How is that possible? Who would know to look here?'

Sarah was nauseous and getting light-headed. Someone else was looking for the diamond and they had known about this clue. She tried to compose herself, but images of her loving family stopped her. Panic was setting in. 'I need to get to the church,' she blurted out.

'When?'

'Now! The clue isn't here, Katrina. That means someone else is looking for the diamond and probably knows about the bracelet. I need to reach that steeple before they do!'

'Sarah, take a deep breath. How do you propose to search the church now, at this hour? People will be about. Certainly the vicar.'

Her head was beginning to ache and, as much as she didn't want to admit it, she knew Katrina was right. The only way she would have a chance at getting into the steeple was in the middle of the night—dressed like a man.

'I will go tonight. I'll pretend to feel ill and stay home while my parents go to the theatre.'

'I cannot take you there tonight. I wish I could, but Julian and I have accepted invitations for this evening. If I tell him I can't go, he will want to know why and—'

Sarah held up her hand. 'You do not have to accompany me this time. It's not far from home. I can go on my own.' She would much prefer to go with her friend, but she had no choice. If she waited, the other clue was sure to be gone. Knowing the man who took this clue might already have the next was making Sarah's stomach turn. She understood Katrina needed to put her family first, however she couldn't help but miss the days when her friend was there for her whenever she needed her.

There was a long pause before Katrina let out a deep breath. 'I do not like the idea of you venturing out alone at night. You know how dangerous that could be.'

'I will be dressed as a man. It will not appear odd to see a gentleman walking alone at night along Piccadilly.'

'Suppose you are set upon by thieves.'

'I will be in Mayfair. All will be well. You'll see.' She only prayed that whoever else was looking for the diamond hadn't already searched St James's Church.

Chapter Seven

Hart was all too familiar with how hard it was to tear himself away from a card table when he was on a winning streak. Vingt-et-un had proved to be his game tonight as he sat in White's, drinking brandy and collecting his winnings. It was tempting to stay, but he had a debt to settle. There was a diamond waiting for him in St James's Church and it would be best if he just fetched it now. The other players at his table did not hide their relief as he excused himself and made his way to the door, accepting congratulations for a well-played night along the way.

Knowing the gate to the church on Piccadilly would be locked at this hour, he took the short stroll down Jermyn Street to try the back door of the building. The stores along the fashionable shopping street had long closed up for the night and the only people he passed along the way were two young bucks making their way to the end of the street where the gentlemen's clubs were located.

Upon reaching the back door, he looked both ways before trying the handle. The door was locked. He took out the key from his pocket and tried inserting it into the lock. It wouldn't fit. There was a chance the lock had been changed since the key was hidden away, or perhaps this key fit another entrance to the church.

To his left, high above a brick wall, was the church's graveyard. One by one he carefully climbed the steps in the darkness and walked past the rows of thin slate gravestones until he came upon the double doors he was looking for. The arched fanlight above them revealed a dark interior. Surprisingly, this side-entrance door was unlocked.

Hart stepped inside, his boots echoing around the empty vestibule with its vaulted ceiling. He turned and tried to insert the key in the lock, only to find it did not work on this door either. He walked to the front door of the church and found the key incompatible with that lock, as well.

The clue on the bracelet was of the church's

steeple. It was possible the image had been used simply to identify the church since each steeple was unique, however Hart believed there was more to it than that.

He found the small black arched door that led up into the tower, and as he began to climb the spiral staircase, he anticipated having the diamond in his hand tonight. Using his pocket lantern, he slowly studied the wooden walls surrounding him for the Greek key pattern. He found none. As he reached one particular turn in the staircase, a faint golden light was visible above. He immediately extinguished his lantern, knowing he wasn't alone.

The rhythmic clicking of the clock mechanism told him how far he had climbed. Not far ahead should be the room that housed the workings of the clock whose faces appeared on all four sides of the steeple. Someone was in that room and he'd wager that was where the diamond was. He had a choice. He could admit to Prinny that he could not get the diamond, or he could discover who from the Home Office had it and then steal it from them.

It was not in Hart's nature to admit failure. If he could not bring Prinny the Sancy, it would diminish him in his friend's eyes. Plus, it was a debt of honour, so really, he had no choice. Hart was getting that diamond, no matter what he had to do.

He crept up the stairs, grateful at not having stepped on any squeaky boards, and peeked into the room. Someone was sitting back on their heels near the clock's mechanism, unaware they were being watched. He recognised that cleric's hat from the night on Theodosia's roof. *Dammit! Was Miss Forrester everywhere?* He pressed his shoulder into the door frame to prevent his fist from hitting it.

Even though he was careful not to make a sound, her head jerked up and her eyes widened. 'You,' she uttered in what sounded like disbelief.

'Miss Forrester, I *should* be surprised to find you here, but as of late you've been appearing at the most unexpected times, so I find that this isn't a complete shock.' He extended his hand to help her up. Once she took it, Hart knew things between them were about to take a very different turn.

'Are you following me?' she asked, eyeing him up and down.

'Don't be absurd,' he replied, pulling her up. 'If I intended to follow you, I would have been looking for someone dressed as a woman, not as my valet on a bad night.'

She adjusted the lapels of her coat, as if her goal in life was to look like a fashionable gentleman. 'Then why are you here?'

There was no reason she would be here unless she also was in search of the Sancy. 'Why are you?'

They stared directly into each other's eyes. If this was to be a contest of who would look away first, he was determined to win.

'Why is it you seem to be making a habit of donning such attire? Not that I don't enjoy seeing you in those trews, but it is a rather bold fashion choice on your part.'

She glanced away. 'Haven't you heard? It's rather dangerous for a woman to walk alone at night.'

'Then perhaps you shouldn't be roaming Mayfair in the middle of the night at all. Admiring the architecture again, are we?'

'Ecclesiastical architecture is inspiring.'

'You're in a clock tower.'

'Your point?'

'You were on your knees when I arrived.'

'I tripped.' She stuck her right leg out from under her black cape and brushed off her thigh.

He crossed his arms, creating space between them. 'Do not think to distract me with those legs of yours.' She didn't need to draw further attention to them when it was taking a lot of effort on his part to keep his eyes on her face as it was. Why was the daughter of the American Minister searching for the Sancy? He could tell from her defiant expression she would offer him no explanation. He himself was not feeling very forthcoming.

'Is someone up there?' a wavering male voice called from the bottom of the stairwell. A small yapping sound, as if from a tiny dog, followed.

Miss Forrester's gaze flew to the staircase in terror. It was probably the vicar or curate, out late walking his dog. He knew the Home Office would not announce themselves.

They were not going to get caught if he could help it. Hart blew out the small lantern she had left on the floor and pulled her silently across the room towards the ladder that led to the belfry.

'Whatever you do,' he whispered in her ear, 'do not step on any squeaky boards.'

She threw up her hands. 'As if I have control over which boards are squeaky.'

'Go,' he whispered in her ear as he poked her back.

His heart pounded as they made their way up to the belfry, where the slight evening breeze blowing through the slatted openings cooled his heated skin. They were trapped, like two birds in a cage. Except his hard body was pressing her soft one into the wall.

His instinct was to protect her and block the view of her should someone find them. All of his attention should be on avoiding discovery. But being this close to Miss Forrester and those legs in the quiet darkness had him thinking about what she would feel like if he took her against this wall—over and over. Bloody hell, he needed to focus and her soft rapid breath on his cheek wasn't making it easy! He pushed his forearms harder against the wall above her head to stop himself from touching her. Then he looked down at her and found she was staring at his mouth. He unconsciously licked his lips.

Immediately, she looked away.

'I entered through the door in the churchyard,' she whispered harshly. 'Well out of sight of the vicarage. This is all your doing. What if he comes up here? Surely we will get caught and—'

He rested a finger against her soft lips. 'If we are quiet, he might leave. Let's just pray he doesn't decide to bring that dog up here.'

The distant rumble of carriages along Piccadilly mixed with the sound of their breathing was deafening. There was a shuffling of footsteps below and a yellowish glow shone from the opening in the floor they had crawled through. Miss Forrester clutched his waistcoat and shirt, grabbing a few of his chest hairs with them. He squeezed his eyes shut with the pain.

Finally, she released a deep breath, the warm puff of air scorching his cheek as the light coming from the room below disappeared. Once more they were bathed in faint moonlight.

As he went to step back, the hairs on his chest were pulled even harder. 'You can let go of me now,' he whispered into her ear. 'He is gone.'

She looked at her hand in puzzlement, as if she hadn't realised she was holding on to him as if he were her lifeline on a sinking ship. When she released her grip, she wiped both her hands on her trews. 'Forgive me.'

'It was probably the vicar. His dog probably

needed to go out,' Hart said, explaining his theory to her. 'I'm sure he is accustomed to making certain the doors to the church are locked. I assume he noticed the side door wasn't locked and came inside to see if all was well. I left the door to the steeple open. It would be reasonable for him to check up here.'

'Then this is your fault.'

'Think about this, darling. If I hadn't been here, you might have had to deal with him on your own. I assume it was you who left the door to the side entrance unlocked.' He peered through the slates of the belfry and could see the figure of a man and his dog heading towards the vicarage. 'How did you accomplish that, by the way?'

'It was unlocked when I arrived.' She looked away and chewed her lip. 'Perhaps he is waiting for us to come down.'

'He is gone.'

'How can you be so certain?'

'I just saw him leave the graveyard for home.' She held out her hand. 'My lantern, please.'

He placed the small collapsible brass-and-glass rectangle in her palm and watched her approach the ladder. It was no coincidence they were both in this church and it was also no coincidence he had found her making her way to the Chinese Bridge in the park earlier in the day.

Why would Miss Forrester want the diamond? How had an American diplomat's daughter come to even learn of its existence? Who was she working for?

'Why are you really here, Miss Forrester?'

'Why are you?'

He wasn't about to betray Prinny's trust and tell her the truth. And from the way she deflected his question and the look on her face, he could tell she was not about to be forthcoming with him, as well.

'I came to admire the views from up here,' he replied.

'And so did I.'

Could she have found the diamond? He needed to search the clock tower thoroughly.

She noticed he made no move towards the ladder. 'You're remaining here?' she asked, narrowing her eyes.

'If we are discovered together, it would compromise you beyond repair.'

She arched a brow. 'You're concerned for my reputation?' Under the circumstances, that seemed to be the least of their worries.

'I have no wish to be obligated to marry you. It's best if we part ways inside the church.'

Her right hand fisted at her side and she raised her chin. 'Very well, I will leave you here. Thank you for your assistance.' She spun on her heels and left with clipped movements.

It was just as well she appeared angry—probably still blaming him for the vicar's appearance. He needed to focus. And Miss Sarah Forrester had a tendency to muddle his brain and torment his body. She was much too tempting and all wrong for him. And he had a diamond to find. Scrubbing his hand over his face, he began to think about why she was searching for the Sancy. Were the Americans involved now, too? Would they send a woman out into danger? Miss Forrester had left without any persuasion, which left Hart troubled. Had she found it?

He went down the ladder, relit his small lantern with his tinderbox and studied every inch of the walls.

Nothing.

He even went so far as to inspect the clock mechanism. He looked at the floor, scanning each strip of dull scuffed wood until he spied the plank he needed…right where he had found Miss Forrester earlier.

'Dammit!'

He dropped to his knee and traced the Greek key design etched into one of the floorboards. Using the knife he kept in his boot, Hart pried up the six-inch-long plank.

The hollow space was empty.

He sat back on his heels and threw his knife across the room, embedding it in the wall. *Damn, she had it!* He had found a key that must open the box that contained the diamond. But *she* had the box. The Sancy was in her possession—but not for long.

Chapter Eight

The handle of the French door that led from the terrace to her father's study turned silently in Sarah's palm, bringing a smile of relief to her face. The familiar faint smell of almond oil mixed with her father's pipe tobacco was comforting after the last few stressful hours.

She lit the oil lamp on his desk and sifted through the few pieces of unopened mail resting in the oval silver tray. Even though she knew she had time before the blackmailer would send word to her father, instructing him where to leave the diamond, she couldn't help obsessively checking his mail whenever she had the opportunity.

Once more she reached into the pocket of her cape and gripped the unopened linen-wrapped packet that she pulled from the floorboards of St James's Church. She was fighting the urge to untie the thin black ribbon and unroll the packet here, but she needed to go to her bedchamber to slip out of these clothes and back into her night-rail before anyone saw her.

At least in her own home she knew where the squeaky floorboards were and she was able to avoid them as she crept up the darkened staircase. Once she was inside her room, she removed her prize from her pocket and unhooked her cape. With a pounding heart, she lit the two lamps flanking her dressing table. Their glow reflected off the window behind them. She took a deep breath, untied the ribbon and unrolled the linen.

A small iron key slipped out into her palm, making her forehead wrinkle.

What was she to do with a key? There were no more clues on the bracelet. She had nothing to open.

Hartwick's arrival at the church had not been a coincidence. And it was no coincidence that he had been in the park with muddied boots earlier in the day. He was the man who had whatever was hidden below the bridge. And since she now had a key, the logical conclusion was that he must have some sort of box that housed the diamond—a box that he could probably pick the lock to, making her key unnecessary.

'Blast that man!'

Sarah clenched her fists so hard, her nails dug into her palms. What was she to do now? How she wished she could stomp to her wardrobe and slam the doors. Instead she allowed her rage to bubble under the surface as she changed into her night-rail and dressing gown. She shoved her clothes into a pillowcase, along with her boots, and pushed them under her bed.

Many women in London would be thrilled to find themselves alone with the Earl of Hartwick. Couldn't he have had the decency to spend his time cavorting with one of them, instead of getting in her way?

Pacing about her room, all she could think about was how much she wished she had reached the bridge before he had. Then she would have everything! Her parents couldn't find out about Alexander's treasonous act. They had suffered enough. She needed that diamond and no one was going to prevent her from handing it over in exchange for those papers.

Why would Hartwick want the diamond anyway? He was reported to be a very wealthy man.

He didn't need it. Or was he secretly in debt? How had he found out about it? And how did he know about the clues on Lady Everill's bracelet? Sarah had witnessed the woman stash it back in her reticule the other night. Had he stolen it from her? Why, oh, why had she not reached the bridge first?

She would be awake for hours if she did not get something to steady her nerves. A glass of sherry from the dining room would do the trick. In the morning she would figure out a way to steal the diamond from him. She knew where he lived. How difficult could it be to sneak in and grab it? He was barely home.

But as she stepped back into her room after fetching the wine, she almost spilled her glass at the sight of Hartwick. He was sitting up on her bed with her pillows propped behind him and his shiny Hessians crossed at the ankle. Against the white linen of her bed, his black hair, black clothes and polished black boots made an ominous sight, even if there was a hint of amusement on his lips.

His words from earlier in the evening played over in her mind.

'I do not wish to be obligated to marry you. It's best if we part ways inside the church.'

Well, she had no wish to marry him either! He was a rake of the first order. And, as if that weren't enough, he was a titled Englishman who would never leave this country to live in America! Not that that mattered in the least. It didn't. He was a rake. A big, arrogant, insufferable—rake! She bit the inside of her cheek to stop herself from telling him so.

Pushing the door shut behind her, Sarah took a much needed sip of wine. If there was one thing she knew about the Earl, it was not to let him see when he unnerved her.

'You're on my bed.'

He surveyed the area around him. 'It would appear so.'

'Why?'

'The only chair in your room did not appear comfortable and, at this hour, I have a tendency to want to be comfortable.'

'I meant why are you in my room? How did you get in here?'

His penetrating gaze travelled slowly down the length of her body, and she tugged the opening of her dressing gown closed.

He glanced to the French doors that led to her Juliet balcony. 'The trellis on the wall of your home is rather handy. It was much too easy to hop over the railing and enter your room.'

'And what led you to believe this was my room?'

'I saw you in the window a short while ago.'

It was obvious from his relaxed demeanour he was in no hurry to leave. The ease of his manner under such improper circumstances was maddening since his presence in her room—on her bed—was bringing fluttering feelings throughout her body. She was a fool. This was a man who thought nothing of entering women's bedchambers. He did it frequently. It didn't make her special. But as much as she told herself that, she couldn't help notice that he looked devilishly handsome at the moment.

She pointed to the French doors. 'Well, now that you've challenged yourself with breaking into my room, you can challenge yourself with finding a way out. Although, I request you do so quietly and quickly so as not to get caught. I also have no desire to become obligated to marry you.'

That last sentence was uttered a bit too forcefully and a small smile lifted his lips. 'I'm glad to hear it,' he drawled. 'No reasonable person should ever consider marriage.'

'Not interested in committing yourself to one woman until death?'

'Something like that.'

The sharpness in his eyes told her that he knew she had found the key. There was no other reason he would be visiting her bedchamber. While he had often teased her, he had never made any attempt to seduce her. Seeing him gloat over having the diamond would not be in his best interest at the moment. She walked across the room to her dressing table and placed her glass of wine down.

The leather of his boots made a soft squeaking sound as he tapped his right foot against his left. As if realising the sound would carry, he stopped. 'Come and sit with me, Miss Forrester. I think you and I need to have a chat.' He patted the bed beside him and brushed a lock of hair out of his eyes.

'We can converse from our various vantage points. I do not need to sit beside you to hear you.'

He arched a dark brow. 'You're afraid you might not be able to resist me while I sit beside you… in your bed.'

Those smooth lips of his curled into another smile, showing his straight white teeth. His arrogance marred his character, but physically she couldn't find one thing wrong with him.

'I know you're too mulish to admit the truth,' he continued. 'So I will state the obvious. You feel safer over there.'

The insolent clod! 'Not every woman in London finds you irresistible.'

'Irresistible?' he said with a chuckle. 'I rather like that word. You look quite fetching in that,' he continued, 'although I will admit I am partial to you in trews.'

'Flattery does not work on me and *I* can resist you.' She would teach him that lesson and took a step towards the bed to prove it.

'Bring the wine,' he said, gesturing to her glass. 'With the night we have had, both of us need it.'

He was correct about that. She picked up the glass and strolled to the bed, sitting beside him once he adjusted two pillows for her against the headboard. She stretched her legs out and mimicked his pose, then realised she had given him a perfect view of her bare feet next to his leather-encased ones. Perhaps he wouldn't notice.

He held out his hand for the wine and took a fortifying sip before handing it back to her. He had noticed.

'One of the things I admire about you, Miss Forrester,' he said, gazing at her legs, 'is your forthright nature.' He looked directly into her eyes. 'It's very rare, in my opinion, to find a woman willing to speak her mind as freely as you seem to do.'

If she was at all honest, she would admit that sitting this close to him on her bed was leaving her rather warm and it had nothing to do with the temperature in the room. She wasn't as forthright as he thought.

'That being said,' he continued, unaware how much she liked his cinnamon-and-leather scent, 'I think we both would agree that finding ourselves together tonight was no coincidence. We were both in that church for a reason.'

She took a sip of wine. 'It's probably a similar reason.'

'I'd venture to say it was for the exact same reason. You just happened to get there before me and I'd wager my finest horse your trip into the church was more successful than mine.'

'And I'd wager my favourite pair of slippers that my evening was just as successful as your jaunt in the park.'

'There is that sense of honesty I admire so. That's why I'm here. It appears we are both after the same thing, however, we each possess a half of the whole.'

She narrowed her gaze on him. Apparently he wasn't able to pick the lock to the box after all, or he would not be in her room. 'And you think I should relinquish my half to you. I don't think so.'

A sly smile curved those lips. 'I wouldn't dream of demanding you give me what you have acquired in a most impressive fashion. Believe me when I say, I have the upmost respect for you. You were brave enough to break into the Everills' town house the night I found you on the roof.'

As she began to offer an excuse, he held up his hand.

'I know now that is why you were up there, so there is no sense in denying it. I came to discuss our mutual interest.'

'Rooftops?'

'Diamonds. Or shall I say one diamond in particular. Let's drop the pretence. It's obvious we both want it.'

She could deny knowing anything about the diamond, or she could find out what he knew and maybe find a way to steal the diamond from him. Hartwick was so carefree. How difficult could that be? 'Are you here to boast about what you have acquired?' she asked, tilting her head.

'I never boast.'

'That is all you do,' she said, letting out a wry laugh.

'That is not true... Well, I don't boast that much. I believe I have something you need.'

'And if I agree you do, what then?'

'I only ask to see what you found.' He shrugged. 'I'm a curious person by nature. Surely you are curious to see what I have.'

'And if I show it to you, will you show me yours?'

A roguish smile changed his rather serious expression. 'I will show you anything you are curious about. You simply have to ask.'

'Rake.'

'Temptress.'

'Flattercap.'

He smiled in amusement before he grew serious once more. 'So will you show it to me?'

She had nothing to lose and now she would be able to identify the stone in his possession when she went to filch it. 'You first.'

He reached into his pocket and withdrew a linen packet tied with a thin black ribbon no bigger than his palm—a packet that looked exactly like hers. This was no box.

'Why the quizzical expression?' he asked.

'That is what you found at the bridge?'

'It is. Do not look at me so. I have no reason to lie. Show me what you found in the church?'

She slid off the bed and went to her dressing table to retrieve the key that she had rewrapped in the linen. He caught the identical packet easily with one hand when she tossed it to him. When he opened it, his eyes went wide.

'I do not understand,' he said, looking up at her. 'You found a key?'

She nodded, chewing her lip. 'What does your packet contain?'

He motioned for her to take it from his hand. It hadn't given her a complete shock when she opened it since the packets were virtually identical.

'How is it possible we both found a key?' she mused.

He shrugged, still staring at the key in his palm with a wrinkled brow. 'There was nothing else in the church?'

'No, it was the only thing inside the compartment under the floorboard. I checked. Are they the same?' she asked, handing him back his key.

He covered one with the other and shook his

head. 'No, there is a slight variation. See. They open two different locks.'

'I don't understand. I had assumed you found a box,' she said.

'And I thought you did, as well.'

How was it possible that the only two clues led to two keys? She began to pace. 'This is nonsensical. How did you know how to find your key?'

'Lady Everill's bracelet.' He pulled it out and held it up so it dangled from his long fingers. The candlelight reflected off the gold. 'I might have borrowed it from the jeweller who was asked to fix it. How did you know to go to St James's Park and search the church?'

'The bracelet.'

'But how? I saw you return it to Lady Everill after the catch had broken during the Dowager's soirée.'

Once more she went inside the drawer of her dressing table and this time removed the folded drawing of the bracelet. She held it up for him to see. 'That evening I had sufficient time alone with the bracelet before I returned it to Lady Everill. I've been using this drawing to find the clues like a treasure map. There must be something I missed when I drew it. Surely there is another clue to the diamond's whereabouts.'

He tossed his legs over and sat at the edge of her bed, extending the bracelet out to her. 'Have a look. Although I must say I've been over it numerous times to see if there's anything I've missed and found nothing.'

She studied the bracelet and once more searched for any hidden compartments. She also found nothing. 'I don't understand. I was told this bracelet would lead me to the diamond.'

'By whom?'

She was not about to share that information with Lord Hartwick. 'Never you mind. Who told you about the bracelet?'

'In the words of an American I'm acquainted with, never you mind. You can keep your secrets and I'll keep mine.'

That suited her just fine. She would never let him know what her brother had done. Not only would it destroy her parents to know, but Hartwick was friends with members of Britain's political circle. What would happen if they found out the son of the American Minister was a traitor? How would that impact her father's position here? What if news spread to Washington?

His piercing blue eyes narrowed on her. 'I believe you enjoy a good competition just as much as I do, Miss Forrester. What if we lay our cards on the table and make a wager? It's apparent both keys are important. What say you to agreeing that whoever finds the diamond first wins both keys. The loser will forfeit their key to the winner.' He tilted his head to the side and a slow smile spread across his lips. 'And what if we make this even more interesting by exchanging the information we already know about the diamond? You're a smart woman. I'm a smart man. Let's match wits.'

'You're a man. You possess the freedom to travel anywhere, at any time. You could leave here tonight and fetch the diamond, even if I might be the one who determines where it is before you. That hardly seems fair.'

It was as if he was seeing her on equal ground through his thick dark lashes. 'Forgive me. That hadn't occurred to me.' He tossed a lock of hair out of his eyes. 'What if we agree we cannot begin searching for the diamond until two o'clock tomorrow morning? That would allow you to leave this house under the cover of darkness as you did tonight.'

'I barely know you and I certainly don't trust you.'

'You have my word as a gentleman. I will tell you all I know and I will wait to search for it.'

While she would never call Hartwick a gentleman in the strict use of the term, he did surround himself with honourable men. And he hadn't managed to get himself barred from society. If anything, he was a man who seemed to be invited everywhere—except the households who had young, eligible daughters.

He stuck his hand out towards her. 'Gentlemen shake hands when they reach an agreement,' he explained needlessly.

She eyed it sceptically, knowing that hand had done more than shake hands with gentlemen. There were times she had seen that hand move seductively along a woman's back as they walked off a dance floor or strolled into a darkened garden. Not that she had paid that much attention to the Earl of Hartwick's actions this past year.

He glanced pointedly down at his hand.

'I am not a gentleman,' she replied, watching him step closer to her.

'But you do look fetching in trews.'

The playful tone to his voice was what she had become accustomed to. It was somehow comforting while she was fighting the fear of losing the diamond to him. If she knew that he had the stone, she might be able to find a way to steal it from him. She took his hand and gave it a firm shake.

A small smile curved his lips. He tried to kiss her hand, but she pulled it out of his warm grasp.

'Why don't you tell me what you know first?' she said, taking a seat at her dressing table.

He sat back on the edge of her bed and laughed softly. 'Do you always need to set the terms or is that something you just do with me?'

It was something he brought out in her. Whenever he was about, she felt this urge to prove to him she wasn't like the other women of his acquaintance. She was different. She was smarter and she liked to remind him she could see through his false pretences. 'I don't know what you mean.'

'I doubt that. I'm wondering if I can trust you, Miss Forrester. I fear I shall reveal all my secrets and you will hold back some of yours, giving you the advantage. I'm wondering if this agreement is indeed wise. Perhaps you should go first. What do you know about this diamond that has you dressing in men's clothing and breaking into buildings?'

She didn't know much. If she said so after he revealed what he knew, he probably wouldn't believe her. That notion wasn't sitting well with her. She shouldn't care what he thought. 'I honestly don't have much to tell. I know it's a valuable diamond of substantial size that is yellow. That is it.'

His brow furrowed and he leaned forward, resting his forearms on his knees. 'That is all? Aren't you aware of its history? Don't you know what makes this diamond so special?'

Slowly she shook her head, hating that he apparently knew more about the diamond than she did. 'What do you know?'

Those appraising eyes studied her before an arrogant smile turned his lips. 'The diamond is known as the Sancy and it's part of the missing French crown jewels. The bracelet was created by a man named Guillot, who is believed to have stolen the necklace the diamond was set in during the French Revolution. He had the bracelet designed in England as a treasure map of sorts for himself and his partner so they would be able to locate the stone after he hid it. Guillot was found murdered, and his landlord took his possessions and sold them to pay his debts. The bracelet was lost for years until it resurfaced recently and found its way to Rundell & Bridge, where it was sold to Lord Everill.'

She leaned forward. 'What of Guillot's partner?'

'His partner returned to France and was arrested on a charge of robbery. Among his papers, French officials found a letter from Guillot with details about the bracelet. You know none of this?'

She shook her head.

'And yet you knew this bracelet would lead you to a very valuable diamond. How?'

'I was told so.'

'By whom?'

If she knew that, she might not need to find the diamond in the first place. She could break into their residence and retrieve the letter condemning her brother as a traitor. 'I'd rather not say.'

He studied her intently. 'There are easier ways to pay for footwear.'

'I will remember that the next time I am tempted to purchase a pair.'

He grinned an infectious smile and held out his hand for the bracelet. She dropped it into his open palm.

'All I know is that this bracelet is the only clue to the stone,' she said, crossing her arms. 'We have two keys and nothing else. So where is the stone?'

He shook his head. 'Obviously we are missing something, but I cannot begin to fathom what.'

The sound of footsteps coming down the hallway broke the silence, and for the first time Sarah noticed streaks of sunlight painting the sky pink. 'Give me my key, please. Neither of us is any closer to finding the diamond than we were at the beginning of this discussion.'

He stood so they were toe to toe and looked into her eyes as if he hadn't heard the footsteps or noticed the changing of the sky—as if they had all the time in the world to stand there facing one another, alone in her room. He ran his hand down her arm until he came to her hand. He raised it to his lips and placed a kiss on her palm before sliding the key into it. The hairs on her arm stood up.

'Thank you for sharing what you know with me.'

The warmth from his lips still danced around her hand, making it tingle. It took her a minute to realise he had said something.

He leaned down and his breath created warm puffs of air in the hollow of her ear. 'You are an impressive woman, Miss Forrester.'

There was a slow touch of his lips against the shell of her ear, the heat of which spread throughout her body. Before she was able to respond, he sauntered past her to the door to her balcony. 'If you find you need to reach me because you found the diamond, send word. I live at Albany on Piccadilly.'

She knew of the building housing London's most elite bachelors and she had already known it was his residence. Katrina must have mentioned it at one time. Why she chose to remember that small detail about him was surprising. And why a rake like Hartwick would live in a building where women were not allowed to cross the threshold was even more perplexing.

He turned to her before climbing over the railing. 'Or better yet, will you be at the Skeffingtons' ball tomorrow?'

'Yes, I'll be there.'

'We should reconvene then to see if one of us has determined where the diamond is located. Perhaps one of us will claim victory tomorrow.'

The early-morning air was cool as he made his way smoothly down the trellis. It was a good thing for him he had a lean, athletic build. If he were a large man, the wooden structure might not have supported him. When he reached the bottom, he looked up at her and tipped his head to bid her farewell. Then he disappeared in the shadows of the back garden and she didn't see him again until he managed to hoist himself onto the stone wall and slide over it into the mews behind her house. Leaning against the door frame, she should have been thinking about all the information he had given her. Instead she was thinking of the feel of his mouth on her palm and wondering what it would have felt like if he had kissed her.

Chapter Nine

Hart walked along the mews on his way home and tipped his hat at the iceman driving his cart along the cobblestones. He had almost kissed her! He was always impulsive. He always did what he wanted. And tonight he had wanted to kiss Sarah Forrester—desperately. But he had no notion if she would welcome his advance or not. And then to what end?

From the moment she sat beside him on her bed, looking tempting in her nightclothes, he had wanted to take her and not stop until they were both spent. And then, when they were too exhausted to move, he'd fall asleep holding her in his arms.

Hart rubbed his eyes. It must be later than he thought. He never slept with anyone. One of the advantages of bedding married women was that they never asked him to stay till morning and he preferred it that way. It was much too intimate. And any woman who tried to sneak into his rooms with the idea of sex and sleeping with him would not be successful getting past the porters that manned the door at Albany. A number of London ladies had found that out. Living in a residence that did not allow women on the premises had been a brilliant move on his part.

Until now—now he wished Miss Forrester would sneak into his rooms wearing those trews she owned that showed her shapely legs. He wanted to know what she wore under that pale yellow dressing gown of hers. He'd seen traces of white linen peeking out near her ankles. How sheer was the linen? And what did she look like all rumpled in the morning with sunlight streaming on her soft skin.

He needed to stop focusing on the temptress and refocus his thoughts back on the diamond. It wasn't long before he was strolling past the porters and up the stairs to his set of rooms. He walked in to find Chomersley asleep on his sofa. No matter how many times he told his valet not to wait up for him, Hart always found him in his drawing room, sometimes asleep, sometimes awake.

He took a blanket from his bedchamber and covered Chomersley before going into his study to look over Lady Everill's bracelet for the hundredth time. The existence of two different keys made no sense. What could they open? It was becoming difficult to keep his eyes open. The night had been long and more eventful than he anticipated when it began.

Crawling into his bed, his thoughts turned to Miss Forrester and her dressing gown.

Hart entered the Skeffingtons' ballroom and wondered if Miss Forrester had found another clue that led to the location of the diamond. He had spoken to Prinny earlier in the day. The Prince Regent had no new clues to offer. The Home Office hadn't uncovered anything as far as he knew. Even visiting the various inns in town where he would always hear rumblings about stolen property proved to be of no use.

He spotted Miss Forrester by the large wall of windows talking with Katrina. She looked quite fetching in a white gown with silver flowers embroidered near the neckline and scattered along the skirt. As she moved, the silver thread sparkled near the swell of her breasts, drawing his attention to her smooth, creamy skin. From what he could tell, she had lovely breasts. They fit her frame well. If only he could see them exposed to the evening air—preferably in his bed—preferably with her arching her back and crying out his name as he pounded into her. Over. And over.

Why couldn't she be a married woman interested in a tumble?

To those around her, she appeared the epitome of a lady at ease in her surroundings, but he could see those sharp eyes periodically scan the room. She was looking for him. The very notion that he was the man she was searching for was unsettlingly satisfying, which was not good—for either of them.

He tossed a lock of hair out of his eyes and stared up at the massive crystal chandelier that was responsible for making her sparkle. The only way he was going to find out if she was any closer to finding the diamond was to speak with her. If he asked her to dance, he could accomplish that without compromising her reputation. And honestly, how many people would notice she was the first unmarried woman he had danced with since Caroline almost ten years ago?

Of course, he assumed she would dance with him. It would be rather humbling if she turned him down. One of the best things about Miss Forrester was that he never knew what she would do. She was an attractive woman, so it was possible all her dances were already claimed. If they were, the idea of coaxing her into the library or any of the other rooms of the house did have a certain appeal.

'I am surprised to find you smiling after you paid so much for that horse of yours.'

Without turning, he knew his father had approached his side. There was no need to face the man as they stood shoulder to shoulder. They wouldn't be talking for long.

Hart diverted his attention away from Miss Forrester and settled his gaze on a gown near her, trying not to give his father any indication who the minx was that put a smile on his face. Although his eyes were fixed on the emerald gown, his complete attention was on the man next to him.

'The money I spent for that fine horse is of no concern to me. I have plenty.'

'Some day your money may run out. Then what will you do?'

'We both know that is not parental concern in your voice. Do not think you can convince me otherwise.'

'I wouldn't dream of it. You have not taken money from me since you left school, for which I should be grateful. I know you have done well with your stable of racehorses and I imagine there are other investments you have, but I am curious—should all that go away what would you do? Would you crawl back to me for help?'

If there was one thing in life Hart was certain of, it was that he would never crawl back to his father for anything. This man should have comforted him as a child when his mother died. He should have encouraged him and provided a supportive environment for him. Instead he had methodically taken away almost everything his son held dear.

Hart purposely relaxed his fingers. He was no longer a boy and he would never allow himself to get close to anyone, ensuring there would be no one in his life his father could manipulate into abandoning him.

His father took a sip from his glass. 'You and

Lyonsdale have always been close…like brothers, some would say. I suppose should you find yourself in dire straits, he would take you in.'

Julian had been the one constant in his life. They had known one another from the cradle. Hart always attributed his father's inability to harm their friendship to Julian's exalted title and fierce sense of loyalty. 'He has been more like family to me than you have ever been, therefore I suppose he would. However, I am resourceful enough that such a thing would never happen. Is that what you were trying to do? You want to bankrupt me, assuming I would beg you for help? I'd rather clean chimneys for my food.'

'I imagine you are too big for that now. Regardless of what you believe, I have no desire to provide for you financially ever again, even if the image of you on your knees would amuse me. I've given you enough in your life. You will not get handouts from me.'

'There are some men who would not view it as a handout if it were helping their own flesh and blood, but we talk in circles. What is it you came here to say? I'm certain there was a purpose behind this informative discussion.'

'I just wanted to remind you that we don't always get what it is we want in life. This last time I relinquished the animal to you, however next time I might not be so generous.'

'That horse cost me over seventeen hundred pounds. One would hardly call that generous of you. But rest assured, I could have outbid you even if you continued your game.' They stared at one another finally, eye to eye, and the cold, calculating depth of his father's brown eyes was another reminder to Hart that he would not miss the man when he perished.

His father turned and looked out across the room. 'She's rather enticing,' he said through a snide smile. 'I'd venture she would be a tasty morsel, wouldn't you say?'

'I have no idea to whom you are referring.'

'You can pretend indifference all you like, but I've noticed your interest in her—and not just on this occasion.'

Hart wasn't given a chance to reply before his father sauntered away.

Immediately, Hart's gaze darted to Miss Forrester, as if by some odd occurrence his father could harm her from all the way across a room simply with some words. There she stood talking with Katrina, oblivious to the man who had sized her up a bit too intimately. He'd be damned if he let any harm come to her at the hands of his father! She would not meet the same fate as Caroline. Of that, he would make certain.

Dammit! If he danced with her now, his father would know he was correct in his assumption about who had held Hart's interest. He would have to refocus his attention on the woman who stood behind her, to... Theodosia! He almost sighed out loud. They hadn't spoken to one another since he slipped out of her bedroom that rainy night over a week ago. While she was a lovely woman and not the type to demand his further attention after their tryst, he really had no desire to spend time with her now, except his father had given him little choice.

Hart always did what he wanted. There was no reason not to. However, tonight, for the first time, he would dance with one woman, while he really wanted to be holding another.

He was coming towards her. Sarah took a breath and tried to pretend she was not noticing every powerful step Hartwick took across the ballroom floor and all the female heads that turned to follow his progress. She tried not to notice how that lock of hair slid over his eye and how he tossed his head to move it aside. And how it slipped back down as he got closer to her. Katrina had said something, but she had no idea what it was. She hoped her smile was an appropriate response and Katrina hadn't revealed someone was gravely ill or had suffered some horrific accident.

Her body hummed with anticipation…until he strode right past her without so much as a glance and instead approached Lady Helmford, who was standing behind her.

He was the one who had suggested they meet this evening to discuss their progress in finding the diamond! He was the one who had suggested their wager! Did that man's passions ever stop long enough for his brain to function?

Her stomach did a queasy flip. What if he had decided he no longer needed her? What if he had found the diamond and didn't need both keys? The blackguard didn't even have the decency to tell her! She was breaking out into a cold sweat just thinking that he might be in possession of the stone.

She angled her ear towards him just as he asked Lady Helmford to dance. The only thing preventing her from tripping him as they walked past was the notion she might ruin her spectacular slippers embroidered with silver thread. He was fortunate she was a woman who appreciated fine footwear.

From the corner of her eye, she noticed a figure approach her little party. He was a well-made man probably in his fifties who had retained his good looks. His light brown hair was cropped very short, highlighting his strong bone structure. One thing that was impossible not to notice was the way he carried himself with confidence in his fine black evening clothes.

He gave them a deferential bow. 'Ladies.' His pleasant voice was deep and smooth, and Sarah tried to recall if she had ever seen him before.

She and Katrina were very close and she knew that slight squint of her friend's eyes meant she was not fond of the man. As he stood discussing the weather with Katrina, Sarah could tell she was avoiding introducing them. When it became apparent he would not leave without making her acquaintance, Katrina somewhat reluctantly introduced her to Lord Blackwood.

'Miss Forrester,' he said, tipping his head in greeting, 'I've wanted to make your acquaintance for some time.'

'Why is that, my lord?'

'Is it so unusual for a gentleman to seek out the introduction of a beautiful woman?'

Oh, lud, not another charmer!

'And I have an interest in America. I own a very successful shipping company and have a number of trade vessels that continually travel between our countries. My pockets are heavy with the generosity of your countrymen.'

Now she understood Katrina's reluctance to introduce them. Out of boredom she looked towards Hartwick and Lady Helmford, who were standing side by side at the edge of the dance floor. They appeared to be having an entertaining conversation. Didn't the woman realise she was just one of many in his long line of lovers?

'Would you care to dance, Miss Forrester?'

Her shoulders sagged. She hadn't been looking at the dance floor as a hint to get Lord Blackwood to ask her to dance. This was all Hartwick's fault! The last thing she wanted was to spend more time with the ridiculously rich man and his tales of how much he enjoyed fleecing her countrymen.

There was no mistaking the disapproving look Katrina gave her. But if she didn't accept his invitation, she would not be able to dance for the remainder of the evening. Most of the men who had reserved dances with her were rather nice. And perhaps this would show Hartwick she wasn't waiting around for him to find her.

She forced a smile on her face, ignored Katrina's glare and allowed him to escort her to the dance floor, where he stopped not far from Hartwick and Lady Helmford. Within moments the beginning strains of the quadrille drifted down from the balcony where the musicians were sitting and they separated in the movement of the dance.

'I understand you had not been on our shores prior to your father's appointment here.'

'Yes, this is my first time here.' She gazed past Lord Blackwood's shoulder, and her eyes met Hartwick's piercing blue ones before they both looked away.

'I imagine you had some trepidation, not knowing what to expect here,' Lord Blackwood said, pulling her attention back to him.

'My brother had travelled to England. I remembered how much he enjoyed his time here.' If she could have banged her head on his shoulder without making a spectacle of herself, she would have. It was frustrating to have moments when your mouth and mind did not work as one. Now was not the time to talk about Alexander with anyone.

'I see.' His brown eyes were studying her closely. 'I imagine London is vastly different from New York.'

'It is, although both are stimulating in their own ways.' There was no need to mention her family's estate was on Long Island, away from the bustle of the city. It might only provoke him to ask her more questions.

'And you also lived in Washington. I hope you were not there during the burning of the city. I imagine it was not a pleasant place to be.'

What a horrific thing to bring up during a dance. 'No, but I have friends who witnessed the destruction as they fled and lost much that night. You know quite a bit about me.'

'I told you I have been eager to make your acquaintance. I am sincere in my interest in you and when I am interested in something I give it my full attention.'

She felt as if she was being inspected like a bit of cloth, as though he couldn't decide if he wanted to use her for a coat or curtains. They were separated by the movement of the dance, and when they came back together she pasted on a smile even though his scrutiny was making her uncomfortable.

'You are an exceptional dancer,' he said, giving her a charming smile.

'And you, as well,' she replied to be polite.

She knew she should make an attempt to think of things to converse with him about, but there was something about the man that made her uneasy and she preferred to dance in silence than encourage further conversation.

When their dance ended he returned her to Katrina's side and bowed politely over her gloved hand. That attractive smile was on his lips once more as he bid her farewell and informed her that he would enjoy becoming better acquainted in the future.

Katrina eyed him as he retreated into the crowd. 'I wish you could have found some excuse not to dance with the man. I do not like him.'

'I really had no desire to sit out the remainder of my dances so I didn't have much of a choice, now did I?'

Before Katrina could respond, Sarah's mother and the Dowager joined them. The diamond tiara the Dowager wore in her hair sparkled like large dewdrops on a sunny day. The grey-haired woman's lips were pursed tightly and she did not look pleased in spite of the impressive jewels that capped her petite frame.

'Sarah,' her mother addressed her with concern in her eyes, 'try to avoid that man in the future. Her Grace has told me tales about him.'

'I assure you I have no intention of seeking him out.'

'See that you don't,' the Dowager stated. 'Lord Blackwood amuses himself in inappropriate ways. He is one to stir up trouble and then step back to watch.'

'Julian has told me things about him,' Katrina broke in, 'and has witnessed the man treat his son horribly.'

The Dowager looked away. 'I don't believe even Julian knows how horrible he has been.'

It was so frustrating to be left out of conversations. 'I don't understand. What son?'

Katrina opened her mouth to reply, but the Dowager jumped in. 'Hartwick will take Lord Blackwood's title when the man expires.'

Sarah looked over her shoulder in search of the man she danced with. 'Lord Blackwood is his father? But they look nothing alike.'

The Dowager's softened expression landed on Hartwick, who was across the room bidding farewell to Lady Helmford. 'He is the very image of his mother. She was a lovely woman. It's a pity she died so young.'

Sarah glanced at her mother, whose attention was fixed on her glass, not meeting anyone in the eye.

'I wasn't aware you knew his mother,' Katrina said, also studying Hartwick.

For all Sarah knew he could be walking around with the diamond in his pocket at that very moment, probably congratulating himself that he was smarter than she was. He would get no sympathy from her.

The Dowager let out a hacking cough, drawing the attention of those around them.

'Would you like me to fetch you some water?' Sarah asked with true concern.

The Dowager shook her head as the coughing began to subside. 'There is no need to fret. You all look as if you are expecting me to expire. When I do, I assure you it will be in a spectacular fashion. My dearest friend, the Duchess of Dunbarton, expired in the middle of Almack's ages ago after dancing with a crowned prince. People still talk about it to this day. That might be why Lord Hartwick never attends assemblies there.' She arched her brow and waited for a reaction.

Sarah was not going to take the bait. Unfortunately, Katrina did.

'What does that have to do with Hartwick?'

'She was his maternal grandmother. Our estates were neighbouring properties and we were very good friends. Hartwick was very close to her as a boy after his mother died. She was the only one who showed him any affection that I witnessed. I imagine being in a place where she took her last breath would be painful for him.'

Sarah refused to feel sorry for him. She simply refused.

'When did his mother die?' The words were out of her mouth before she could stop them.

'When he was about seven. Such a tragedy. To her, the moon and sun set just for him. One windy day she fell from a cliff on their estate and was killed on the rocks below. Poor boy was devastated. Didn't speak for weeks. I don't think he ever got over her death. I don't think one ever completely does from the loss of a parent when one is so young.'

'Or the loss of a child,' Sarah's mother muttered.

'This is true,' the Dowager agreed. A sense of

melancholy hung in the air before she seemed to recall her story. 'Lord Blackwood did nothing to help his son.'

'Perhaps Lord Blackwood did not know how to help his son grieve? Or he was grieving himself,' Sarah offered, knowing very well how difficult it could be to stand by helplessly and watch those around you suffer through their grief.

The Dowager looked her directly in the eye. 'Lord Blackwood couldn't care one wit for his son's grief or that he lost his wife.'

Sarah rubbed the back of her neck, flattening out the hair that stood up with the Dowager's comment. She scanned the ballroom for father and son, but saw neither.

During the carriage ride home, Sarah was so convinced Hartwick had found the diamond that she wanted to toss up her accounts. He'd had numerous opportunities to speak with her this evening and hadn't taken one of them. Obviously he no longer needed her key. She would not allow him to toss their wager aside. If he found the diamond, he should have the decency to tell her. Then she could devise a plan to steal it from him.

It was a mystery why he even wanted the diamond. From what she observed, he appeared to be a very wealthy man. Was the diamond another impressive item he wanted to collect? He owned a fine stable of racehorses, had affairs with beautiful women and now he would have a large yellow diamond that was probably worth a small fortune. But perhaps he had large debts she knew nothing about. He certainly had secrets. Didn't everyone?

When they entered the house, her mother rubbed her forehead and informed her that she was heading to bed. The discussion of death tonight had scratched at the grief that was still but newly healed. Her mother would need some time alone before she would return to herself again.

There was little chance of Sarah falling asleep unless she found something to settle her mind. A good book might help. They kept the family's collection of books in her father's study. From the thin band of light streaming out from under the door, she knew he was still awake.

She gave a soft knock and walked inside when his muffled voice bid her to enter. He was seated at his desk, where he was huddled over some official looking document. 'How was the ball?'

'It was lovely. They all are,' she said with a shrug.

He gave a low chuckle. 'Now I know you are tired if you expect me to believe that.'

That small tease made her smile—the first one since she realised Hartwick had left the ball without seeking her out. 'Are you still working?' she asked, approaching his desk.

He pinched the bridge of his nose and looked like he was trying to stay awake. 'I thought I'd finish making some notes before I retire for the night. And you? What brings you in here?'

'I thought I'd get a book to read before I fall asleep.'

'If you'd like to fall asleep, I can give you some of my paperwork. I find I need coffee to slog through the latest batch of correspondence from Washington.'

She smiled at his jest before she couldn't help glancing at the empty silver tray.

'Your brother would often read when he found he could not sleep,' her father remembered. 'I often wondered how many times Alexander would find it necessary to reread the books he took with him on his voyages.' He had a faraway look in his eyes and a sad smile. As if recalling where he was, he turned to Sarah. 'I imagine the men traded books aboard the ships. Wouldn't you think?'

'I imagine so,' she said, trying to offer a comforting smile. Alexander would often sit with her on her bed when they were children and read to her on stormy nights. It was as if he knew she had trouble sleeping when she had to lie there alone, listening to the cracking and booming of the sky.

'Were you surprised he wanted to go to sea?' she asked, running her finger along the polished surface of his desk.

He shook his head. 'He always loved the ocean. Even as a very young boy, I would take him to see the ships in the harbour.'

'I remember when he went to sea for the first time. Mama cried so much. I expected her to beg him to stay.'

'It would have been easier on her...on both of us really, if he had remained close to home, but his interest was elsewhere. What kind of father would I be if I prevented him from pursuing what he loved? And we know his time at sea was important. The people of Baltimore were saved that night by men like your brother—men who were willing to sacrifice their own lives for the safety of others.'

She wanted to tell him the truth. But she couldn't find the words. And anyway, his heart was weak and they had almost lost him when he was grieving over Alexander. Was he strong enough to withstand the truth?

She moved beside him and kissed the top of his head. His soft hair tickled her nose. 'You have always been—and continue to be—the finest of fathers. Do not ever forget that.'

Grief was still there in his eyes and probably always would be to some extent. They said one never completely moved past the death of a child. Even if that child had been a man when he died.

She would find a way to steal that diamond from Hartwick. Her father and mother would never learn of Alexander's betrayal. It was her duty to make certain of that.

Chapter Ten

Hart stood in the back garden of the Forresters' town house and eyed the trellis that led to Miss Forrester's bedchamber. The windows of her room were still dark. What was taking her so long to return home?

A light was on in the lower left corner of the house, illuminating the small terrace about twenty feet from where he stood in the shadows on the grass. Knowing most of these town houses were laid out in a near-identical fashion, he assumed it was Mr Forrester's study. The man needed to hire himself another aide-de-camp if he was working this late into the night.

There was no sense in continuing to wait where he was when he could just as well make himself comfortable in her room. He had climbed about six feet off the ground when the distinct sound of someone clearing their throat came from behind him. He froze. Closing his eyes in exasperation, he jumped to the ground. When he turned his eyebrows rose at the sight of Miss Forrester, dressed in her fine gown, with moonlight shining off the silver lady's pocket pistol pointed at his chest.

Would this woman ever do anything predictable?

She tilted her head and recognition lit her eyes. 'What do you think you're doing?' she whispered harshly.

'I would think no explanation was necessary. I was on my way to your bedchamber when you rudely interrupted me.'

'Rudely interrupted you? You have no place in my bedchamber or in my garden for that matter.'

'Oh, I disagree. You and I have matters to discuss away from prying eyes.'

'Shall I call on my father to give us his opinion? He is just over there,' she said, tipping her head towards the terrace while she continued to point the pistol at him.

'You won't call for him and risk me informing him about your habit of donning men's attire and traipsing about London at night. In addition, I doubt you want to be forced to wed.'

'Wed? To you? Don't be absurd. My father knows I would never consent to marry an Englishman and he wouldn't force me to marry you. He might, however, choose to use this gun on you himself.'

'About that gun—don't you think it's time you put it away, now that you know it's only me attempting to scale the battlements of your castle?'

She chewed on her lip as if she truly couldn't decide if she wanted to shoot him or not. Finally, she lowered the gun and stepped closer, pulling him further into the shadows along the building. 'You said we would speak during the Skeffingtons' ball about the diamond. Instead you ignored me and danced with Lady Helmford. What makes you think I want to talk with you now?'

It was difficult not to smirk. 'You noticed I was dancing with Lady Helmford.'

'Do not flatter yourself. There is no reason for me to be jealous of Lady Helmford.'

'She was in my arms.'

'Being in your arms is the furthest thing from my mind.'

'You're staring at my lips.'

'I'm trying to read them in the dark.'

'The sound of my voice is not sufficient for you to know what I'm saying?'

'Oh, do hush before I decide to pull that pistol out of my pocket.'

'Why do you carry a pistol and wherever did you acquire one?'

'My father gave it to me prior to boarding the ship that brought us here. He was concerned for my safety. And I carry it with me because I am trying to locate a rather large diamond. One never knows who one will encounter while doing so.'

'Have you managed to locate it?'

Her eyes narrowed slightly. 'No, I assumed you had found it when you didn't approach me tonight.'

That was a relief. 'My enquiries have brought no new information to light.'

It was difficult to determine if she believed him, which was odd. Miss Forrester was usually very easy to read, but there was something about her demeanour. A sense of dread crept along his skin. 'What did Lord Blackwood say to you tonight?'

'I don't see how that is any of your concern. I did not ask what you and Lady Helmford discussed.' She held up her hand as if to stop him. 'And before you tell me, I really don't want to know.'

'I know the true measure of the man. That is why I am enquiring.'

There was a distinct pause. She was considering what she would say to him, which was nothing like the impetuous Miss Forrester he knew. 'We spoke of nothing, as one does during a dance.'

'He is a man who enjoys manipulating those around him. Do not allow his easy manner to fool you. He is dangerous and ruthless in getting what he wants.'

If he had warned Caroline about his father, things might have turned out differently for both of them. He would not make that same mistake with Miss Forrester. With her, he would do everything he could to protect her. He needed her and her key to get the diamond.

'This may sound melodramatic to you,' he said, 'but I strongly urge you to stay away from him. He has no morals and is not the type of man an unmarried woman should have any association with.'

She crossed her arms. 'Some might say the same about you.'

'They might, but it wouldn't be entirely true.'

'You are trying to tell me you have morals?'

'It might surprise you to find out I do have

some. If I didn't, it would be very easy for me push you against this wall and kiss those pouty lips of yours.'

The sash of the window of her father's study closest to them lifted and she went to put her hand over his lips.

'If you put your hand over my mouth to hush me, I will lick you,' he whispered.

Her hand froze mere inches from his lips.

'I can very easily speak in hushed tones, Miss Forrester. You, on the other hand, have a tendency to become rather lively at times. I will make this brief. I propose we continue with our wager until one of us finds the diamond. Do you agree?'

'I agree. Should you locate the diamond, pass a note to Katrina for me and I will pass her a note for you should I find it first. I think she is our best option for communicating with one another.'

She was right. It would be too risky for Miss Forrester to use one of her own servants. And he regularly visited Lyonsdale House so his presence would not be remarked upon. Katrina was discreet and knew what mischief her friend was up to.

'Does Julian know about your clandestine activities?'

The chestnut-coloured tendrils at her neck

swished from side to side, skimming her skin as she shook her head. 'I have asked her not to tell him.'

'But yet she is aware of my interest in the diamond.'

'No, I have not told her yet. However, I assure you, she can keep a secret.'

No one should know he was looking for the Sancy. Hell, he hadn't even told Andrew and he had helped him steal the bracelet! He rubbed his eyes.

'She will not breathe a word of this. I can assure you of that.'

'I hope you are right.'

He should leave. There was nothing left to discuss. And yet he couldn't walk away. She was stirring something inside him—something more than wanting to take her right there in the darkened garden against the wall of her house—although that thought had merit. He refused to mull over what it was. Instead he decided to kiss her.

As he took a step closer, she took one back. 'I should go inside. I'm ruining my slippers by standing in the grass with you.'

'I'm certain you have other pairs.' He took another step.

Their bodies were almost touching. If she decided to retreat it would place them in plain view of her father's occupied study. She held her ground and reflexively licked those irresistible lips.

He ran his fingers through his hair. 'I need to kiss you.'

'You've never needed to kiss me before.'

'This is the first time I've mentioned it.' He skimmed the tips of his fingers across hers, needing to touch her in even the smallest way.

There was a catch in her breath.

When he lowered his head, she didn't move away. Her faint lilac scent drifted towards him as he leaned forward and kissed her. It was a slow and savouring kiss that made the rest of the world fade away.

He had imagined what it would feel like to kiss her. But now that he knew the taste of her lips, the way the soft, plump skin felt between his teeth as he nipped at them, Hart realised kissing Miss Sarah Forrester was not something he would easily forget.

He tugged her closer to deepen the kiss. Her breasts pillowed against his chest and he knew if he was thrusting inside her this is how they would feel. He was getting hard.

With her prickly nature he thought she might step on his foot, but instead she trailed her fingers up his back and cupped his neck as if she didn't want him to stop.

Miss Forrester was kissing him back—the same Miss Forrester who loved to remind him that she did not find him the least bit attractive or charming. And while he always liked kissing women, she elevated the experience to an entirely different level of enjoyment.

He skimmed his fingers up the faint ripples of her ribcage and palmed her right breast. Urgently he trailed kisses along her jaw and down her neck to the upper swell of her breast. Dragging his tongue along the neckline of her gown, he savoured the slight saltiness of her skin. Her breathing was erratic and her fingers gripped the back of his hair.

He tried to lower the neckline but it wouldn't budge. He wanted to tear the silk apart and suck hard on that nipple that he knew must be straining against her stays needing his touch. Frustrated, he kissed back up her neck and finally to those full, parted lips—lips that he was envisioning doing wicked things to his body. He was claiming her with his kisses, because he couldn't do it any other way.

A soft moan escaped her lips. He was not the only one who was desperate to know what it would feel like to thrust himself inside her over and over. She wanted him. She might deny it, but he knew the truth. That was why he had kissed her. That was what he had needed to know.

He smiled against her lips.

She stepped on his foot.

Chapter Eleven

Sarah had often wondered what Hartwick's kisses would feel like. Now that she knew, she wished she had remained ignorant. He kissed like a man who knew her body even better than she did.

She wasn't prepared for the way he made her feel. He kissed much better than the two other men who she had allowed the privilege of kissing her. Each time his tongue glided across her own, it sent shivers up and down her spine. Her breasts felt fuller and tighter as if they were straining to remain in her stays. And, as if by some kind of magic, his hands brought a tingling feeling between her legs even though they had not been below her waist.

He made her feel incredibly desirable. She wanted it to go on all night.

Until the bounder had the nerve to smile while he kissed her.

That smile brought her back to reality. He had done all of this to prove that she wanted him, just like all the other women in London—and she had. Stepping on his foot gave her a bit of satisfaction and helped return her sense of dignity.

When he pulled his head back, that small smile was still on those skilful lips. 'I thought you might do that.'

'Kiss you? Let's clarify, *you* kissed *me*.'

'I was referring to stepping on my foot. And to clarify—you kissed me back.'

Lord Hartwick really was the most arrogant man she had ever met. 'Stop being so uppity.'

A small, low laugh was his response. 'You must admit, that was one fine kiss...or kisses, if you want to be exact. I'll be reliving the experience for quite some time.'

'Doesn't it become tedious repeating the same statements over and over to the women you know?'

His brow wrinkled and he jerked his head back. 'I've never said that to anyone before and I confess, it leaves me wondering if it would be best to avoid you entirely in the future. You, Miss Forrester, are a danger to a confirmed bachelor like myself.'

There was sincerity in his eyes. Something she hadn't expected.

'You should go,' she said, crossing her arms to create some distance between them.

His eyes never left hers and she had the distinct impression he was envisioning what he wanted to do to her at that very moment. It was getting hard to breathe and she could not tear her gaze away from his seductive blue eyes.

'I'm going to kiss you again,' he whispered.

'I think that would be best.'

Oh, she was in trouble now. That kiss was even better than the first.

The next day, Sarah strolled with Katrina on the pathway that ran alongside Rotten Row, well before the fashionable crowds descended on Hyde Park. There had to be a way to bring up Hartwick without sounding like a love-struck girl. Which she wasn't. What woman with any brain would allow herself to fall for the likes of Hartwick?

'For someone who called on me and was eager to go on this walk, you're unusually quiet.' Before Sarah could think of a response, Katrina pulled

her back by the arm. 'Has your father been con-
tacted?' she asked with concern in her voice.

It was a simple question, but it filled her stomach with butterflies. She needed to stop thinking
about that impertinent man whose kisses left her
breathless and concentrate on finding that blasted
diamond! Her family needed her and she needed
to put them first. 'No, no other letter has arrived.'

Relief washed across Katrina's expression as
they resumed walking. 'You said Hartwick was
the man who found the clue under the bridge. Are
you worried he might have found the diamond?'

'No, I'm not worried and after speaking with
him last night, I do not think he's any closer to
solving this puzzle than I am.'

'Last night? When last night? Not once did I see
him in your company and you left before I did.'

'He slipped into my garden after the ball so we
could speak. He wanted to know if I had found
the diamond and he wanted to be certain I was
interested in continuing with our wager until one
of us finds the diamond.'

'And you're not sure you want to do that?'

She wasn't sure she wanted to be anywhere
near the likes of Lord Hartwick in the future, but
she didn't have much of a choice. 'No, I do want

to continue the wager. I think it's wise to be informed of his actions.'

'Why do I have the distinct impression you are not telling me everything that occurred between you and Hartwick last night?'

Was she truly that transparent? Over the last year she had voiced her contempt to Katrina about the women who foolishly fell over each other to catch his eye. She had always said *she* would never consider a man like him. The man she would fall in love with would be utterly and completely devoted to her and her alone. Not that she thought there was the slightest chance she would fall in love with the Earl of Hartwick. She never would. But it was still embarrassing to admit she had let him kiss her—more than once!

She looked down at her Pomona green half-boots peeping out from her skirt with every step. 'Hartwick and I kissed.'

Katrina stopped walking. There was no sense in stopping, as well. Katrina would catch up.

Within minutes she was back at Sarah's side. 'How? I always knew you found him attractive, but… How?'

'I believe you know how it is done. More important, I do not find Hartwick attractive. I have always found him to be the most insufferable, arrogant man who has ever lived.'

'The lady doth protest too much.'

'Shakespeare? You are using a quote of Mr Shakespeare's when we are discussing Hartwick? I'd wager the man can barely read.'

Katrina arched a sceptical brow.

'I am simply stating my opinion of him.'

'I see. And after all this time knowing him, and disliking him, what prompted you to kiss him?'

Sarah fisted her hands at her side. 'He kissed me,' she stated firmly.

'Why am I not surprised? I imagine you slapped him.'

Sarah chewed her lip. 'Not exactly.'

'What exactly did you do?'

'I kissed him back.'

A roar of laughter came out of her graceful friend. 'Why? You just said you think he is insufferable and arrogant.'

'Because he kisses very well,' Sarah admitted with her jaw clenched.

Katrina laughed again, covering her mouth as she tried to stop.

'I'm glad I can serve as amusement for you.'

'Oh, don't be so peevish. It was just a kiss. You

were the one who told me I should kiss Julian to see what it felt like. You've kissed other men. Certainly Hartwick's kisses aren't *that* good.'

Sarah had no idea what her expression revealed, but it sent Katrina into a fit of laughter all over again. When she finally stopped laughing, her friend pressed her fingers to her lips. 'Oh, dear, they were, weren't they?'

Sarah rubbed her brow as if she could scrub away the image of Hartwick kissing her goodbye one final time. 'I need to find a way to stop thinking about kissing him. What did you do when Julian had you all flustered like this?'

Katrina shrugged. 'I kept thinking about him. I honestly liked recalling his kisses.'

'But I have a diamond to find and that man and his kisses are not letting me do that,' she stated in complete frustration.

'Tell me about the other men you've kissed. Perhaps if you give them more consideration, you'll see there is nothing extraordinary about Hartwick.'

It was worth a try.

'Well, when I was sixteen my father employed a groom by the name of Jerome. He was a few years older than me and quite handsome—the kind of man you could admire while you watched him split firewood. I would often go riding just to have him hold my hand as I stepped on the mounting block. One evening when I was walking through the fields, I found him lying in the grass and watching the clouds drift by. We talked for a time and, just as the sun began to set and the sky turned pink, he kissed me.'

'That sounds like a lovely first kiss.'

'It was. He was. It left me breathless. But shortly after that, he left our home to return to his family near Philadelphia. I think he was worried my father would find out. I was very sad when he left, but I was so young.'

'Anyone else?'

Sarah looked away. 'I might have kissed Mr Merriweather.'

'John Merriweather?' Katrina sputtered. 'Your father's aide-de-camp?'

'That's the one.'

'But John Merriweather is so…so…boring.'

'Yes, well, his kisses were, too.'

'What possessed you…?'

'You know I have no wish to marry an Englishman and settle here. I thought perhaps if he kissed well enough, I might consider encouraging his attention. If I married him, I would certainly settle close to my parents.'

Katrina looked like she was holding in a smile. 'John Merriweather?'

Sarah waved her off. 'It was shortly after your wedding. I must have been overtaken with the romance of it all.'

'Anyone else?'

'No, that is all of them.'

'Do you feel any better?'

'Not in the least,' she replied with a sigh.

'Maybe you're thinking about Hartwick and his kisses because finding the diamond is proving to be too difficult.'

That was completely logical, and Sarah was holding on to that notion as hard as she could.

They continued walking, both lost in their own thoughts, until Katrina spotted Lady Holt and Miss Winthrop walking towards them. She had recently become friends with the widow and her companion when she had discovered they had similar literary interests. Although Sarah liked the two women, making polite conversation with new acquaintances was not something she thought her brain could do at the moment. So when Katrina suggested they join them for a bit, Sarah begged off and walked to the iron rail that edged the bridle path.

She stared out at the few riders and carriages with unseeing eyes, knowing she was a fool for wondering if Hartwick was thinking at all about the time she had spent in his arms. A shadow fell upon her. The seated figure of a man on a large stallion loomed from above.

'Miss Forrester,' drawled Lord Blackwood with a tip of his hat, 'what a lovely surprise finding you here. May I say you look stunning in primrose?'

He should have waited for her to acknowledge him before approaching. It appeared Lord Blackwood thought he was above the rules of civilised behaviour.

'Forgive me, my lord, I had not noticed you on the bridle path.'

He smiled at her subtle poke at his lack of propriety as sunlight bounced off the gold buttons on his blue coat. Everything about his appearance, from the clothes he wore, to the shiny top boots on his feet, to his fine black Arabian horse, spoke of money. 'Well, it appears I'm not the only one to flout convention. There is the matter of your solitary walk in the park,' he countered. 'But I confess, I do adore a woman who does as she wishes.'

'But as you can see, I'm not alone,' Sarah said, looking over her shoulder to where Katrina stood talking with her friends.

'Ah, I see. I should have known you would be with Her Grace. The two of you are quite dear to one another.'

What a keen observation from a man she had just met the night before. 'We are.'

'Were your families very friendly in New York?'

Her eyes narrowed. 'No, we lived in two different parts of the state.'

She felt the strongest urge to redirect the conversation away from her. 'Do you typically ride here at this hour? I would assume you would be busy with your business affairs.'

'I'm on my way to see a colleague of mine. I prefer travelling inside the park. The views are infinitely better here.'

The smile that slid across his lips made the hair on the back of her neck stand up, but she smiled politely, not letting him see that he unnerved her.

'I wonder how many times you've said something similar to the women of this town.'

'Are you always this direct?'

'I see no reason not to be.'

He swung his leg around the back of his horse

and came to stand inordinately close to her, holding the reins to his beast. Every nerve in her body pricked to attention, although she did find comfort in the iron rail between them.

'I find Americans so delightfully unpredictable.'

'Do you know many Americans?'

'A fair number, but you outshine them all.'

Sarah wanted to roll her eyes.

He tipped the brim of his hat, shading his eyes from the sun. 'Perhaps you would do me the honour of allowing me to escort you on a drive through the park so we can further our acquaintance.'

Whatever had she done to make him think she wanted to spend more time with him? 'I'm aware what such an act would convey to society,' she said, feeling her brow wrinkling. 'I'm not willing to make that statement with a man I barely know.'

There was a twist to his lips as if he enjoyed a challenge. 'I look forward to trying to change your mind.' His gaze travelled past her right shoulder.

Katrina approached Sarah's side, eyeing Lord Blackwood in the fashion befitting a duchess looking down on a marquess. He tipped his hat to her in a deferential greeting.

'Lord Blackwood,' she said, sounding as if she

would prefer not to have to address him. 'I hope you do not mind if I steal Miss Forrester away. The hour is growing late and we must return home.'

'But of course.' He hoisted himself easily onto his stallion and smiled down at Sarah. It was a pleasant smile, but there was something in his eyes she did not like. 'Ladies, I bid you good day.' He turned his horse around and kicked it into a gallop.

'I wish you would not converse with him,' Katrina said, eyeing his progress to the park's entrance.

'I didn't have much of a choice. He approached me before I even realised he was near.'

They walked back to Katrina's house, discussing the books Lady Holt and Miss Winthrop had recently enjoyed, which gave Sarah a reprieve from thinking about Hartwick or his father. But that reprieve was short-lived, because as they crossed the park in Grosvenor Square, Sarah spotted Hartwick's horse hitched to a post outside Katrina's home.

'Does a day go by when that man does not call on your husband?'

Katrina followed Sarah's gaze and smiled. 'He

is not in my home every day. Julian is the closest thing to family Hartwick has and it's beginning to feel as if he has become my brother.'

'Do not wish that on yourself. The man is a nuisance.'

'Says the woman who kissed him.'

Sarah nudged her shoulder into Katrina.

'If his horse is outside, it means he is here for only a brief visit.' Katrina eyed the animal as they walked closer to her home. 'What did his father have to say to you?'

'Just flattery nonsense and he asked if I'd care to go for a drive with him in the park.'

Reynolds opened the door for them before Katrina even knocked.

Katrina dismissed him with their bonnets and gloves before giving Sarah a pointed stare as they stood in the deserted marble entrance hall. 'Tell me you will not be doing anything so foolish.'

'Why does it not surprise me that statement is addressed to Miss Forrester?' Hartwick drawled, sauntering down the hall with a smug smile, his black coattails fluttering behind him. His eyes travelled over Sarah's body much too slowly, making her tingle inside.

'Skulking about, I see,' she commented in what she hoped was a bored tone.

'It's one of my many talents. Shall I tell you about the others?'

'I think I know all I care to about you.'

Katrina watched the two of them and shuffled restlessly. It must be time for her to nurse Augusta again.

'Go, Katrina,' Sarah prodded. 'I'll find a way to occupy myself.'

Her friend appeared hesitant to leave them alone. Sarah realised she might be unwilling to leave them alone after Sarah's admission in the park and she felt a warm flush spread across her cheeks.

'Very well, I won't be long.'

Hart smiled at her friend as she climbed the stairs. The moment Katrina was out of sight, he turned and licked his top lip.

'Do you even know how to be subtle? Everyone will know we kissed if you continue to behave like that,' Sarah exclaimed.

'Like what? That is how I always behave. And do you really expect me to believe you did not tell Katrina about last night.'

'I don't know what you mean.'

'She knows what happened between us in your garden. I could tell the minute she hesitated about leaving us alone. I never took you as one to kiss and tell.'

Sarah crossed her arms, feeling uncomfortable for the first time about confiding in Katrina. 'And you expect me to believe you do not talk about the women you kiss. All of London knows who you've been kissing.'

He gave her his most charming smile. 'No, they don't. I assure you, if they did they'd be quite surprised. I can keep a secret when necessary.'

'You won't tell Lyonsdale?'

'God, no, he'd be dragging us both to the church, convinced the evening did not end so innocently. Since neither of us want that, I don't intend for him to find out.' He stepped closer, the scent of leather and cinnamon drifted in the air, reminding her of being in his arms last night. 'What happened between you and me, Miss Forrester, should remain our secret.'

Her mouth went dry at the thought of kissing him again and she wet her top lip. His gaze rested on her mouth.

'I've thought about last night,' he said in a low

voice, stepping closer. 'I wish I could kiss you right here.'

'Here in the hall or here on my lips?'

'Are there other parts of your person you'd like me to kiss? I find I'm rather agreeable to the idea.'

'One kiss was enough, Hartwick.'

'It was not one kiss and I think we both know it will never be enough, Miss Forrester.' He took a loose tendril of hair and tucked it behind her ear, caressing the shell with his fingertips before lowering his hand.

The gesture sent a ripple of awareness through her body. 'Behave.'

'This is me behaving. If I weren't, I'd be dragging you to that alcove, pushing you against the wall and kissing you senseless.'

'Why do you assume *you'd* be the one making *me* senseless? I might surprise you.'

'I'd love to see you try. Shall we?' He arched a brow and with a teasing smile took a step towards the alcove under the stairs.

Why was it so difficult to resist his challenges, even when he was teasing? However, instead of the alcove, she grabbed his hand and pulled a surprised Lord Hartwick into the small yellow drawing room to their right.

'You know, you're quickly becoming my favourite person in the entire world,' he said with a grin, while he watched her quietly close the door behind them.

'I could say the same about you.'

'You could?'

'I'll let you know after this.' She grabbed the lapels of his coat and crushed her lips to his, kissing him as if it would be their last—which it would be. They couldn't continue to keep kissing. But he did it so well!

His mouth was hot and there was a faint taste of brandy on his tongue. She spun them around and pushed his back against the door. The kiss was unapologetic and demanding. And from the moan that left his lips and filled her mouth, it was affecting him just as strongly as it was affecting her.

She tugged his coat off his shoulders and he quickly shrugged out of it, all the while never breaking their kiss. His fingers dipped into the lace neckline of her gown and yanked it down. When he was able to raise her breasts out of her stays, he broke the kiss and let out a sigh.

He lowered his head to her chest and trailed his tongue down and around her nipple before taking it into his hot mouth. The sensation of him sucking on her was like nothing she had ever felt before. As she dug her fingers into the hard muscles of his arms, she could feel those muscles flex through his linen shirt. At some point he must have spun them around, because now the door was at her back, and she was thankful to have something to lean on.

'I wanted to do this last night,' he said, kissing his way to her other breast while his hand caressed the outside of her thigh through her gown.

'Why didn't you?'

'Your damn dress was too tight.'

Never again in her life would she wear a dress with a bodice that was so well fitted. With every suck on her nipple there was a pull between her legs, as if they were connected by an invisible thread inside her. She wanted to take her hand and rub between her legs to stop that tingling sensation, but she was afraid he would notice.

Suddenly Hartwick was caressing the inside of her thigh. The inside! How had he got his hand there without her even realising it? The pads of his fingers traced circles towards the area that was making her so restless. The first time his fingers slid across her, she jumped from the unusual sensation. But the second time, her hips followed his movement and she wanted to tell him to do it again.

'Damn, you're so wet,' he groaned against her breast.

Her face heated with embarrassment. She tried to push his hand away. 'Sorry.'

He wouldn't let her. Instead he moved his mouth to her ear and slid a finger deep inside her, making her moan. 'Don't ever apologise for that. I want you wet.' He inserted a second finger and began to thrust them in and out of her while he nipped at her neck. The sensation had her grinding herself against his hand. It was as if he knew her body better than she did.

'Tell me how it feels,' he whispered in her ear.

He wanted her to form words? Now? She was having trouble recalling her name. 'Incredible,' she groaned, closing her eyes.

He trailed his hot tongue along the shell of her ear. 'You are so tight.' He shifted his fingers inside her.

She wasn't sure what he did, but now she could barely breathe. It felt as if she was on the edge of a precipice wanting to jump off.

'You're driving me mad. I've thought about this lying in bed at night.' He slipped his fingers out and began to stroke her slowly. 'I've imagined spreading those lovely legs of yours apart. My mouth is where my hand is and I'm dragging my tongue across you. Then while I'm licking you, I slide my fingers inside.' The minute he thrust his fingers back in, her legs began to tremble.

'I've thought about doing those things to you many times and do you know what I've done while I've imagined that?' he whispered into her ear.

She swallowed hard and shook her head, unable to speak as he worked his fingers.

'I've stroked myself to completion.'

He crushed his lips to hers, swallowing her cry of release as she broke apart in his arms. This was what her body was straining to do. And this was what he knew she needed.

Her eyes fluttered open as she pressed the back of her head into the door, needing something solid to bring her back from the cloud she felt she was drifting on.

He was watching her intently. 'I've tried to envision what you'd look like when you come countless times. You look even more beautiful than I imagined.'

That simple statement washed away any embarrassment she was feeling. She brushed his skilful lips with the tips of her fingers and he kissed them.

'I'm yearning to taste you,' he said, removing a handkerchief from his waistcoat pocket, 'but not from my fingers.'

'Are you always so bold with your speech?'

'I find with you I am. I hadn't intended to tell you any of that or do any of that.'

'Why did you?'

He took a deep breath and, with a creased brow, put on his coat. 'I have no idea.'

She fixed her skirt and watched him adjust his cuffs. After what happened between them, it was surprising she could look him in the eye. And yet she found it impossible to look away from him and his warm smile.

They had let their passions get the better of them. They couldn't let it happen again. 'We can't keep kissing. If we continue to do this, we are bound to get caught.'

He let out a long, resigned breath. 'You're right. It must be the last—the only—time we do that. And we should probably leave now before the

Dowager finds us,' he said before he froze and watched her adjust the bodice of her gown. 'You have no idea how badly I want to assist you with that.'

'If you keep talking that way, whoever sees us next is bound to know what we've been about.' She opened the door and peeked out into the empty hallway. It was safe for them to leave.

He rubbed his brow and followed her. 'Very well, why don't you tell me about what you and Katrina were discussing when you arrived. But I beg of you, do not tell me it involves your lovely legs in trews.'

'She was telling me she thought it unwise for me to go for a drive with your father in Hyde Park.'

His body went dangerously still and his eyes grew dark and hooded. 'My father? You didn't tell me he asked you to go for a drive last night?'

'He didn't. He approached me in the park today.'

The anger rolling off him was almost palpable. 'Why would you encourage an acquaintance when I told you to stay away from him less than twenty-four hours ago?' he bit out.

'I did nothing to encourage the encounter. He approached me before I even spotted him. After we talked briefly he asked if I'd like to go for a ride in the park with him.'

The vein near his right temple appeared. 'And what did you say?'

'I told him no.'

'Exactly how did you say no?'

She put her hands on her hips in response to his demanding nature. 'I believe I told him that I knew what a drive like that would convey and I had no desire to make that statement with him.'

'Why?'

'Because I barely know him,' she replied as if it should be blatantly obvious. 'I also have no desire to be in his presence. There is something about his manner that leaves me disconcerted.'

Hartwick gripped her arm then immediately released it, as if he was surprised by his own action. 'Has he made any inappropriate advances to you? Has he touched you in any way?'

'Of course not. I've spoken to him in a ballroom and a public park, hardly the places he would do something so forward.' Even though the conversation had been polite, the way Lord Blackwood had stood over her in the park had felt almost threatening, but from the controlled anger rolling off Hartwick, she didn't think it wise to mention that.

'I must go,' he said abruptly. 'Stay away from him.'

He strode towards the door, but she grabbed his arm, pulling him back. She had never seen him like this. 'Where are you going?'

'I've a pressing matter to attend to,' he all but snarled before storming out the door.

Chapter Twelve

Hart rode to his father's house as if the hounds of hell were on his heels. It was his worst nightmare come to fruition. His father was planning on using Miss Forrester in one of his sick twisted games and it was taking every bit of Hart's control to keep his anger from exploding on everything and anyone in his path. Over the years he had learned that his best defence against his father was a calm demeanour. He was usually able to disguise his true feelings with a devil-may-care attitude. This time, he was having no luck.

When Hart was young, his father would immediately dismiss any tutor his son grew attached to. Being away at school had been a reprieve for him. During those years his father had exhibited no interest in him at all. After graduating from Cambridge, he had immediately set up his own household using money he won through gambling. All his life, all he had ever wanted was to be free of his father's control. Investing in racehorses gave him a means to do that.

Yet the man found a way to extend his reach and Caroline had suffered greatly for it. Hart had wanted to marry her. And his father had gone to extreme measures to make certain that would not happen. He wasn't certain why the man was fixated this time on Miss Forrester. He only knew he would not allow his father to prey upon her. He was putting an end to this game. Now.

It had been years since he'd entered his father's home. Would he even be admitted inside?

He lifted the ring of the shiny brass doorknocker and rapped out some of his anger. Within moments, the door was edged open by Newcomb, his father's butler. The condescending glare on the man disappeared the moment he realised Hart was standing before him.

'My lord,' the elderly man exclaimed, his expression shifting rapidly from a welcoming smile to concern, probably because he remembered the last time Hart was here he'd come to blows with his father over Caroline.

'Is my father home?'

'I shall see if he is receiving,' he replied, escorting Hart towards the Gold Drawing Room to wait.

The room hadn't changed since he was a child and he could recall playing in it with his mother. The memories were faint—the smell of her perfume, the look of her embroidered shoes as he hid under the sofa while she laughed as she searched for him. This was one of the few rooms of the house that held good memories.

Ten minutes had gone by and still there was no sign of Newcomb. It was apparent his father was home. If he hadn't been, Hart would have been notified immediately. It was just one more of his father's games. Well, he had never played by his father's rules. And he wasn't about to start now.

Storming out of the drawing room, he took the chance his father was in his study. A nervous Newcomb caught up to him in the hall.

'Can I be of assistance, my lord?'

Hart waved him off as he continued towards the room he had always been summoned to as a child.

Newcomb was fast on his heels. 'My lord, my lord,' the butler called to him in a state of nervous panic. 'I'm certain you will not be waiting much longer.'

It was a woman. It had to be. Would he be cursed

forever with interrupting his father doing things he'd rather not see? But when he threw open the door and braced his stomach, he was surprised to find his father was alone, looking out the window at the back garden. He eyed Hart over his glass of wine as he took a sip.

'Forgive me, my lord,' Newcomb almost begged the Marquess as he hurried to stand beside Hart. 'I told him to wait.'

His father's eyes narrowed on the butler before shifting his attention back to Hart.

'I grew bored,' Hart stated offhandedly.

With a nod of his head, his father silently dismissed Newcomb.

This room had also not changed. Every inch of the walls and ceiling were painted to give the effect of being inside the Coliseum. On all four walls of the fresco, hundreds of people in Roman garb were depicted in various poses sitting in the stands that surrounded the room. Some were looking down at the room's inhabitants in scorn, some in amusement and some were too busy performing various sexual acts to even notice. Above them, the gods of Olympus looked down in judgment from a circle of clouds on the ceiling. Hart hated this room.

Silence stretched between them, as it had since Hart was a boy. He'd be damned if he would be the first to break it this time.

'I wondered how long it would take you to realise I wasn't going to send Newcomb for you,' his father finally said. 'What is it you want?'

'You and I need to talk.'

His father took a seat at his large mahogany desk and gestured to the chair across from him.

Hart had sat in that chair many times as a child to be reprimanded for some deed. He'd even named it the Chair of Despair. 'I prefer to stand.'

The faint wrinkles by his father's eyes deepened as the man studied him. 'As you wish.' He leaned back and placed his feet on his desk with his ankles crossed. The shine from his Hessians competed with the gleaming wood of the desktop.

'Stay away from Miss Forrester.'

A sly smile slid across his father's mouth. 'I was not aware the woman was under your protection.'

'You know she is not.'

'And yet here you are, warning me away from her.'

'Oh, I haven't even begun to warn you away from her.'

His father took a slow sip and his watchful eyes

narrowed. 'I take it your presence here means you're aware I spoke with the lady today. That was quick.'

'I was at Julian's when she arrived at Lyonsdale House with his wife. It came up in conversation. I'm not sure why you have developed a sudden interest in the lady, but I firmly advise you to curtail it. She is the dear friend of the Duchess and the daughter of an American diplomat. You will not toy with her the way you did Caroline.'

The sly smile on his lips made Hart want to punch him. 'Are you certain you wish to discuss Caroline with me? You were not interested in hearing how I amused myself with her the last time you were here. That day your only interest was in drawing blood.'

Hart crossed his arms to prevent himself from reaching across the desk and throttling the man a second time. He purposely relaxed his fingers so his father would not witness them digging into his biceps.

He knew exactly what had happened between Caroline and his father. He knew Lady Helena Wentworth had befriended her at his father's request. On the night of Caroline's sister's engagement ball, Helena had helped his father seduce the innocent Caroline. Her parents found out and were going to cast her out once Lord Blackwood refused to marry her, but Caroline's sister had begged them not to.

He had been ignorant to all of this. At the time of Caroline's sister's engagement, he had been in Dover, collecting information on a conspiracy against the Prince Regent. Two weeks later when he returned to London, he had been met with the news of Caroline's death from a fall down the stairs in her parents' home. He knew what had happened because her sister had given him a note she had found addressed to him in Caroline's room. The tear-stained letter explained all of it and she had apologised for what had happened between her and his father. He would never know if she had been carrying his father's child. He would never know if her fall was an accident. He suspected it wasn't because she had written him the letter.

'You were planning on asking for her hand, were you not?'

It was just as Hart suspected. 'What have I ever done that warrants the way you behave towards me? The way you treat those close to me. Tell me,' he spat out.

His father studied his glass that he swirled on the desktop.

'Tell me! What would cause a father to take away what his own flesh and blood holds dear? No man does that. You behave like a spoiled child who needs to be the only one with the finest toys. You lie and cajole because no one would give anything to you freely. Why my mother ever agreed to marry you is a question I have asked myself for years. She was better than you. She was everything that is good in this world. And you are nothing!' There was a sense of relief in saying those words—words that he had wanted to say for so long.

His father abruptly stood and kicked his chair back. 'You think her a saint, but she was nothing without me. Nothing!' He was growing red in the face. 'Without me she would not have had all of this. Her family had debts when I married her. I never promised to be faithful. I never promised even to like her. Yet your grandfather begged me to marry her. Did you know that? I saved them! Me and my money!' The veins in both his temples were visibly throbbing.

Hart had never witnessed his father lose control like this. It was the first time he had mentioned his mother to the man since he was seven and he watched them lower her coffin into the ground. On that day, his father had warned him never to speak of her again.

Hart clenched his fists so hard it was a wonder his fingers weren't breaking. 'And you were happy to remind her of that every day of her life. I remember. I was there. I heard. You're such a bastard!

'I am not the bastard here!'

'What did I ever do to you to warrant the way you have treated me? If you're not the bastard in this, then who is?'

'You are! You are not my son!' his father screamed. The admittance of this revelation seemed to shock him almost as much as Hart and he rubbed his hand over his mouth.

As if the words held the force of a thousand blows, it pushed every last breath out of Hart with a sudden rush. 'What?'

His father's throbbing veins were still visible. 'You want to know why I care nothing for you? Why I have never cared for you? I'll tell you. Because that harlot mother of yours could not accept my mistresses and took a lover of her own. She spread her legs for another man. And I've been reminded every day you have lived that she played me for a fool! Me! She thought I would never find out. But you are proof that she did!' The man was visibly trembling with rage as he raked Hart with his glare.

'You're lying.'

'You have no notion of how badly I wish that were true.'

'How do you know I am not your son?'

There was a hesitation, as if he was debating with himself if he should tell Hart the rest. 'Because I had not bedded her in months,' he spat. 'Then, miraculously, she is with child. You are not mine and I have never considered you so.' If it wasn't for the crazed state the man was in, Hart would have thought this was another game.

'Then who is my father?'

Blackwood finished off his wine in one gulp. 'She wouldn't tell me, no matter how hard I tried to beat it out of her.' His face contorted in anger. 'So you see, you are a bastard. A bastard no one wanted. You thought I wanted you because I needed an heir. I'd rather the line pass to some feckless cousin. You don't deserve any of it! You want to know why I dismissed every tutor you grew attached to? You want to know why I bedded that girl? It's because you don't deserve happiness. I haven't been happy since the day you were born.'

Hart's legs felt weak, but he raised his chin and held his ground. 'Why tell me this now?'

The man shook his head as if he could not explain his unprecedented outburst. 'I will not denounce you, if that is what you fear.'

There was only one thing Hart feared and he still had enough rational thought left to recall what brought him here in the first place. 'I don't care if you denounce me, but I'm warning you,' he said through his teeth, 'stay away from Miss Forrester. There is no reason to drag her into this vendetta of yours. She means nothing to me.'

'Don't think you can fool me. I know what I see when I watch the both of you.'

'Your mind is playing tricks, old man. This is your only warning. Stay away from Miss Forrester.'

He strode from the room to the front door. He needed to get out. It was becoming difficult to think clearly.

Hart had walked around aimlessly for hours, trying to make sense of this revelation. All his life, the man had treated him with derision or with no care at all. While he was away at school his friends' families would send packages to them with knitted scarves and gloves and their favourite treats. Not once did he ever receive anything from home. The fathers of his classmates would periodically arrive at school to check on their progress. The only time his father saw the inside of Cambridge was when he himself had attended it.

It had been painful.

The only consolation he'd had was knowing that as much as his father despised him, he would have been pleased he was a boy. Now he didn't even have that.

The idea of going home to his empty set made him cold and clammy. Even after the loss of his mother he had never felt this alone and confused. He needed to be in Lyonsdale House. He needed to talk to Julian.

The door to Lyonsdale House opened halfway as Reynolds guarded the entrance. Hart had known Reynolds all his life and he always followed the butler's directions when he called, regardless of the room he was placed in to wait. This time he pushed past him before Reynolds could even say if Julian was even home.

'I will wait for him in his study if he isn't here. Do not think to dissuade me on this.'

He stormed down the hall with Reynolds hurrying after him. He was so fixed on his thoughts, he didn't even notice passing Sarah and Katrina as they stepped into the hall. When he opened the door to Julian's study, he was met with his friend's surprised expression from where he sat at his desk.

Before Reynolds had a chance to explain Hart's presence, Julian waved him off with a lift of his hand. 'What has happened?' he asked when the door closed, concern evident in his expression.

'I don't even know where to begin.'

'That's a first. Would you care to sit?'

'No. I find it's best if I keep moving.' He paced back and forth in front of the desk.

'Brandy?'

Hart shook his head. A case of it would not change the fact he was a bastard. Julian came around, sat at the edge of his desk, crossed his arms and waited.

'I just came from my father's…rather, Lord Blackwood's house.'

'You shouldn't have gone to him,' he stated firmly. 'I told you I would help you if ever you needed funds.'

'I have plenty of blunt. I went on my own accord.'

Julian's brow wrinkled. 'About?'

'I needed to resolve a matter, although I may well have made the situation worse. I have no way of knowing.'

There was more of course—so much more. It was apparent Julian would wait until Hart was ready to explain. Hart braced himself for his friend's reaction. If it were true, he would have to grow accustomed to saying it.

He stopped pacing a few feet from Julian and looked down, finding it easier than looking at his closest friend.

'I'm a bastard.' The words were like acid on his tongue.

'What did you do now?' Julian muttered in exasperation.

'That's not what I meant,' he said through his teeth.

'I'm not following.'

'I'm a bastard… A by-blow… A chance-bairn!' His voice was rising with every word. 'He told me.'

Julian stood frozen. 'Your father told you this?'

'Bloody hell! Have you not been listening? He took great pleasure in informing me of it!'

'Are you certain you heard him correctly?'

Hart picked up a book from Julian's desk and threw it against the wall. The unusual display of temper made Julian stand up.

'It is not something one misinterprets!'

'Surely he is trying to provoke you. Why tell you now? After all he has done in the past, one would think he would have used this to his advantage before now.'

'I'm not sure. I got the sense that he regretted telling me, more as if he wanted to take his shame back than to spare me any hurt.'

'Do you think it's a lie?'

Hart shook his head. His father's rage had been so raw, so honest. Hart knew it wasn't a lie.

'Do you believe he will use this against you? That you will not inherit?'

'He has publically claimed I am his son. My mother is dead. What could he say now? What evidence could he give?'

'So this was just for your own edification.'

'He was explaining his lack of affection.'

'I see.'

It was obvious Julian's ridiculous sense of propriety was preventing him from asking the question he was dying to know.

'I don't know who my father is. It seems she never told… Blackwood. Probably afraid of how he would retaliate against the man. So whoever he is or was, she protected him to the end.'

'Which shows she had genuine affection for the man.'

'Or wished to prevent the scandal my father's actions would incur.'

He turned away from Julian to avoid the pity in his friend's eyes and strode to the window. 'Damn him! And damn her for not letting me know!'

He stared out the window at the world that had not changed for anyone in it except for him. His world had changed completely with just a few words. 'I don't even know who I am…what I am. What does this make me? Am I the son of a footman? Some gentlemen? Or a tradesman's son?'

'You are still the man you always have been.'

'Oh, that is rich! You saying that. You, who almost married someone else to protect your family's esteemed lineage!'

'Do not bring my wife into this,' Julian ground

out. 'And, yes, I struggled with the fact she is American, but I realised none of it mattered because I fell in love with her. If anyone should be able to convince you not to concern yourself with lineage, it should be me!'

And yet Julian wasn't helping. Julian, who could trace his lineage back hundreds of years to men of outstanding merit and honour, would never know what it felt like not to know who you were or where you were from. Whenever Hart needed reassurance, he would turn to his friend. He should have found some comfort, but now he feared coming here had been a mistake.

'I want to help. I only wish I knew how,' Julian said softly.

Hart turned to him and looked him in the eye. 'I know you do.'

'We can go a few rounds if you think it will release some of your anger?'

'It's more like rage. Are you sure you're up for it? It might get bloody.'

'I can take it.' Julian pushed himself off the desk. 'Let me fetch my coat. Don't break anything while I'm gone.'

It was too late. Hart was already broken inside.

Some day he would be the Marquess of Blackwood in the eyes of the *ton*, but who was he really? Who the bloody hell was he?

Chapter Thirteen

The door to Lyonsdale's study opened abruptly, almost sending Sarah and Katrina careening into the room from where they were standing with their ears pressed against the door. The last thing Sarah saw before he quickly closed it was Hartwick's back as he faced the window.

'What are you two doing?' Lyonsdale demanded, eyeing them slowly.

'I would think it obvious,' Katrina replied. 'We were sitting in the next room trying to have a conversation when we heard the commotion in your study.'

He folded his arms and arched his brow. 'If it was going on in my study behind closed doors, it was private.'

'I was listening because I was concerned for *your* well-being.'

He gave an exasperated huff with a slight smile. 'I'm off to fetch my coat. We're going to go a few rounds. It might release some of his anger. Do not go in there. He is in no state to speak with either of you.' He pointed his finger at both of them in warning and strode off down the hall.

Katrina and Sarah eyed one another.

'I'll go in,' Sarah said before Katrina had the chance.

Muffled yells and banging were not sounds that ever travelled through the walls of Lyonsdale House, as far as Sarah could tell. Reynolds had appeared quite shaken until Katrina dismissed him with the reassurance that Hartwick would never harm her husband. When Sarah had placed her ear to the door, she'd been able to distinguish Hartwick's voice.

'He took great pleasure in my shock that I'm not his son! I'm surprised he waited this long to tell me!'

They had looked at one another in obvious surprise. There had followed more muffled talking, which Sarah had assumed was Lyonsdale. Not long afterwards the door had opened.

'I think I know him better, Sarah. He's a frequent visitor to my home,' Katrina said.

'That's why I should be the one to speak with him. He may be more guarded with you for fear of offending you.' She knew with all certainty he had no qualms about offending her.

Katrina went to reply, but Sarah immediately slipped into the room. Taking an uneven breath, she rested her back against the massive door.

This was why she needed to be in here. She needed to see the state he was in. His shoulders were hunched as he rested his hand on the window frame and stared out at the back garden. It always appeared as if nothing and no one could affect him—as if he was above all the petty problems in life.

But this was no petty problem. This was an enormous revelation. And as he stood with his shoulders hunched, he looked broken. Slowly she walked towards him, not knowing what to say.

'I hope you've brought brandy with you,' he muttered, still staring outside. 'A glass might be wise before we have at it.'

'Brandy will not help.'

His head snapped around and those piercing blue eyes narrowed on her. 'What are you doing here?'

'Visiting.'

'I meant in this room. Go away, Miss Forrester. I have no wish to spar with you.'

'That's a relief. I find I have left my sharp tongue at home. I would hate to disappoint you.'

He faced her and that lock of hair fell over his eye. She was close enough now that she brushed the thick silky strands away for him. As she moved her hand to do it again, he jerked his head back.

'Julian went to fetch his coat. We're going out.'

'I know. I'll sit with you while you wait.'

'There is no need.' It was evident he was trying to remain polite but was hanging by a thread.

It would not be wise to push him, but she had the strongest urge to offer him comfort. She sat down on the sofa by the fire and looked over at him. 'Would you care to join me?'

'I prefer to stand.'

'It's your choice.' She folded her hands in her lap, taking in Lyonsdale's study. She had never been in the room before. It was a decidedly male space with substantial pieces of furniture and a portrait of an unsmiling gentleman over the fireplace. She assumed it was the Duke's father. Her gaze finally landed back on Hartwick, who was watching her silently.

'Did Julian ask you to stay with me for fear I will do damage to this room or myself?'

'No. Actually he specifically told me not to come in here when he found me outside listening with my ear to the door.'

He closed his eyes and shook his head before dropping down beside her. 'Do you ever follow directions?'

'When the directions coincide with what I wish to do… Otherwise I find them tedious.'

He stretched his booted feet out. 'Why are you here, Sarah?' he asked softly, staring at his crossed ankles.

The intimate use of her given name on his lips for the first time made her heart flip. 'There is something you need to be aware of.'

'If you've found the diamond, now would not be the best time to inform me of it.' He rested his head back and stared at the coffered ceiling.

She resisted the urge to stroke his forehead. 'As much as I would love to have said as much, that was not what I was about to say.' She turned her entire body to face him, giving him her full attention. 'I'm aware that here in Britain you place great emphasis on who your ancestors are. Here, heritage and pedigree define a person.'

'If your observation was intended to help, I should inform you that I think you might be making me feel even worse than I did before.'

'Let me finish,' she said firmly. 'That concept of placing one's worth on who came before you is very odd to me, and even though I've been in London almost two years it is one of your principles I could never agree with.'

He eyed her while his head continued to rest on the sofa.

'In America, we judge a man by his actions and his accomplishments, not those of his father or his father's father. The worth of a man is here.' She poked his chest above his heart. 'It is not in his blood. It is not in what was handed down to him. It is in what he has made of himself—what he stands for—how he decides to conduct his own life.' She gestured about the room. 'The gifts of a fine family are just pretty rooms. Where I come from, it is more impressive if the man built the room than if he were given it.'

He leaned closer and those eyes—those eyes that could be so observant and amusing and devilish—were intently focused on her.

She needed him to understand. 'Who your parents are has no bearing on the man you've become. *You* determine that.' She stood up, looked down at him and pushed that lock of hair out of his eyes. 'I think you've done fairly well on your own.'

'*Fairly* well?' he echoed.

'You don't expect me to give you a true compliment, now do you? I fear if I did, your head would not fit through that doorway when you decided to leave.'

His lips rose into a slight grin, which raised her spirits considerably. If she could get him to smile—even just a little—than it had been worth coming in here.

She leaned over and kissed him. It was soft and brief, meant to offer comfort, not stir his passions.

'Think about what I said. Some of your British ways may not be the best.'

It wasn't easy to kiss a man and forget about him after he looked like he might fall apart before your eyes. The entire rest of the evening that Sarah spent at the theatre with her parents, she began to realise how much she actually liked Hartwick and it mattered to her that he was in pain. When he put aside his bravado and showed her his true nature, he was hard to resist.

He would eventually find his own way to make peace with this revelation, but there was an ache in her heart knowing that he would do it without her.

As she passed his residence on her way home from Drury Lane, she scanned the darkened windows of the building and wondered which ones belonged to his set. Had he returned to Lyonsdale House when his match was over to seek the comfort of his friend, or had he sought out a woman instead? The thought of him with another woman turned her stomach.

It was late when she arrived home and she was having no luck pushing Hartwick from her mind. She needed to stop thinking about him and instead try to figure out a way to find the diamond. Soon the blackmailer would send word to her father where he should leave the stone. Her priority should be her family.

In her dressing room, her maid helped her into her night-rail before she dismissed her for the night. She entered her bedchamber, clutching the book she hoped would settle her jumbled thoughts enough so she could fall asleep.

'What are you reading?'

The book fell to the floor.

Hartwick was sitting cross-legged on her rug in front of the fire in the same black clothes he had worn earlier in the day, looking lost and tired. A part of her had hoped he would come to see her. She wasn't proud of that part. They had no future together.

'It's a collection of poetry by Mr Keats,' she replied, picking it up and placing it on the table beside her bed. The best course of action seemed to be to pretend his presence in her room was commonplace, which, if he kept this up, it would be.

He toyed with the fibres of the carpet. 'I needed to see you. Needed to talk with you.'

Her heart gave a funny flip. She lowered herself down across from him, crossing her legs and tucking them under her yellow muslin dressing gown, unconsciously mimicking his pose. Their knees were almost touching as she waited for him to continue.

The rug held his undivided attention and it appeared as if he had forgotten she was there. 'I like this room,' he said after some time, finally looking up at her. 'It smells like you…like lilacs.'

Sitting this close to him in the firelight, she saw the shadows under his eyes.

'I like this room, too,' she said, chewing on her lip.

'I imagined more shoes.' He surveyed the room before his gaze landed back on her rug. 'Are any of these furnishings yours?'

'The house was leased to my family fully furnished. However, the smaller bits about the room are mine.' She needed to pull him away from his solemn thoughts. 'You live at Albany, don't you? Was your set of rooms already furnished?'

'No, I bought my set empty. I brought all my furniture with me when I took up residence.'

'That must have made it feel like home rather quickly. I'm sure that was comforting.'

There was sadness in his eyes. 'I'm not sure any place I've ever lived has felt like home in the comforting sense.' He gave a shrug. 'They're just buildings I reside in.'

What a terribly sad way to live. 'You've felt that way about all of them?'

He nodded. 'I take it your experiences have been different?'

'I take comfort in being at home. I am especially fond of the home I lived in as a child.'

'What was it like?'

'My family still owns it. It's in New York, not too far from the Newmarket Racetrack in Salisbury.'

'Racetrack?'

'I thought you might find that of interest,' she said, smiling at how well she knew him. 'The home is small by your standards but comfortable. When I was a child my father raised Narragansett Pacers there. It is surrounded by green pastures that rise and fall with gentle hills. Stone walls run along our borders and the sun shines there more than it does here.'

'Narragansett Pacers?'

'They are saddle horses that are quite prevalent back home.'

'Do you have brothers who are managing the business for your father?'

Now it was her turn to play with the rug. 'No. My father has hired a gentleman to manage the estate and the horses. My only brother, Alexander, was in the Navy and died during the war.'

'You have my condolences.'

She met his careful eyes and wished she could have said something noble about Alexander.

'Were you and your brother close?'

'At one time. It was just the two of us. He was six years older. When I was little I would follow him around our land and we would devise games to pass the time. He taught me how to climb trees, hop fences and ride horses.'

'He sounds like an ideal brother.'

He was at one time.

'I think I would have liked to have had a brother.'

'I wish I could have given you mine.'

'A kind gesture.'

Not as kind as he thought.

'I know what it is to lose those you love,' he said in a faint whisper. 'My mother died when I was seven, my grandmother when I was ten. It taught me love is a useless emotion. The people who mean the most to you only leave you in the end.'

What a sad way to see the world. 'Do you truly believe you can stop yourself from feeling certain emotions?'

'*I* can.'

'But you are close to Lyonsdale.'

'I have known him all my life. Julian is the one exception. You seem at peace with your loss.'

She'd thought she was, until that letter had arrived. 'It was difficult, getting word of Alexander's death after he had been at sea for two years. There were times I would have to remind myself he was gone forever and would not be coming through our doors after a long journey. When you don't have the opportunity to say a final goodbye to someone...when the last time you saw them they were in good health and lifting you up to hug you goodbye, it's hard to reconcile that their light doesn't shine somewhere in this world.' She shook her head. 'And when you have no body to bury...' Her voice was cracking now. It was bringing back all the pain she'd felt when she read the letter from his commanding officer, speaking of how Alexander had died a noble death that night at sea, defending the people of Baltimore. After reading the first two sentences, her mother had broken down in violent sobs and tossed the letter aside. Sarah had picked it up to read the rest.

'I'm sorry,' he said, brushing a tear from her cheek.

She dabbed under her eyes. 'The grief was much worse for my parents. My mother retreated to her room for months. I thought she would never come out. My father was a senator at the time. He threw himself into his work. Barely slept or ate. His heart suffered for it and we almost lost him.' He held her hand, comforting her when she should have been tending to him.

'But they seem to have adjusted.'

'They have. While my mother was finding her way to cope with Alexander's death, I tended to my father and his health returned. I don't think his heart will ever completely recover, but he is much better now. It took time and tears and talk, but I was able to find the one thing that helped both of them accept his passing. My parents firmly believe his death served a greater purpose. They find comfort believing his noble sacrifice helped to save the lives of the people of Baltimore. That his death was a necessity.'

'And you? Do you believe that?'

'I have accepted his death.'

He stared down at their hands, locked together. 'My mother's death served no noble purpose. She went for a walk, slipped off a cliff and left her child in the care of a monster.'

She combed her fingers through the hair by his temple, her heart breaking for the little boy he once was. 'Reverend Thomas says, "Through pain we discover how strong we really are."'

'Pretty words said by a man who did not grow up with my...with Blackwood. Is it really true Americans do not judge a man by his family?' From his expression, it was apparent this was why he had come to see her.

'I don't look at you and think of your family. I see you for who you are and the experiences I have had with you.'

'Do you miss being in America?'

'I do miss the open land. Town can feel confining at times.'

'Have you not visited the countryside much since you've been here?'

'Only a few times.'

'You should see more of it. There is nothing like the English countryside. I think you would like it. You should ask Katrina to open one of their houses. Then you could visit with her there.'

'Are you trying to rid yourself of me? Are you trying to have me remove myself further and further from the diamond?' she teased.

'It feels as if I haven't thought of that diamond in ages.' He rubbed a loose tendril of her unbound hair that was resting along her neck between his fingers and let out a sigh. 'No, Sarah, I find I have no wish to be rid of you…none at all. I'm not sure why that is.'

His words tugged at her heart. There was sincerity in them—and in his eyes—in those eyes that didn't lie. You could tell a lot about a person if you looked in their eyes. And while women would swoon discussing the colour of his, she always found what they revealed about him at any given moment to be what she liked best about them.

'Why do you want the diamond?' This question had plagued her since he had discovered her at the church. He was a man of wealth. Why would he need the Sancy? Was he being blackmailed as well, or was he looking for one more thing to add to his list of accomplishments?

'Let us put aside the diamond for tonight. I find I have no wish to consider things that separate us.'

She had no idea why he had chosen to be with her tonight. She just knew she was glad he had. 'Is there anything I can say to help you through this?'

He shook his head. 'Just being here has settled my mind somewhat. Although I don't believe I will ever feel quite like myself again. It's difficult to put into words.'

'This is all very new to you. In time you'll come to realise you're the same man today that you were yesterday and the same man you were when we met for the first time. I'm sorry to say you are just as annoying now as you were then. It appears your lineage has no bearing on the man you truly are.'

A small smile crossed his lips as he looked up at her. Slowly he lifted their joined hands and kissed her wrist. The velvety warmth of his lips scorched her skin like a branding iron.

'And here I thought you were starting to like me.'

'Whatever gave you that notion?'

He leaned closer. 'Because you like to kiss me.' His hands gently cupped the back of her neck to draw her towards him and then he took her lips. It was a slow kiss—a leisurely kiss—a kiss that made her feel as if there was nothing else in the world he would rather be doing at that moment than kissing her.

With each breath they moved closer and closer until Sarah found herself on her back with Hartwick above her, propping himself up on his elbows. Her dressing gown had opened and she could feel the buttons and seams of his clothes through the linen of her night-rail. When he began rubbing his lower body against hers, he created such delicious friction that she matched his movements to make certain he wouldn't stop. It was making her insides tingle.

Suddenly he broke the kiss and threw himself on his back beside her with his forearm over his eyes. His ragged breathing matched hers. 'Forgive me. You know what I want to do to you.'

She did now and was having fluttering feelings between her legs just thinking about it. 'I have an idea.'

He raised his arm and looked at her. The warm glow of the firelight gave her a perfect view of his firm smooth lips. 'I am not a man who believes in marriage. It's not for me. But know this, if we continue, it will torture me to stop. I won't be able to taste you without needing to take all of you. Not tonight. Tonight I want to lose myself in you so neither of us knows where one ends and the other begins.'

He was being honest with her. He wasn't trying to bed her and then leave her to believe this would lead to more than he was willing to give. At least he was honourable enough to believe there was no sense in marrying a woman if he could not be faithful. She couldn't fault him for that.

He wanted her and she wanted him, too. Would she ever find an American man who stirred her the way he did? It wasn't just the way he could set her aflame with the mere sweep of his gaze. There was something else. He touched something deep inside her. What if this was her only chance to be this close to someone she felt so strongly about?

She leaned over him and lowered her mouth

so it was a fraction of an inch away from his. 'I don't expect you to marry me, but I don't want you to stop.'

Their breaths mingled. He opened his mouth to speak, but she silenced him with another kiss. A soft purring noise came from deep in his throat. She straddled his hips and slipped off her dressing gown.

He brushed his fingers up her calves, taking the linen along with him. 'I've dreamt about you like this.'

'I want to know what you feel like.' The knot of his cravat was easily undone. She unwrapped the linen and slid it out from under his neck and tossed it aside. She never imagined a neck would be tempting but his was. Leaning down, she traced her finger and then her tongue over his skin, which was slightly salty and warm.

'Let me get out of these.' His deep voice reverberated against her lips as she kissed his neck.

There was no hesitation or sense of shyness about him as he stood above her. His eyes held hers as he slowly unbuttoned his coat and peeled it from his body. The buttons to his black waistcoat needed his attention and he looked down as he undid them. But as he went to slip out of it, he looked deeply into her eyes through that lazy lock of hair.

She shifted to her knees when he slowly pulled his shirt out of those black breeches that could have been painted on his muscular legs. Was he purposely going this slowly? Didn't he understand she wanted to see him...now! When he grabbed the back of his shirt and pulled it over his head, her mouth went dry and there was an audible catch in her breath. She needed to suck in air because the sight of Hartwick without his shirt was breathtaking. Nothing could have prepared her for seeing him without his shirt, wearing skintight black breeches and black Hessians in the glow of the firelight.

His strong shoulders curved towards his biceps and there was a faint dusting of hair across his chest. He stood like a man who was comfortable in his skin and had nothing to hide.

Unable to stop herself, Sarah stood and took a step forward so they were mere inches apart. She felt his eyes on her as she watched her own hands move up his arms, feeling the muscles of his biceps flex as she skimmed over them on the way to his shoulders. The hair on his chest was springy and slightly coarse and stopped at the top of his ribcage. There were ripples of muscles crossing his flat stomach that she traced softly with the pads of her fingers until she brushed along the thin line of dark hair that extended from under his belly button to the top of his breeches.

She wanted to see the rest of him. Did he look like the statues of the nude men in the museum? Before she was conscious of what she was doing, she gave a slight pull to the waistband of his breeches. A devilish smile curved those smooth firm lips and he arched a challenging brow while placing his hands on his hips.

There were six buttons on the fall of his breeches. Could she be so bold as to undo them? Part of her knew she should feel embarrassed by her forward actions, but he was looking at her with intrigue and a smouldering passion that made her feel emboldened and free to explore his body.

Was she daring enough to unwrap the rest of him? She chewed her lip and eyed those buttons. Six little soldiers guarding what the whispered rumours said was something very impressive indeed. His devilish grin grew a bit wider.

If he could see the intimate parts of her, it seemed only fair she should cast her eyes on him. She was biting her lip now as one by one she undid the buttons. When it sprang forth it was definitely bigger than the statues in the museum—much bigger. And it was stiff and pointing up towards her as if it was straining to reach her. She raised her hand to feel it and it twitched. It actually moved on its own.

She met Hartwick's aqua-eyed gaze with astonishment and he let out a soft chuckle.

'Forgive me. I couldn't resist.'

'You did that? You can do that?'

He rubbed his lips together in an attempt to suppress a grin and nodded. 'I can do many incredible things with it. I'd love to show you all of them, but tonight we'll only do a few.' His eyes grew dark. 'You can touch me, Sarah.'

Biting her lip, she reached for him. This time she stroked his velvety soft skin with her finger from the tip to the base and back again. She noticed a bead of wetness at the tip and pushed it around with her finger. If he liked that she had been wet for him, Sarah assumed this was something good. If she had any doubts, his unsteady breaths were her reassurance.

He swallowed hard and adjusted her hand so it was wrapped around him. He felt hard and stiff when she slid her hand up and down along his length. His fingers curled into her hips through the linen of her night-rail and suddenly his hands were cupping her jaw and he was devouring her mouth in a kiss. The firmer her grip as she stroked him, the harder he became until he grabbed her wrist to stop her movements. They were both breathless.

'Lie down for me.' It was out of his throat like a low growl, making the apex between her thighs flutter.

She did as he asked, lying on the red-and-gold rug, the warmth from the nearby fire heating her skin. Or maybe it was the look in his eyes as he stripped out of the rest of his clothes, lowered himself to the rug and crawled slowly to her like a beast stalking its prey. His eyes never left hers, even when he was sliding her gown up her calves, over her knees and up her thighs. It wasn't until he had spread her open that his gaze dropped and he wet his lips before lowering his mouth to her.

The moment his tongue gave that first long, slow lick, her entire body came off the rug with a jerk. His eyes locked with hers as his hot breath blew against her wet skin. This time when he lowered his mouth to her, he held her hips down so she couldn't move. 'If there is anything you do not like, tell me and I will stop.' She could see the devilish smile lifting his eyes. 'However, if there is something you particularly enjoy, you should tell me that, as well.'

She was trying to breathe and comprehend what he had said. It wasn't easy with his mouth on her again. She couldn't have formed words even if she'd wanted to. He tended to her like she was his favourite treat, savouring her. And when he also slid a finger inside her, an appreciative soft moan snuck out of her lips.

That was all the encouragement he seemed to need.

'Hart,' she said on a breath.

If he stopped now, she would cry. Whatever he was doing felt amazing. All it took was a slight change in the position of his finger and he took her over the edge.

His breathing was as ragged and raw as hers, as he brought his lips to her ear. 'I need you. Right here. Right now.'

There was a feeling of emptiness inside, the likes of which she had never felt before. She needed him to make this ache go away. If they were doing this, she wanted to feel his bare skin against hers. She pulled her night-rail off and tossed it aside.

'Sarah, you have no idea what you do to me,' he growled, positioning himself so they were face to face. 'I know how to do this so there will be no child.'

She nodded, trusting he knew what he was doing. He was staring deeply into her eyes and hesitated until he ran his fingers through her hair and gave the slightest tug, arching her neck as he thrust himself inside her. Their eyes never left one another as he moved his hips back and entered her again.

The first thrust inside her had been painful, but as he slid in and out of her now, he was relieving some of the aching and longing she had been feeling.

'You feel wonderful,' she whispered breathlessly.

He gave her a warm smile, which was all the encouragement she needed to say it again. She felt like she was racing to that precipice again, until he rolled them over and she was now on top of him.

'Ride me,' he whispered.

Her confusion must have been evident in her expression, because he helped her straddle his hips. She was now in control of how deep and how fast he entered her. This also was a perfect position to kiss his neck and run her tongue along his collarbone. She liked being on top.

'Should I move faster?' she asked against his ear, coming down hard and full over him.

'Do whatever feels right,' he said through clenched teeth.

Bloody hell! How did she do that? Hart knew she was a virgin. It was apparent from the wince she made when he entered her for the first time. And yet she was able to knot him up so tight he was convinced he wouldn't be able to pull out in time.

She flattened her palms on his chest, bit her lip and threw her head back. Her long, wavy chestnut hair cascaded around her shoulders. These actions were instinctual. There was no false artifice to them. This was Sarah, taking all of him and relishing every single moment of pleasure. He had never seen anything so beautiful. Being touched by her made him feel more alive than anything ever had before, as if he had discovered a new sense of passion he didn't know existed.

She was tight and slick. The friction between them was incredible. He had always used French letters with all of his lovers, ensuring there would be no child. This was the first time in his life he chose not to use them. With Sarah, he wanted nothing between them.

This feeling of needing to be this close to her was terrifying, yet for the life of him he didn't want this to end. But he didn't want to have a bastard, especially not now, and he knew he had better make certain he could pull out from her in time. And if she continued that incredible grinding motion, he wasn't certain he could do that. Encouraging her to straddle him was a bad idea.

He flipped them.

She tried to flip them back, but he wouldn't let her. His thrusts were harder and faster.

Within minutes he could feel her body tremble and her nails dig into his back. 'Hart...'

He held off just long enough for her legs to stop shaking before he grabbed himself and shot his seed on her stomach.

Kneeling between her thighs, he was practically gasping for air and his heart was drumming hard in his chest. It would be a miracle if it slowed down any time soon. He managed to clean her off with his neckcloth before he collapsed down beside her on the rug. Their mingled laboured breaths amid the popping of the logs seemed inordinately loud.

Dammit! Sex with Sarah Forrester was the best sex he had ever had. She was going to be impossible to forget.

She was staring at the ceiling with her hand on her heart. Her breathing had yet to slow. 'Is it always…?'

'It's never like that.'

There was hurt and embarrassment in her eyes when she looked over at him.

'No. No, Sarah, not in a bad way. It was good. Too good.'

'Oh.' She started chewing her lip again. 'This *is* bad, isn't it?'

'That might be an understatement.'

She propped her chin on her hands that were resting on his chest and looked into his eyes. 'Do you wish we had not done that?'

'I do not regret a moment of what just happened.' Did she? 'Are *you* regretting what we have done?' He had felt so alone and lost tonight. He should have gone back to Julian's. His friend had been his anchor in many storms in the past. Hell, he could have gone to White's and immersed himself in cards. But lying in his tub after going a few rough rounds with Julian, the one place he knew he would find peace was with Sarah. With her very American perspective on how she viewed the world, Hart knew she would bear no judgement on him. He had needed the reassurance that the circumstances of his birth had no bearing on the man he was. With her forthright nature, he knew her words would be true.

It was dangerous to depend on her when he was feeling this vulnerable. It was dangerous to depend on her at all. But he needed her just this once. Just this once he needed to be near her and feel as if all would be well in his world. She'd made him feel that way this afternoon in Julian's study. He had needed to feel that way again tonight.

And he finally felt that way right now lying beside her, sharing this moment. Except his stomach dropped—he knew that this had to be the last time he turned to her. This had to be the last time he held her in his arms. The thought she might be regretting what had just happened between them was making it hard for him to swallow. He had taken her virginity. He had never done that to any woman. And as wrong as it was, he would do it all over again given the chance. He'd wanted to be her first, more than he had wanted anything in his life. *Her only.*

'Do you regret this, Sarah?'

When at last she shook her head, his chest felt lighter.

'No, I don't. But I do want to do it again…with you. And we can't. We really shouldn't. It would be bad.'

He was glad she clarified her comment. He would hate to think he was responsible for turning Sarah into a wanton who would be visiting the beds of a number of young bucks in London before she had to go home to America—and she would be going home. Going back to America. Living an ocean away.

It was sobering and it reminded him that it was best to end things now.

He played with a lock of her hair and twined the curl around his finger. 'I agree. It wouldn't be wise to keep doing this, as much as I want to. We'd probably get caught eventually. No matter how careful we were. And eventually I won't be able to withdraw from you in time, or I wouldn't want to because I'll need to know what it feels like to leave something of myself inside you.'

'Are you always this honest in bed?'

'Honest, yes. This forthcoming, no. You are easy to talk to. I don't know why. Over this past year, I have frequently found you irritating.'

She gently flicked his chin with her finger. 'You did not. I was the one who found you irritating. You and your hair.'

'What is wrong with my hair?'

'Look at it. That lock always falls in your eyes. I would think it would get rather tiresome having to do this all the time.' She gave what he believed was a rather exaggerated imitation of the way he tossed his hair out of his eyes. 'Why do you continue to have your hair cut so if it obstructs your view of the world?'

'I like it like this.'

'It's annoying.'

He took that lock of her hair and brushed his lips with it, staring into her eyes that were the exact colour as his favourite cognac. 'You're rather lovely in bed. You say such sweet and endearing things.'

It was obvious she was fighting the urge to laugh. 'We aren't in bed.'

He placed his hand behind his head and glanced around at their clothes scattered about the floor, the rug they were on and the fire that needed tending. 'Then I will excuse you this time, darling. Next time I'll take you on a bed and you'll need to do better.'

It was out of his mouth before he could stop it. He shouldn't be talking of taking her again. He shouldn't have taken her this time. He could not marry her. His brain knew that. But he hadn't lied when he said he didn't regret it. He never would—however, this had to be the one and only time.

Sarah started chewing on her lip. 'There is a bed just over there.'

He tipped his head back and saw the very comfortable tester bed she slept in. He should leave. The longer he stayed, the greater the chance of them being discovered. He couldn't do that to her. But she was just too tempting. 'Well, since we both agree tonight will be the last time we do this...'

Her small smile shone in her eyes.

'Is the door locked?' He arched his brow.

'I've taken to locking it since a certain gentleman has been making a habit of sneaking in here.'

'Dastardly fellow. Whatever will you do about him?'

She sat back on her heels and held out her hand. 'I have an idea or two.'

Chapter Fourteen

Sarah was sore and it was all Hart's fault—him and his big, big idea.

'We don't have to lie down,' he'd said.

'You can just lean over the bed,' he'd said.

Well, after having him inside her twice last night and now having to pretend she wasn't sore while standing politely in the Everills' drawing room, she was hoping he was at least a little uncomfortable today. It only seemed fair. At least tonight's event was a musicale and there would be no dancing involved.

Her mind kept drifting to the time they spent together. Not once had he made her feel self-conscious about her curiosity. Not once had she felt as if she should hide the way her body was reacting to his. He had been absolutely lovely with her and it made her heart ache knowing she would never find another man like him. When she married—if she married—she would pretend she was untouched. However, it would be difficult not to compare her wedding night to the one night she had spent in the arms of the Earl of Hartwick.

She tried not to sigh as she glanced around the elegant room. The candlelight sparkling off the crystal chandelier did wonders for the diamonds worn by the fashionable ladies around her. She stood not far from the door with her friends Olivia, the Duchess of Winterbourne, and her sister, Victoria, while they waited to be called into the music room along with the other guests.

They were in the middle of discussing the latest play to open at Drury Lane when Sarah sensed the moment Hart entered the room. She looked past Olivia's shoulder and watched him make his way through the guests to join a group of gentlemen across the room that included Olivia's husband. He hadn't mentioned he was invited, although, to be fair, she hadn't told him she was attending the musicale tonight either. How was she ever going to be able to appear composed with him here after what they shared last night?

Victoria gently nudged her arm and nodded towards the group Hart was standing in. 'You seem surprised to see Lord Hartwick here?'

Oh, lud! Was it that obvious she was panting after him already? How would she survive the rest of her time in London if everyone noticed her interest in him each time they were in the same room?

'I wasn't aware he was that well acquainted with the family.'

That was good. It showed vague interest and seemed like a feasible thing to wonder about.

'I would surmise the invitation was extended at the request of Everill's niece. I've noticed she has shown as interest in him since her husband passed. Someone should inform the poor woman he only has an appetite for married women.'

It wasn't easy to smile back at that observation but Sarah tried. Thankfully Olivia resumed recounting the performance she had attended last night, drawing Victoria back into their conversation.

Over Olivia's shoulder she saw Hart scan the room, then those soft lips of his rose into a conspiratorial smile as his eyes met hers. His fixed attention was making her feel warm.

The Duke of Winterbourne turned and said

something to him, pulling his attention away from her momentarily to reply. But as soon as the Duke and his brother, Lord Andrew Pearce, began speaking again, Hart's eyes were back on her. This time they travelled slowly over her body.

Victoria excused herself to say hello to some friends, leaving Sarah and Olivia alone. But they weren't alone for long. Both of them were surprised when Olivia's husband joined them with Hart by his side. Was he trying to torture her with his presence?

Sarah had only spoken to the Duke on a few occasions. He always struck her as a very formidable man. It might be his impressive height and broad frame. Or the way he barely spoke. Or it might be that he had only recently reconciled with his wife and Sarah had become very fond of Olivia.

He addressed her first as they stopped across from them. 'Good evening, Miss Forrester. I hope you and your family are well.'

She gave a polite curtsy. 'They are. Thank you, Your Grace.' She attempted to smile politely at Hart and he nodded a proper greeting. This was good. She could behave as if nothing had happened between them.

The Duke turned his attention to his wife, giving Sarah a chance to study his angular features as he stood next to Hart. There was a sharp contrast between the two men. The Duke had neatly trimmed, light brown hair and wore an expertly cut black tailcoat with a pale blue silk waistcoat. Hart was dressed all in black as usual and that lock of his jet-black hair was draped close to his eye.

'I need you to settle a wager Hartwick and I have,' he said to Olivia. 'He believes Mr Lawrence's portrait of Prinny for the Waterloo Chamber will have him on horseback. I told him he was wrong but he insists. Could *you* please tell him that he is wrong?'

Olivia's brown eyes narrowed as she looked between the two men. 'You wagered over this?'

'Forty guineas. It was his idea,' the Duke said as if he saw nothing wrong with making a wager over such an odd detail.

She let out a sigh and shook her head. 'I'm sorry to say, Hartwick, the portrait does not include a horse or any animal for that matter, in the event you both thought to wager over whether it had a dog.'

'You're certain?'

It was the first time Sarah had heard Hart's deep

voice since he bid her goodnight before climbing over the rail of her balcony last night. Her insides did a funny flip.

'I'm quite sure,' Olivia replied with a nod.

'Well, that doesn't seem at all like a portrait worth hanging in a room commemorating the battle and our victory.'

'Except Prinny wasn't at the battle,' the Duke replied in exasperation.

Hart looked eagerly at his friend. 'I wager at least one of them is on horseback.'

Winterbourne closed his eyes and shook his head while rubbing his brow. 'No.'

'You suck the joy out of everything. It's a wonder you and I have remained friends as long as we have.'

'I've tried to get rid of you. You never seem to take the suggestion.' There was a teasing glint in the Duke's eyes that startled Sarah. She would have never imagined he was one for humour.

'Yes, well, one of these days I shall leave town and ride off to the countryside, and you shall be rid of me. I find town can become so confining at times. Wouldn't you say, Miss Forrester?'

Her words from last night… What was he about? Was that a flush spreading up her neck?

She cleared her throat to find her voice. 'I find I feel the same, my lord. While I do enjoy town, there is nothing like the fresh country air.'

'And being able to ride,' Hart said wistfully. 'There isn't much chance for you to ride while in town, I imagine.'

'I think one can find opportunities to ride if one is eager enough,' the Duke said more to his wife than to Hart.

Olivia began to choke on her sip of wine. Poor thing—Sarah hated when she swallowed and it went down the wrong way.

'Do you ride, Miss Forrester?' Hart raised his brows, looking somewhat angelic.

She had last night. *Twice.*

'I do.'

'Do you enjoy it?'

'Very much so.'

Hart's lips twitched. 'I couldn't agree with you more. There is nothing quite like a good ride to get one's heart racing. Do you prefer to gallop or canter when you ride?'

They had agreed last night that it would be the last time they would be together. She should not flirt with him, but it was impossible not to. 'I find I prefer neither exclusively. If one only gallops or canters, the ride can be rather singular in its en-joyment.'

'I agree. One never wants to be singular in one's enjoyment.'

Her insides were tingling and it was getting warm. He was such a rogue.

Olivia turned to her. 'I had no idea you enjoyed the countryside. Since you've come from Washington, I assumed being accustomed to town life you would have preferred that.'

'Oh, I do enjoy town as well, but I do miss the countryside.'

'The countryside does have its appeal,' Winterbourne said, nodding sagely. 'One cannot swim in town.'

'True,' Olivia replied. 'And there is nothing as stimulating as a refreshing swim in the country.'

While it didn't seem unusual for Sarah to have learned to swim, it did surprise her that a woman of Olivia's station would have learned.

'My only objection to going out to the country-side is that it is such a bother,' Sarah said, recall-ing her endless ride to visit Katrina at Lyonsdale's grand ancestral home. 'The carriage rides can take so long.'

'They're not that bothersome,' Olivia and the Duke said in unison and then both looked away.

This gave Hart an ideal opportunity to eye Sarah through his dark lashes. It wasn't a horribly overt look, but in the depths of those blue eyes she knew he was also having a difficult time not thinking about last night.

'Well, we've intruded on your conversation long enough,' he said, tossing that lock of hair out of his eyes in a rather exaggerated gesture. 'Thank you for settling the wager for us, Your Grace.'

'Yes, Hartwick is right. Miss Forrester, it has been a pleasure.' Winterbourne gave her a polite dip of his head. 'Olivia.'

Her friend smiled at him and watched her husband cross the room once more. 'Men are such strange creatures.'

Sarah couldn't agree more. Was Hart trying to get her all flustered? She shouldn't be thinking about last night. Not here. Not now.

It was almost time to begin the evening's entertainments and Sarah's mother and the Dowager Duchess joined them by the door.

Her mother eyed her with concern. 'You look flushed.'

Oh, lud! She should just avoid Hart completely from now on. 'It's warm in here. That's all.'

'You haven't been yourself all day. I hope you have not caught something.'

Something. Someone. It was semantics at this point.

'I told you. It's warm in here.'

'Perhaps you should get some air on the terrace,' the Dowager suggested.

'I'll go with you,' her mother offered, taking a step forward.

'Let her be,' the Dowager countered. 'We will keep a seat for you with us in the back row so no one notices when you return, my dear.'

'You're only suggesting we sit back there because you're planning on falling asleep during this performance and you don't want anyone to see,' her mother said through a smile.

'That's true, but we don't have to let the entire room know that. Do go on, Miss Forrester. Enjoy the quiet while you can.'

Sarah could feel the heat radiating off her skin. If she walked past Hart now, she was sure everyone would know what had happened between them last night. She would escape to the terrace from the ballroom. Excusing herself, she made her way out of the drawing room just as an announcement was made for everyone to move to the music room.

The ballroom was located in the next room, so she didn't have to walk through crowds of people to get inside. The room was vacant and her faint footsteps were the only thing to break the silence—that was until the sound of heavy footsteps behind her made her turn around. With the bluish light from the full moon streaming in through the windows and doors, she spotted Lord Blackwood walking slowly towards her.

'Miss Forrester, I had no idea you favoured empty ballrooms, as well. If I'd known you were here, I would have ventured into this room sooner,' he said, giving her a polite smile.

'I just walked in, but I'm sure you're aware of that.'

She hadn't seen him since she arrived and had been grateful for his absence. She knew Hart had gone to see him after finding out that he'd approached her in the park. Whatever Hart had said to him that day had prompted Blackwood to reveal the truth that had devastated him. She was not feeling very cordial at the moment.

'You have found me out,' Lord Blackwood said,

adjusting his cuff. 'I admit I followed you in here. What a lovely sight you are, much better than any of the others in attendance this evening.'

His constant comments about her appearance were becoming irksome. 'I am not one to fall for false flattery, my lord. And you should know better than to place yourself with a lady when no one else is about.'

A sly smile lifted the corners of his mouth. 'I do adore your forthright nature. I think I would enjoy taming that spirit of yours.'

'With one breath you say you adore it and the next you say you want to tame it. What makes you believe I want to change?' she replied, lifting her chin.

He took a predatory step closer and Sarah held her ground, refusing to show that she found him intimidating. A cold sweat travelled along her body.

'I assure you,' he drawled, 'one can find pleasure in pain.'

He was talking nonsense and she resented the small smile that curved his lips when she felt her brows wrinkle at his comment. His tall stature blocked her view and made her feel as if the walls were closing in on them. She was foolish to have entered this ballroom alone when it was empty. It was all her fault that someone could come in at any minute and assume the worst.

'Excuse me, my lord, but I should return to my parents and the evening's entertainments.' She went to walk past him and he grabbed her arm.

'I can provide you with entertainment here. There is no need to return just yet.'

She looked down to where his fingers were pressing into her arm. 'Please remove your hand.'

'You're a rather tempting woman. Has anyone told you that before?'

She narrowed her eyes. 'I will ask you again to remove your hand.'

He took another step closer and she could feel his hot breath on her cheek. His other hand firmly cupped the back of her neck and he forcefully smashed his lips into hers. There was nowhere to go with his substantial size in front of her bearing down. She remembered something Alexander had taught her years ago and she lifted her knee and slammed it into his groin.

His fingers released their grip as he doubled over. 'You bitch!' he ground out.

'If stopping you from kissing me makes me so, then I suppose I am. Think about that the next time you try to lay a hand on me.' With trembling hands, she rushed to the door.

She was a few feet out of the room when Hart flung open the terrace door, charged across the ballroom and tackled the unsuspecting man to the ground. With Hart's first blow to the jaw, the right side of Blackwood's face slammed into the parquet floor.

'I told you to stay away from her,' he ground out, landing a second punch.

Blackwood seemed to come to his senses before Hart threw the third punch. He tried to push Hart off, but he was straddling the man's knees. He tried to hit Hart's face, but Hart blocked him and threw another punch. Hart pounded into him several more times, each time successfully blocking the man's counterpunches, until he grabbed Blackwood by the throat with both hands and squeezed with all his might.

Blackwood's eyes were bulging and he worked furiously to break Hart's grip. His mouth was open in a silent scream or an unsuccessful gasp for air. Hart could kill him right now. All he had to do was keep squeezing and the man would be dead. It was what he had wanted since he was a boy. One more minute and it would be over.

'A man's worth is measured by what he has made of himself—what he stands for—how he decides to conduct his own life.'

It was Sarah's voice he heard in his head. Could he kill someone, no matter how repulsive they were? Is that the kind of man she thought he was?

He released his grip and stood, kicking Blackwood's legs aside.

'I am better than this. I am better than you.' The words came out clipped with clear distinction, assuring Blackwood heard them over his wheezing and gasping for breath.

'For the last time, I want you to stay away from Miss Forrester.' He clenched his hands at his side to restrain himself from choking the man again.

Slowly Blackwood staggered to his feet, wiping the trail of blood from his split lip. There was fire in his bloodshot eyes—fire and venom. 'What you want doesn't matter to me. It never has.'

They had lived apart for years. Why was this man still obsessed with destroying him? Suddenly it came to him.

'But that's not true, is it? What I want matters so much that you've tried to destroy anything I hold dear. That is your weakness,' he spat out. 'I am proof of your weakness. Yesterday I wondered why you never cast my mother out the way other members of the *ton* have done when faced with a similar situation. I couldn't understand why you didn't send her to the continent to deliver me and arrange to have another family take me in and raise me as their own. Devonshire did that to Georgiana. Why didn't you do the same?'

Hart raised his chin. 'Now I know. You're ashamed of my existence because it reminds you that my mother refused to push your indiscretions aside and did not crumble into a ball when you rejected her. Some man took a liking to her. And he took what was yours and you don't know who he is. If you banished her, you knew word would eventually get out and everyone would know. Your pride could not endure the humiliation. And it is humiliating to know you were a cuckold. Isn't it?'

Blackwood was breathing heavily like a dragon about to shoot flames. Hart wasn't afraid. He knew how to destroy him now.

'But worst of all, you know the man who had your wife could be anyone. You know that someone here knows your secret and it is killing you that they are laughing at you behind your back.'

'Do not assume to know me.'

'But I do. I lived with you. I watched you. I know what you have done to try to destroy me in order to feel better about yourself. Stay out of my life. Do not attempt to approach Miss Forrester or her family or anyone else in my circle. If you do, I will shout about my parentage from the rooftops of London. It matters not to me. My reputation is not pristine and I would welcome the public separation from you. I would rather be known as a bastard than as your son.'

They stared at one another, their chests rising and falling with angry breaths.

'I am done with you,' Blackwood finally said.

'It's about time! Perhaps I'll sell off your family estates or carelessly lose them in card games when you're gone. You thought to hurt me with all you have done. The pain you have caused me has made me stronger and now I can do much worse.'

Blackwood lunged at him as two footmen entered the ballroom and pulled them apart.

'My lords, please.'

Blackwood tugged his arm free of the footman holding him and glared at Hart before storming off towards the French doors that led to the garden and the mews beyond. It was just as well he left that way. His bloodied presence at the Everills' musicale would have been the talk of the *ton* for weeks.

Checking his appearance in a nearby gilded mirror, Hart tossed that lock of hair out of his eyes. It was surprising he couldn't see any blood on his clothes. The fact that he was in his customary all-black attire probably helped.

He needed brandy and it didn't take much persuasion to have one of the footmen fetch it for him. It wasn't the finest he had ever tasted. Heaven knows it wasn't from the year of the comet, but it would do.

The strains of a violin drifting down the hall told him how to find the music room. It was brightly lit with numerous candelabras on gilded stands and an enormous crystal chandelier above. Apparently Lady Everill was proud of this room and wanted to make certain everyone could see all the details, from its cream-coloured walls with gilded trim to the ornate gilded plaster images of various musical instruments in each of the four corners of the ceiling.

From the doorway, he scanned the room, searching for a vacant seat. Julian's grandmother was seated in the last row immediately to his left and had just removed her reticule from the chair next to her. He leaned down close to her ear. 'Is that seat taken, Your Grace?'

She looked up at him. 'No, my boy,' she replied before covering her mouth with a yawn. 'But here, let me sit at the end of the row.' She moved, allowing him to take the seat she had vacated.

As they settled into their chairs, he noticed Lady Everill sitting directly in front of him. He leaned over to the Dowager. 'What is her ladyship doing all the way back here?' he whispered.

'She never stops talking,' she whispered back, 'and Mr Ebsworth refuses to sing here if she sits in the front. Poor Mrs Forrester, I assume she wishes she were deaf in her right ear about now. I don't believe Lady Everill has stopped talking to her since they sat down.'

To Lady Everill's left sat Mrs Forrester with her brown hair done up fashionably with emerald-studded combs. He restrained himself from looking for Sarah. The Dowager was too observant. She would notice.

'I see you brought your own way of enduring this evening's performance,' the Dowager whispered, gesturing to his glass of brandy and interrupting his thoughts about Sarah lying under him by the fire.

When he held his glass out to her, she patted her blue silk reticule that rested on her lap. 'Oh, I came prepared. I have a flask of gin with me. I find it goes surprisingly well with most punches served.'

He started to chuckle, but managed to turn it into a cough.

The Dowager let out a delicate yawn while covering her lips. 'Dear boy, I am much too delicate to snore, however, if I do so, please give me a nudge.'

He nodded with a smile and took a sip of brandy. Sitting back in his chair, he swirled the warm liquid fire with his tongue and looked over to his left.

And almost spat his brandy on Sarah.

Inches away from him, she was staring at him as if she couldn't believe how long it was taking him to realise he was sitting next to her. He looked back at the Dowager who was sitting upright with her eyes closed. Could one really fall asleep sitting up?

Sarah leaned over, the faint smell of lilacs drifted on the air. It reminded him of the way her room smelled when he first walked into it a few nights ago. He never realised how much he liked the smell.

'She does that a lot,' Sarah whispered. 'It's why we are sitting back here.'

'I wouldn't be surprised if she is indeed awake and straining to hear what we are saying to one another at the moment.'

Sarah leaned past him and eyed the Dowager. 'No. I truly believe she is asleep. Do you really think she is sly enough to even out her breathing to support such a hoax?'

It was true. The woman's breathing was rhythmic, but he still wasn't convinced. He leaned closer to Sarah, pressing the side of his leg against her thigh. The heat from their bodies spread to his groin. Damn, it was impossible to be near her now without touching her. He needed to stop thinking about how incredible she looked lying naked on her rug or how it felt when he was inside her. He needed a distraction. Thankfully he had his brandy. Except the drink made him recall why he needed it and Sarah's encounter with his father.

He placed his lips near her ear. 'How are you faring after your encounter in the ballroom?'

Her shoulders stiffened. 'How do you know...?'

'I was out on the terrace and witnessed you bring him to his knees. Remind me not to anger you in the future.'

'You were out on the terrace?'

'I was. I hadn't realised it was you with him until you kneed him and stormed out.'

She leaned past him and eyed the sleeping Dowager before pursing her lips together in a thin line. 'He deserved that.'

'He did. I can assure you he will not be approaching you again.'

'Yes, I believe he understood my warning.'

He combed the lock of hair away from his eyes with his fingers. 'No, I spoke with him.'

Her eyes widened. 'What did you say?'

'I made certain he is aware, should he approach you again, that I will tell the world about my parentage. He is ashamed of my mother's affair. His pride is too great and could not withstand the derision were the world to know. Do not worry, he will never harm you.' He caressed the hand that was hanging down between their chairs and hooked his little finger around hers, confident that with the wall behind them no one would see.

She leaned her head towards his and kept her voice to a faint whisper. 'When you left last night we agreed that was the last time you and I would give in to this attraction between us, yet tonight you decided it was appropriate to flirt shamelessly with me in front of our friends. You need to stop doing that.'

He wasn't about to point out that she currently had her finger wrapped around his during a very public musicale. It was a pleasurable, affection-ate gesture and he didn't want it to end. And no one could see them. Perhaps it was the danger of getting caught with their secret that made flirt-ing and touching her in public all the more entic-ing. 'Do I need to remind you that you did indeed flirt back?'

'You shouldn't have approached me when I'm with my friend for the sole purpose of flirting.'

'Perhaps I wished to remind you of last night.'

'There is no need to remind me. It is seared into my brain.'

He really did adore the way she spoke her mind. If he wasn't careful, it would be his downfall. 'I shall be reliving last night when I close my eyes for the final time.'

She squeezed his finger hard. 'Stop flirting with me.'

'Why? No one can hear. And you have to admit it is much more entertaining than this musicale.'

She pursed her lips together to try to hold back a smile.

'Very well,' he said begrudgingly, knowing she was right. 'It's probably wise for us to grow accustomed to conversing in front of others the way we did before. I vow to behave myself from now on.'

She eyed him as if she wasn't certain he could comply. He would prove to her that he could. There had been times he had resisted his passionate urges with other women. This should be no different. He had no desire to get married, to fall in love with someone and become dependent on them for his happiness. In addition, Sarah had stated quite plainly last night she had no wish to marry him and he knew she always spoke her mind. An affair with the unmarried daughter of the American Minister was out of the question. This needed to end now.

But as they sat there listening to Mr Ebsworth sing, their fingers were still locked in the only embrace they could manage.

There was a break in the programme while the musicians changed their sheet music and Mr Ebsworth approached the side of the pianoforte. The murmur of voices around them was at a low hum, yet they were content to sit silently beside one another. He was afraid if he opened his mouth, Sarah would accuse him of flirting with her—which, at the moment, he most likely would.

The voice of Lady Everill rose above the others. 'They did not take this long to remove a link from the bracelet. I do not know what is taking them so long to fix the clasp on it.'

He froze.

'But why would you have a link removed?' Sarah's mother asked.

'The bracelet was too large for me. One would think it was made for a man's wrist. And the image was not to my liking.'

Both he and Sarah stared at one another before jumping to their feet. Hurrying with careful movements to get around the Dowager, they headed for the door. Once in the hallway, Sarah grabbed him by the arm and pulled him to the deep, narrow alcove behind the staircase. Their bodies were practically touching in the small shadowed area.

'Did you hear—'

'I need to do this first.'

She never got to finish her question because he crushed his lips to hers in a kiss. He really needed to stop being so impulsive. There must have been orange in the Everills' punch because he could taste it faintly on her tongue as they deepened the kiss. He needed more and slid his hand up her side to cup her breast and give it a gentle squeeze.

She pushed lightly against his chest. 'You said you would behave.'

'I'm trying.'

'Try harder. You're making it impossible to act with propriety.'

The distinct sound of footsteps approaching was like a bucket of cold water on the passion simmering between them. He spun her around in his arms, shielding her with his body.

She spun them back and tried to peek out from their hiding spot.

Before she had the chance, he spun her back quickly and pushed her up against the wall so she could no longer move. Whoever it was kept walking, but their presence was enough to bring both of them to their senses. He had a diamond to find, and they had finally located another clue to help them do it.

'You heard Lady—'

'There's another link,' she whispered back, grabbing his hand. 'That's the clue we've been missing. Once we find it, it won't be long before one of us has the diamond.' Her body was practically vibrating with excitement.

He wondered yet again why she needed it. It was just as well he didn't know. He couldn't risk being swayed by her reason—he would be torn between his own need to honour his debt and his desire to give this glorious woman everything she wanted. She was open and forthright, and if he asked, he suspected she would tell him the truth. He could already feel doubt begin to creep into his heart, along with confusion and indecision. He ruthlessly put a stop to it. He was one step closer to settling his debt with Prinny and now, more than ever, he needed to prove his worth to the man. Now, when his own sense of who he was had been thrown into question by Blackwood's revelations. If, as Sarah said, he would be judged on his actions, then he needed to know he had honour, that he was a man who paid his debts. The diamond was his.

He combed the lock of hair out of his eyes. 'The link must be here. We are in the house and Lady and Lord Everill are occupied entertaining their guests. It's the ideal time to search for it. I'll get it and we can look at it together.'

'Why should you be the one to go and find the link?'

'Because I am adept at finding my way around a woman's bedchamber in the dark.'

She pursed her lips together in a thin line. 'I have had experience in that, too, you know.'

'Well, I know where women hide their jewels.'

'I *am* a woman,' she replied with clenched fists. 'I—'

She covered his mouth with her hand. 'You need to stop talking.'

His tongue travelled across her palm and she shook it out.

'Sarah, your absence will be noted. You must return to the music room. *I* will go. I will meet you back there once I find the link. We can study it together and as per our wager, the first one to find the diamond will win both keys.'

She let out a sigh and massaged her forehead as if it were giving her pain. 'Very well, you go. But I need your word you will return with it, that we will examine it together.'

He took her delicate hand and placed it over his heart. 'On my honour. You have my word. I will not run off without giving you a fair chance to study it. Now, hurry back to the music room before the Dowager thinks I am tupping you behind a curtain somewhere in this house.'

'Why would you believe she would think you and I were doing that?'

He arched his brow. 'You have met the woman, have you not?'

She nodded thoughtfully. 'Oh, you're probably right.'

Chapter Fifteen

Sarah couldn't stop tapping her foot and it had nothing to do with the song Mr Ebsworth was singing. What was taking Hart so long? She had been in this house before. She had been in Lady Everill's room. She knew where the woman kept her jewels. He should have retrieved the link by now. Could he have run off without showing it to her as they agreed? No, he wouldn't do that, would he? Unless his reason for searching for the diamond was something even more compelling than her own, something that would make him break his promise. If she had been the one to find the final clue, she would have kept the terms of their wager… Wouldn't she?

For the fifth time she casually glanced over her shoulder to look for him. This time he finally was standing in the doorway.

And he wasn't alone.

Even though the woman's face was turned away from her as she whispered in Hart's ear, Sarah knew it was Lady Helmford—the same Lady Helmford who lived a few doors away from here—and the same Lady Helmford that Hart had been visiting the night they met on the rooftop after Sarah had searched this very building for the bracelet.

Bile rose in her throat at the thought of him with that woman. She tried not to picture them together. But now that she knew the intimate details of some of the things he enjoyed doing, it was hard to push aside the image of him between the woman's thighs. She was well aware of his notorious reputation. Their interrupted encounter under the stairs had left them both frustrated. She'd felt his hard length against her hip when she had been in his arms. Had he found his release with the Countess?

Just as she was about to turn around and pretend to concentrate on the music, Lady Helmford whispered something else to Hart and he gave her a devilish grin and shook his head, that lock of hair falling over his eye. She had probably asked him if he'd had enough of her. Her glance dropped to the sleeping Dowager. She also knew what kind of a man Hart was. The woman was right. He probably *had* taken a woman behind a pair of curtains in this house—except it wasn't Sarah!

He had been gone much too long. Now she knew why and she wanted to cry.

She jerked her head towards the front of the room and pretended to concentrate on Mr Ebsworth's voice.

Men are clods.

Men are scoundrels.

Men can't keep their trousers buttoned!

Those weren't the words he was singing. But those were the words she sang to herself in her head.

When Hart finally got around to sitting down next to her, he had the nerve to smile as if nothing was amiss. If only he knew how close he was from having her elbow shoved in his gut.

'I've got it,' he whispered in her ear before flashing her that charming smile of his and tossing that ridiculous lock of hair out of his eyes. 'Why are you looking at me like that?'

'Like what?'

He narrowed those piercing blue eyes and studied her through his thick black lashes. 'Like how you are looking at me right now. Is anything troubling you?'

'No.' She brushed the wrinkles out of her skirt and raised both brows in an attempt to soften her expression. He didn't need to know she had been contemplating ways of tripping him and Lady Helmford. If she did it to both of them on the same night, would it appear suspicious?

He went to hook his little finger around hers, but she moved her hand.

'You're certain nothing is amiss?'

'I am fine.'

Which should have told him she wasn't, if he truly cared and knew her well enough. If he knew her well enough, he would know what was wrong. She wouldn't have to explain it!

She crossed her arms. 'Why were you gone so long?'

'It is much easier to manoeuvre your way through a house when all the occupants are either asleep or out. It takes skill and time to do it when servants and guests are walking about.'

She glanced back at Lady Helmford, who gave her a friendly smile from where she continued to stand by the doorway.

Sarah turned back around. 'Where is it?'

'It's in my waistcoat pocket. Would you like to fetch it out for me?' he asked with a wicked glint in his eyes.

She chose to ignore his question. 'Are you certain it is still there? Perhaps it fell out? Or someone took it?'

His dark brows wrinkled. 'No...it is exactly where I placed it.' He glanced over at the sleeping Dowager and past Sarah to the five vacant seats next to her. 'I can show it to you now.'

From out of the corner of her eye she saw Lady Helmford make her way to her seat that was a few rows in front of them. When the lady sat down, Sarah turned her palm over in her lap. She watched Hart reach inside his waistcoat and drop a small gold square into the pale pink silk covering her hand. They both leaned down as she turned it over, exposing the painting on porcelain of a tombstone with the initials J.H. and a woman weeping beside it. Before she was even able to process the mourning image, he leaned over to her ear.

'It's in the churchyard of St James's Church.'

She glared at him. If she could shoot fire from her eyes, she would have incinerated him. 'You looked at this already. That is unfair,' she shot back.

'No, I didn't. It just came to me. My mind analyses things quickly.'

And hers did not? What kind of an insult was that?

'Don't look at me like that,' he said, curling her fingers into her palm to cover the link. 'It is logical that the clue leads there. The first led to St James's Park. The second, the belfry of St James's Church. It is logical that the tombstone will be found in the churchyard of that church.'

It made complete sense. She tightened her grip around the link, the edges of the gold digging into her palm. If the diamond was in the graveyard, he had won the wager. 'What if it isn't?'

'If you can think of another place to look, go ahead.'

His reasoning was sound. She would probably have guessed the same given the chance to study it. That insufferable man! He had looked at the link while he retrieved it. She just knew it. That would have given him plenty of time to formulate the whereabouts of the gravestone before sitting down next to her. He might have even been thinking it through when he was tupping Lady Helmford.

'You studied this already and stole the advantage,' she said, fighting to keep her voice at a whisper. But could she honestly say that she would not have given in to the temptation to look at the link had she been the one to retrieve it? Her parents' happiness meant everything to her...but so did her honour and keeping her word. She huffed in frustration. How had this situation become so tangled?

'On my honour, I did not. I recognised the shape, saw the Greek key border and put it in my pocket. I could have kept my suspicion to myself and gone to find the diamond on my own.' His brows drew together in anger.

'Why didn't you?'

'I am asking myself that very question right now.'

'You already looked at it because you want to boast about finding the diamond first.'

'You don't really believe that I would do that to you, do you?'

'I have no reason not to believe it.'

His head jerked back as if she struck him. 'Sarah.'

'Do not "Sarah" me. There is no guarantee your guess is correct. Until we are certain, you are not getting my key.'

His mouth thinned, appearing as if he was holding himself back from speaking.

Eventually he rubbed his hand across his lips. 'Very well, meet me at the entrance of the church-yard at three o'clock. Most people will be abed by then and the streets should be quiet. You will see that I am right and the diamond is there.' His voice was low and clipped.

'I will be there.'

'I will count on it. And, Sarah…bring your key.'

She lifted her right foot, but he stood abruptly and walked out of the music room before she had the chance to step on his shiny black shoe.

The full moon shone bright on Jermyn Street as Sarah stood against the brick wall of the church-yard with her hat pulled down low, waiting for Hart. She had been lucky so far. The street had remained deserted. He had said to meet at three. It was ten minutes past. The thought that he could have be detained by Lady Helmford made her clench her fists.

Looking to her left and then right, she finally saw him strolling along the pavement as if he had not a care in the world, swinging his gold-tipped walking stick. Even though he was some distance away, she recognised his gait.

When he reached her side, he tipped his hat in greeting. 'Good evening, old boy. Fancy meeting you here.'

She narrowed her eyes in response to his sarcasm. 'You're late.'

'I needed to change my attire.'

'I changed and yet I still managed to arrive on time.'

Hart arched his brow and leaned closer. 'Is there something in particular you wish to say to me?'

She wanted to ask him if he had been with Lady Helmford, but he was not her husband—or her fiancé. He wasn't even courting her. They had both agreed any physical relationship they had couldn't continue past last night. She conveniently ignored the kiss they had shared at the musicale.

'Unlike you, I do not have the luxury of returning home whenever I wish,' she bit out. 'The later it gets, the greater my chances of being seen by one of the servants in my home when I return.'

He tipped his hat to her again in a cool manner. 'My apologies. Do you have your key?'

She curled her fingers around the warm metal

in her pocket, praying she would not have to hand
it over to him, and nodded.

His eyes narrowed on her. 'Sarah, why do you
want this diamond so badly?'

She looked away. 'The reason I want it has no
bearing on anything. You and I both want it. We
cannot both have it and it cannot be split, so the
reason why doesn't matter.' She finally looked
him in the eye. 'Unless you have changed your
mind about wanting to find it.'

'You will give me no explanation?'

He had cheated her out of finding it and was
probably coming from Lady Helmford's bed. He
didn't deserve to hear the truth. She shook her
head.

His annoyance at her reply was evident in his
expression. 'I still want the diamond.'

It had become fairly easy to read him when she
looked in his eyes, but right now there was a look
she couldn't decipher.

'I have a proposition for you,' he said.

'Go on.'

'I'm of the firm belief that the diamond is hidden away in there, but I have not found it yet. I am
willing to give you a chance to search the graveyard as well to find it. This way we are on equal

ground and no one can be accused of unfair play. Whoever finds it first, wins our wager.'

He was giving her this chance. She would be a fool not to take it. 'Very well, I accept your proposition.' She held out her hand and he shook it, as one would a business partner.

'Shall we proceed?' he asked, gesturing to the stone steps leading up to the churchyard that was high above Jermyn Street.

With a quick nod, she marched past him. Her focus needed to be on the diamond and her family. The thought of digging into someone's grave was making her ill and she wasn't completely certain she could do it. What if the diamond was amongst the bones of some poor, dead soul? Would their ghost return to haunt her? With her hand firmly on her stomach to hold in the contents, she took to the stairs.

Chapter Sixteen

The sight of Sarah stomping up the steps in front of him, knowing she was wearing those trews and boots under that black cape, should have been enticing. It wasn't. She was angry with him. It was plain to see. Well, he wasn't at all pleased with her either.

How dare she assume he had lied to her about studying the image on the link before he showed it to her! And yet, through his anger, guilt churned in his gut that he had glanced at the image before putting it in his pocket. But he had only done so to make certain he was removing a link that was once part of the bracelet.

He had the type of memory that could capture an image once he saw it and retain the details of that image for days afterwards. It was one of the reasons he was so good at cards. He simply would remember all the cards that had already been played.

It was possible that some part of his brain had been trying to figure out where the gravestone was when he was on his way back to the music room. He hadn't intentionally done it.

When he'd spied Theodosia in the hall, she had proved an excellent diversion to keep his mind off the knowledge that he and Sarah would soon be at odds once again. Theodosia had a wicked sense of humour and they had chatted amicably before returning to the music room. She had enquired about seeing him again, since she had not heard from him since he left her room that night in the rain. He had politely declined, saying he was considering a period of abstinence for a while. Theodosia had smiled warmly, wished him well and said she hoped he had better luck at it than she had.

When he walked back into the room, he'd been looking forward to being close to Sarah again, but something had changed. She'd been distant and very suspicious. She'd even had the nerve to accuse him of cheating on their wager. It was an insult to his honour that did not sit well with him—for many reasons. Not least of which that he *had* glanced at the image on the link.

As he reached the top of the stairs, he found her waiting for him in the shadows, looking out over the rows of graves nestled under the trees. The backs of the arched tombstones were visible in the bright moonlight.

He sucked in a breath of the cool night air as his heart started pounding. It was the thrill of the chase. All his life he had proved his worth by winning—and winning came naturally to him.

Looking at Sarah, he tried to hold back his smile. 'We are in search of someone with the initials J.H., if you agree that is how the clue should be interpreted?'

She reached into her pocket and stared down at the link in her hand. 'It appears to be the logical assumption.'

'How shall we divide the stones up? I'll leave it to you.' He should have been the one to decide since it had been his idea to look here. But if he allowed her to select which rows they each checked, she could not accuse him of scouting out the graveyard beforehand already knowing where the tombstone was.

She looked pale, or maybe it was just the light

of the moon. She swallowed and shifted in her stance. 'I'll take the back six rows and you take the front six. That divides it up evenly.'

With a nod, he sauntered to the first grave. *Well, Lady Mary Marow, you are not the one I need. Or you, John Seaton. Or you, Arabella Seaton.* He was moving down the first row at a rapid clip.

This would be over in minutes. In minutes, one of them would find the diamond and the other would give up their key. Why on earth could she need it? Her family appeared to have a comfortable amount of wealth. Why did she seem so determined to get her hands on it, as if finding this diamond was the most important thing to her?

He slowed his pace.

Across the rows, she trudged along from stone to stone. There was no energy to her movements—no excitement in her demeanour. Something was wrong. This wasn't the Sarah he knew. The Sarah he knew thrived on trying to best him.

He pictured what she would look like when he told her he had found the diamond. He felt his stomach turn. He needed this diamond to settle his debt to Prinny. But what would it cost him?

She glanced behind her and they stared at each other across the silent graveyard.

This was it between them. He felt it in his bones and she knew it, as well. What they had shared together, whatever it was, was dying a quick death. After the diamond was found, he would have no reason to seek her out. There were no more chances of them running into each other over the clues that needed to be uncovered. There would be no secret conversations about who had an idea of where the diamond might be hidden. She would go back to being someone he very rarely saw at his friend's house or across a ballroom.

She had already told him she would not marry him. He couldn't go on having sex with her without eventually wanting to spill his seed inside her. It was Sarah. It would be inevitable.

This was it.

When she turned back to continue her progress, he broke out into a cold sweat.

Aside from a few close friends, the people in his life who had come to matter to him had always been taken away. Always. He'd be a fool to believe anything different.

Hart never thought much about divine providence. But now he closed his eyes and took an uneven breath. He would leave it to fate. If he was meant to find the diamond first and hurt Sarah in the process, he would. It was as simple as that.

But when he tried to walk on, his feet felt as if they were rooted to the ground like a mighty oak. She was already on the second row of tombstones. Apparently she had no reservations about finding the diamond before he did. Taking another breath, he walked to the next grave.

The loud curse left his lips before he could stop it. Her head snapped up and she ran towards him.

J.H.

It wasn't a name. The image on the link from the bracelet was an exact replica of the stone. There was no second guessing between the graves of people who shared the initials J.H. This was it. His walking stick fell from his hand. He dropped to his knee on the damp grass and traced the letters with his finger as if he couldn't trust his own eyes.

Sarah reached his side. Her hand flew to her mouth as she let out a gasp. She hadn't run far to reach him, but you would never know that by the way she was breathing. Falling to her knees next to him, she stared at the gravestone and her hand started to tremble.

This was precisely what he hadn't wanted to see. Her reaction was painful to watch. She was clearly upset and he was the one who had done that to her.

'Sarah—'

'You won.' She swallowed hard. 'You found it.'

'It's possible the diamond isn't here.'

She finally looked him in the eye. 'It's here.'

He pulled out his knife from his boot and she scrambled to her feet. 'What are you going to do with that?'

What did she think he intended to do? Stab her for her key? 'I'm going to dig for the diamond.'

'Now?' Her eyes went wide.

'We are alone. It's late. I would think you would agree this is the ideal time to dig for it.'

She rubbed her forehead. 'You have no qualms about defiling someone's grave?'

'Defiling someone's grave? How far down do you think I'll have to dig?'

She visibly shuttered. 'I can't watch.' She spun on her heels and began to walk away, rubbing her arms.

'Don't go far. I will need that key of yours.'

He began to scrape away at the grass closest to the stone. Soon he was digging into soft, damp dirt thanks to the rain earlier that day. About six inches down, a scrap of dirty oilcloth caught the tip of his knife. Slowly he pushed the dirt away with the side of his blade and dug around what appeared to be something wrapped in brown oilcloth about the size of his cupped hands. He lifted it out of the ground and looked over at Sarah's back.

'I have it.'

She peered around her shoulder as if in pain. When she looked down at the package, she let out a breath and walked to his side. He filled in the small hole and wiped the blade of his knife on the inside of his coat.

'We can take this back to my set at Albany and open it there. It is only around on Piccadilly and I'm certain since you are in men's attire there will be no trouble escorting you inside. I fear if we stay here for too long someone will spot us.'

She shook her head. 'That will take too long and I have to get back home.' She glanced around. 'We need to do it now.'

A part of him, a very small part, hoped he wasn't holding the diamond. There was a chance this was just another clue to its whereabouts. He continued to tell himself that as he sat back on his heels and placed the package on his lap—and as he cut the cord that held the package closed.

But when he unwrapped the oilcloth and looked

down at the square mahogany box, he knew he was holding the Sancy in his hand.

She looked around once more and knelt near him with plenty of space between them. Earlier in the night they could barely keep from touching one another. Now an ocean might as well have separated them.

'You found it.'

Her admission should have pleased him. He had won their wager. Under normal circumstances he took great satisfaction in winning—but not tonight. There were two small keyholes on opposite ends of the lid. That would explain the need for the two keys. He took his key out of his waistcoat pocket and unlocked one of the sides.

This was it. This was what he had wanted. And yet he felt his life would never be the same after he opened this box.

He held his hand out for her key and she placed it in his palm without one word of protest. Her key was a perfect match for the other lock.

Only the box wouldn't open. Dammit, what had he missed? He tried turning the right lock and then the left, but the lid wouldn't move. He tried turning the left side first and that did not work either. Was there some other clue they were missing?

'Try turning both keys at the same time.'

She held the box steady for him as he took her suggestion. The click from both chambers brought a smile to his face. 'How did you know to do that?'

'I took a guess,' she said with a shrug.

Well, that was a damn good guess. He lifted the lid and there, nestled in white silk, was the Sancy. It was a multifaceted, shield-shaped stone whose colour, in the moonlight, was difficult to determine. But he knew from Prinny's description that it was a pale yellow. Lifting the heavy stone from its nest, he placed it in Sarah's palm.

She looked down at it with pain in her eyes. In less than a minute, she handed it back to him and stood. 'Congratulations, my lord. You've won.'

My lord? Was this how it was going to be between them? Hadn't their time together meant anything to her?

'What will you do with it?' Her voice was but a whisper.

'I have a debt to settle. The Sancy was the payment.' He should be feeling satisfied, but looking at the sadness she was attempting to hide from him was painful. 'Sarah, what would you have done with the stone if you had won it?'

She shook her head. 'It doesn't really matter, does it? You have won.'

'Sarah, we need to talk.'

'I need to leave. The hour is getting late and soon the sun will be up. I must return home before anyone sees me.'

She was doing the honourable thing. She wasn't trying to cajole him or beg him to give her the stone. There were no tears. She was honouring the terms of their wager. Sarah Forrester was an admirable woman. He put the diamond back in the box and locked it up. 'I will walk you,' he said, standing.

She met his gaze directly with eyes the colour of his favourite 1811 cognac. He would miss those eyes.

She shook her head. 'No, it wouldn't be wise for you to accompany me.'

'It's not wise for you to be walking around Mayfair at night…even if you are dressed like a man.'

'It never bothered you before.'

But it did now—deeply.

He knew that once she turned around he would lose her. And he realised he would never be quite the same when he watched Sarah Forrester turn and walk away.

Chapter Seventeen

Sarah hurried past the gentlemen's clubs on St James's, across Piccadilly and up Berkeley Street on her way home. Unshed tears rimmed her eyes, making it difficult to see, and a deep sense of despair hung over her. She continued to ask herself what else she could have done to get the diamond. In her heart she knew there wasn't anything. Hart had given her that extra chance to find it. She knew how competitive he was, so the gesture surprised her. But he had won it fairly. What kind of person would she be if she somehow went back on their agreement and tried to steal the diamond from him?

Now she had nothing to exchange for the letter.

As she walked along the gate surrounding Berkeley Square, a tear slid down her cheek. She brushed it away quickly, afraid that once one tear fell, thousands more would follow. It was understandable to be this upset over the loss of the diamond. She would be forced to face her parents in the morning and tell them everything. And yet there seemed to be something else lying heavily on her heart.

She ran through her garden and, instead of entering her home through her father's study as she had the other two nights she had been disguised as a man, she climbed her trellis, needing the comfort of her room as quickly as possible. Except when she climbed over her petite iron rail and stepped into her bedchamber, her eyes immediately went to the red-and-gold rug by the hearth and she broke into silent sobs. Clasping both hands over her mouth, she sank to the floor. She had lost everything...the diamond...her chance at protecting her family...and the man she loved.

She knew it now. She loved him. But her pride was too great. She would never beg Hart to carry on with what they had shared that night in her room. He was a man who did what he wanted when he wanted. After witnessing him with Lady Helmford, it was obvious the man wanted more than Sarah. And he was an English lord, so they were destined to live an ocean apart.

She was a fool for allowing herself to fall for him even just a little bit. He filled her heart when she was with him and knowing she didn't have any place inside his was crushing. After throwing aside her hat, she lowered her head to her knees. Their time together was over and she was going to have to find a way to accept that.

But thoughts of him and the idea of telling her parents about Alexander kept her up most of the night in tears.

The next morning, walking downstairs, she was almost tripping over her own two feet from exhaustion. The scents of warm bread, chocolate and coffee were getting stronger as she passed Bayles on the way to the dining room. When she realised what was in his hand, she stopped suddenly and turned around.

'Have some letters arrived?' she asked needlessly, staring at the small stack.

'Yes, miss, I was just about to bring them in.'

She stuck her hand out. 'I'll do it.'

Bayles looked between her and the stack in his hands. After all this time, their very English butler still didn't know what to make of her forthright manner and unconventional way of doing things.

'They are just letters. I assure you my parents will not mind if I am the one to deliver them.'

'I have not had the opportunity to sort them by recipient.'

She waved her hand casually. 'I don't mind doing that.'

Reluctantly, he placed them in her palm, and she waited for him to disappear down the hall before she thumbed through them. Her stomach dropped.

There, in the pile, was a small letter addressed to her father by the almost-rudimentary hand that she recognised. Slipping it into her pocket, she stole away to the drawing room.

The letter was brief, instructing her father to place the diamond in a box under the bench in the pavilion in St James's Square in three days. Once he had the diamond, the letter implicating her brother would be left in the box the next day. She had run out of time.

'There you are,' her mother said, entering the bright yellow room as Sarah quickly slipped the note back into her pocket. 'I was on my way to see what was keeping you. You're as pale as a ghost. What has happened?'

Sarah pasted on a smile and shook her head. 'Nothing. I did not sleep well.'

Her mother took her hand. Concern was etched on her face. 'Come with me to the dining room. A nice cup of chocolate might be just the thing to help. And I have received good news. Your father has just informed me that Captain Van Syke will be in London this week. He is a rather dashing young man and very kind. Do you remember him from the summer ball President and Mrs Monroe held before we left for London?'

'Are you going to tell me you will be inviting him to dinner?'

Glancing at her from the corner of her eye, her mother smiled. 'It would only be the gracious thing to do since he is so far from home.'

'Mother—'

'Is it so terrible that I want you to find a nice husband?'

It wasn't. Sarah knew her mother was throwing men her way because she loved her and wanted her to be happy. Unfortunately, she didn't think she would ever be happy with any man aside from Hartwick.

Her mother was a good, caring person and didn't deserve to have her wounds of grief re-opened. There had to be something Sarah could do. There had to be one last thing she could try before she had to tell her parents about Alexander. It was time to meet this danger head on. It was time to do whatever it took to prevent them from learning about her brother's treasonous act.

Hart yawned loudly as he was escorted down the hallowed halls of Carlton House on his way to see Prinny. He had gotten no sleep last night—not one wink. Part of him wondered if sleep would come once the diamond was in Prinny's possession.

He was shown into the dining room that was adjacent to the conservatory that overlooked St James's Park, an interesting location since the first clue in discovering the whereabouts of the diamond had been found there. His friend sat at the head of the table, resplendent in his fine attire for the day, digging into a pie of some sort with abandon.

Prinny gestured with his fork to the chair to his right. 'Ah, won't you join me, my boy?'

Hart dropped down and leaned his head back to rest on the top of the red velvet chair.

'You look as if you haven't slept all night. Whoever she was, I hope she was worth it.'

The statement made Hart's chest hurt and he

rubbed it as if somehow that would help. Various bottles were in front of him in crystal decanters. Even if he were to drink the lot, it wouldn't ease the pain of losing Sarah.

'Take whatever you wish,' Prinny continued, as an empty crystal glass was placed down by Hart from one of the liveried servants.

He just moved it to the side. Prinny took note and stopped eating to eye him suspiciously.

'I am beginning to believe this is not a social call.'

Hart shook his head, not having the energy to answer.

Prinny sucked some morsel of food from his teeth and watched him. Waving his meaty hand, he dismissed every servant from the room and lowered his fork. 'You have it.' It was a statement, not a question.

Hart rubbed the package containing the Sancy that was wrapped in white silk and was in the pocket of his long black coat. He needed to turn it over to settle his debt and prove to Prinny he could find it. That was why he had spent all this time searching for it. That was why he should be thrilled he had found it.

'I do.' It came out morose, although Prinny didn't seem to notice.

A broad smile pushed up Prinny's full cheeks and he reached for a glass of champagne. 'Capital! I knew you could do it!' He leaned on the table towards Hart and lowered his voice to a conspiratorial whisper. 'Tell me where it was hidden.'

Hart rubbed his eyes as if it would erase the pain he had seen in Sarah's face when she realised she had lost the diamond—pain he was responsible for. 'A graveyard.'

'How marvellously sinister! Well done. Well done!' He downed the entire glass of champagne and smacked his lips. 'Well, let's see it.'

'What do you plan to do with it?'

'I intend to hold on to it until I need funds. Then perhaps I will sell it. Discreetly, of course. Maybe I'll ask you to facilitate a sale for me some day.'

Hart hesitated slightly before placing it on the table. Prinny tore into the silk like a child receiving their favourite treat after being deprived of it for months. He held the substantial stone up to the light. The pale yellow diamond sparkled in the sunlight streaming through the windows from the gardens.

'Stunning,' Prinny said, letting out a breath.

It was and handing it over should have been a wonderful feeling, but Hart just felt sick.

'Well done,' Prinny said again. 'I knew you would find it.'

'How? How did you know I would find it? Why did you single me out to do this?'

'It's that brain of yours. You are smart and cunning. I had no doubt trusting you with finding this diamond would get me what I wanted. Going after what you want and getting it is in your blood. It is who you are.'

Hart fell back, stared up at the ceiling and scoffed. 'If only that were true.'

Prinny studied him while he poured himself more champagne. 'You don't believe you were born for the kind of work you do? Winter has remarked he can count on you to provide sound intelligence to keep me safe and he relies on your uncanny ability to analyse clues. You've done very well for yourself with those horses of yours. It's inside you.' He poked him in the arm. 'In your blood.' He sat back and turned his attention again to the diamond.

It was the second time he had referred to Hart's blood. 'What do you know of my blood?' he replied offhandedly. He was tired…tired from lack of sleep, tired from wondering if he should have given the diamond to Sarah and tired from not knowing who he really was.

Prinny froze momentarily and then waved his hand casually, not looking Hart in the eye.

Hart sat up and leaned over the table between them. 'What do you know?'

Prinny lowered the diamond to the piece of white silk on the table and picked up his fork, still not looking at him. Hart would be damned if he didn't get answers. He grabbed Prinny's hand before the man started to attack his pie again.

'What. Do. You. Know. About. My. Blood?'

'I have no notion what you are talking about.'

He purposely caught Prinny's eye. 'I think you do. I've risked my life getting information to keep you safe. I found that damn diamond for you! You know something about my past. About my blood.' He saw it. He saw the guilt in Prinny's eyes. 'You know who my father is.'

The colour drained from the Prince Regent's face and the fork he was holding clattered to the table. He picked up his glass, but the champagne sloshed around so much he put it back down.

Hart tightened his grip. 'Tell me what you know.'

'Blackwood is your father. Why would you think differently?'

'Because I know the truth and so do you.'

Prinny jerked his wrist out of Hart's grip and stood up. Walking over to the windows overlooking his garden and St James's Park beyond, he rubbed his sweaty brow. Hart stood but didn't move from his place at the table. Although he wanted answers, he wasn't certain he was prepared to deal with the truth. And he had no doubt that Prinny knew the truth.

'Come here, boy. I will not be discussing any of this from across a room.'

Hart grabbed the bottle of champagne, took a long swig and crossed the room with it. He placed it on the base of the life-size marble statue of a barely clothed woman tucked into the nook beside the window and combed the lock out of his eye.

Prinny stared out the window. 'How did you find out?'

'Blackwood told me.'

That caught Prinny's attention and he turned to Hart. 'That's surprising. He told you this recently?'

'He did. Although he doesn't seem to know who the man is who took his wife. But I think you do.

You and my mother were intimate friends. I came here with her as a child. I think she told you and you didn't have the decency to tell me any of this.' His voice was harsh and he was trying to remain calm as he fisted his hands at his sides.

'Perhaps we should sit down.'

'No.' He stepped in front of Prinny, preventing him from walking away. 'You will tell me now. I don't need to sit.'

'Maybe I do.'

'You will not move from this spot until you tell me.'

'No one speaks to me that way, *boy*. I do what I want, when I want. I am your regent!'

'Is that all you want to be to me? Fine! I thought we were friends. But I see I was mistaken.' He spun around and stormed towards to the door, needing to get far away from this man and that diamond that had cost him so much.

'Do not turn your back on me!'

'You never had issue with it before,' he bit out as he continued walking. 'You never requested I treat you as if I'm just one of your subjects.'

'Because you're not.'

'No. You have shown me today that is all I am.' He took two more steps and then he stopped. His breathing was heavy as he looked back at Prinny, who had not moved from his spot. He marched back to him. Every muscle in his body was strung tight as they stared at one another. Then he saw it in his eyes. 'Tell me it is not so.'

Prinny did not move.

'Tell me!'

'It only happened once.'

It was taking every bit of restraint he had not to plant his fist in Prinny's face. 'Once was enough, it seems.'

'Your parents were at a house party I was attending out in Sussex. Blackwood had been found in a rather compromising position with one of the maids. Your mother was mortified. She had always been a dear friend. I found her in the dovecote that afternoon and tried to console her.'

'By getting between her thighs? You thought that would help? How could you seduce her when she needed a friend?'

Prinny raised his hands in a placating gesture. 'It wasn't like that. It just happened. Surely you of all people could understand that?'

'The hell I can! I can keep my damn trousers buttoned. I'm not going around London preying upon unsuspecting women. I've taken necessary precautions to prevent any woman I've ever been with from conceiving a bastard. Don't think to compare me to you! Or are you going to try to convince me my mother was some whore who begged you for it?'

Prinny leaned over him as if he would strike him with his hand. 'You watch your mouth. Your mother was a fine woman. A fine woman. I'll not have you disparage her.'

'So it was you. You saw an opportunity in her distress and you took it!'

'Don't paint me as the villain in this. Things happen. It wasn't anyone's fault. It just happened.'

'You mean *I* just happened. *Me.* You took my mother up against a wall in some dovecote in Sussex and *I* happened.' His anger was like fire burning through his body. It was taking all his self-control not to smash his fist into Prinny.

'If you want me to say I regret what happened that day between your mother and me, I won't. I don't regret it. And I have never regretted for one moment that you are my son.'

Just hearing the man call him his son made him want to vomit. 'And you never thought to tell me this.'

'Blackwood claimed you as his son. How could

I tell you otherwise? I swore to your mother I would never tell anyone.'

'I'm not just anyone!'

'No. No, you are not,' he said softly.

'Who knows about this?'

'They are dead now.'

'Who knows?' he demanded.

'Your mother, of course, and your grandmother. It is why she would bring you to visit me as a child after your mother passed. I have always treated you kindly. I have always treated you like a son. Which is more than you can say for Blackwood.'

All the implications of this revelation were assaulting him at once. Each time he had provided Winter with information that kept Prinny safe, he was actually protecting his own father. And he had known Princess Charlotte. Although she wasn't around court very much, they had been introduced and had spoken on a few occasions. He had attended her funeral and mourned her death along with the rest of the country. She had been his sister!

Bloody hell! That meant that King George was his grandfather! He pushed his palm into his forehead to prevent his brains from shooting out.

Prinny stood less than a foot away, silently watching him.

'I will never forgive you for this,' he said on a strangled breath.

'For being your father?'

'For keeping this from me for all these years.'

This time when he stormed towards the door, he didn't look back.

A short while later he found himself wandering aimlessly along Piccadilly and wondering why his life had been turned on its head. He felt completely betrayed.

No longer would he help Winter protect the royal house. He was finished and he would let his friend know his decision tonight. Prinny was his father. And he wasn't feeling the least bit charitable towards the man at the moment. He wasn't certain he ever would.

He had royal blood in him. He had aunts and uncles he was barely acquainted with. None of them would ever know he was a member of their family.

He was deeply and profoundly alone.

In the past when he was at his lowest, he would turn to Julian. Julian had always grounded him in some way. But lately his friend's calm, level-headed presence hadn't been what he needed. In all likelihood, today wouldn't be any different.

He wanted Sarah. He wanted to tell her everything. And knew her reaction to the news that he had royal blood would be entertaining, if nothing else.

But he couldn't tell her. He couldn't go to her. And he needed to stop thinking about her. Things were over between them. She didn't want him. She didn't want to marry him and had made it clear that after losing the diamond to him, she wanted nothing more to do with him.

He had to get away—far away from London. He considered going to Paris, but that only made him think of Sarah and the Sancy. And the fact she probably hated him for getting the diamond.

Florence. He would go to Florence where he didn't speak a word of Italian, but certainly he could hire an interpreter. It would be warmer and sunnier from what he heard. Italy it would be.

But before he left, he would get his things in order and visit Julian one last time.

Chapter Eighteen

Three days later

'She isn't even a year old,' Julian said with a quizzical brow, eyeing Hart as they stood outside his home on Grosvenor Square.

Hart combed the lock of hair away from his eyes with his gloved hand. 'I'm aware of that.'

'She doesn't even know how to walk yet.'

'Your point?'

Julian cleared his throat and rubbed his lips. 'Have you thought this through? Thoroughly thought this through?'

'Just take it.'

'It's too much.'

'I want her to have it.'

'She can't accept it.'

'I insist.'

The front door to Julian's enormous house

opened and Katrina hurried down the steps, adjusting her wrap. 'I thought that was you, Hartwick.'

'Hart has brought a present for Augusta.'

'That is very kind of you,' she said, looking down at his hands. Confusion crossed her brow. 'What is it?'

Julian gestured towards the impressive, four-year-old colt in the street with its fine black coat shining in the sun.

Katrina barely glanced at it before she was looking at Hart again. 'It's lovely.' She could have at least paid *some* attention to it.

'He should be,' Julian replied. 'This is the thoroughbred Hart bought at Tattersall's recently.'

Her eyes widened and she looked back at the horse. 'But didn't you pay...?'

'Entirely too much,' Hart said, fiddling with the reins in his hand.

'Hart is leaving for Italy and, since he will not be here for Augusta's baptism, he is giving her this horse as a gift. I told him she cannot accept it.'

'You're leaving?' Her voice went up an octave. 'When?'

'Kat, did you hear what I said? He is giving Augusta a thoroughbred racehorse that cost a small fortune.'

'Yes, yes, I heard you,' she said over her shoulder while facing Hart.

Something was wrong. Hart had never seen her behave like this.

'I think we should convince him it's too generous a gift to give her.'

She turned back around to Julian. 'Yes. You are right. I will talk to him. Why don't you go inside and finish working on your speech?' She shooed him with her hands. 'Go. Go. Go.'

Julian stood his ground. 'What's going on?' he asked, eyeing her suspiciously. 'Why are you trying to talk to him without me?'

'I'm not.'

He crossed his arms. 'You most certainly are.'

'It's nothing.'

'If it's nothing, then tell me.'

She bit her lip.

'Don't think to distract me, Kat. What is going on?'

Hart's stomach dropped and he broke out into a cold sweat. 'This is about Sarah, isn't it?'

'Sarah?' Julian said, looking between the two

of them. 'What about— Wait.' He turned to Hart. 'When did she become Sarah to you?'

'We can't talk about this out here.' Katrina turned back towards the house. 'I'll send a footman out to hold your horse. You're going to need it. Meet me in the Crimson Drawing Room.'

A few minutes later the three of them stood in the drawing room behind closed doors.

'I can't believe you kept this from me,' Julian muttered to his wife, pinching the bridge of his nose.

'I only took her to the Everills' house that one time so she could search for the bracelet. That was the only time I helped…aside from St James's Park. But that was during the day and Sarah wasn't dressed like a man. And then there was the time I helped her draw Lady Everill's bracelet.'

Hart was waiting for her to tell Julian about his part in this. Each time she opened her mouth, he thought she would accuse him of somehow cheating Sarah out of the diamond.

'And she left here, dressed as a man,' Julian all but shouted. 'While I sat in this very house, she left my house dressed as a man. And you allowed this?'

Katrina twisted the fabric of her skirt. 'Well,

we were discreet, weren't we? You didn't know until I told you.'

'This was my grandmother's idea, wasn't it? I'd wager she even gave Sarah the clothes.'

'Don't be ridiculous. They are the clothes Sarah had made for the Finchleys' masquerade last year. And your grandmother knows nothing of this. So I suggest you keep your voice down before she does.'

'I am aware she can be impetuous at times. But this is foolish.'

Julian's assessment of Sarah irritated Hart. He wanted to defend her in some way.

'I know that,' Katrina continued. 'I tried to stop her, but she would not hear of it. I told her I would go with her and she said this was something she had to do alone. But I am worried for her. That's why I wanted to talk with Hartwick.' She turned to him in desperation. 'You need to find her. She is going to meet the blackmailer. It's not safe for her to do it alone.'

Blackmailer? She was being blackmailed to find the diamond? Oh, God, what had he done?

'Why didn't you come to me with this?' Julian asked, taking her hand. 'Why go to him?'

'Because you are asking me questions,' she said

impatiently with her nostrils flaring. 'He is not. And he is trustworthy. He kept our secret when you and I met in Richmond before we were married. I feel guilty telling both of you, but I am afraid for her safety. She was to turn over the diamond today, but she wasn't able to get it. So she went to leave an empty box there instead.' Katrina glanced at Hart and he knew she was aware he had won the diamond. 'She plans to wait to see who goes to retrieve it. What frightens me is that she refused to tell me what she plans to do next. You know how impetuous she can be.' She bit her thumb.

Hart took a step towards her. 'What will happen when she doesn't hand over the diamond?'

Katrina's brow wrinkled. 'She didn't tell you? I assumed you knew.'

He didn't even know she was being blackmailed. Dammit! He should have pressed her to give him an answer. He could have asked her and she would have told him eventually, he knew that. He'd been selfish, so selfish, because he'd known that finding out her reason for needing it would have changed everything. His damn honour! What did that matter now? Blackmail was personal. What scandalous things had Sarah done? And now she was placing herself in danger. He could not let anything happen to her.

'Where did she go?'

'She went to St James's Square.'

He dodged around Katrina and went for the door. He'd be damned if he let Sarah face her blackmailer alone.

The birds chirping in the branches above Sarah were beginning to grate on her nerves. Couldn't the noisy flock congregate somewhere else? She had been sitting on this bench in St James's Square for what felt like hours and her gaze hadn't wavered from the pale stone pavilion to her right. The only thing in the three-sided enclosure was a stone bench that stretched from one side to the other with a box underneath. In that box she had placed her small empty box—the box she hoped would lure her blackmailer out to fetch it.

In her peripheral vision she saw a dragonfly land on the black wool covering her knee. At least it was silent, unlike those chattering birds above her. At the sound of crunching gravel on the path behind her, the little creature and the birds flew away. She tipped her head down, praying whoever it was didn't pay much attention to her as they walked by. She had never dressed in men's attire during daylight hours and was worried if anyone looked close enough it would be obvious she was a woman. No one she had passed on her way had given her a second look. Hopefully it would stay that way.

Only this person did not pass her bench. They sat down next to her. She kept her eyes on the pavilion, hiding her entire profile. It was difficult to remain calm on the outside, when your instincts were screaming at you to run.

'Cross your ankle over your knee. You'll look more like a man.'

She knew that low, deep-throated whisper without even having to look.

'Go away, Hartwick.'

'No.'

'I'm busy.'

'So am I. I'm busy making sure you look like a man. Now, adjust your legs.'

She wanted to glare at him, but refused to alter her gaze.

'Do it.'

With a crisp movement she adjusted her leg the way he directed. It felt odd and she felt completely exposed in this position. Lud, he was annoying.

'I see you're raising some kind of breeze,' he said matter-of-factly.

'What makes you think I'm up to mischief?'

'You mean to tell me you've decided you prefer trews to gowns? I commend your bold fashion choice. Let me know if it becomes fashionable.'

'Please go away.'

'I know why you're here. Facing your blackmailer alone isn't wise. I've come to offer my services should you need assistance.'

She glanced over at him in surprise before she caught herself and turned back to the pavilion. 'How did you...?'

'Katrina told me.'

She uttered a very male-sounding growl. Was there no one she could trust?

'Don't be angry with her. She is concerned for your safety. She didn't reveal it all. I still don't know what you are being threatened with.'

She wished she could see if he was lying. 'I appreciate you coming here because of her concern. But you really don't need to trouble yourself. You can go back to her house and inform her I am quite well.'

'I'm not here because of her. I'm here because of you. I knew you'd need some assistance in pretending to be a man. You forget, I've seen you in those clothes before and, darling, you need the assistance.'

She hit her crossed foot into his knee. 'I've done fine so far.'

'Have you ever gone out like this in daylight? You look too enticing in trews and you're in need of a good valet. Those clothes are in a shambles. At least you had the wherewithal to wear a long coat this time.' He plucked at her sleeve. 'Wait a moment. Is that Julian's coat?'

'Maybe.' She tugged her arm away from his, trying to focus her attention on the pavilion, but being this close to him with his familiar teasing nature was breaking her heart. She hit him again with her foot. 'Leave.'

'No. Come now, what harm is there in two chaps sitting side by side, enjoying a day in the square admiring the ladies?'

'What ladies?'

'How long have you been staring at that building?'

'Since I arrived here.'

He made a *tsk* sound. 'Look at me.'

Was he joking? She might miss the blackmailer.

He leaned closer. His warm breath fanned her ear. 'Sarah, look at me.'

She shifted her gaze, intending to do so for a second. But once she looked at him, she couldn't turn away. She had missed his expressive eyes— eyes that were now focused on the pavilion.

'If you are going to operate covertly, you can't make what you are doing obvious. It's better if the two of us sit here. It will appear as if I am looking at you, when in fact I am looking for anyone entering that building. You were being too obvious. Your blackmailer may have noticed.'

'I was being discreet.'

He rolled his eyes and continued to look past her. 'He may decide to arrive tonight,' he offered. 'It would be ideal to remove the diamond in the cover of darkness.'

'The gate to the square is locked at sunset. And I would think he would not want to risk anyone else discovering it. The instructions were to leave the diamond under the bench in the morning. I'm assuming he doesn't want to wait much past noon to retrieve it.'

They sat in silence for a bit longer. Hart stared past her and Sarah tried her hardest not to stare at him. But she couldn't help taking in how his dark brows and thick lashes sharply contrasted to his bright blue eyes. And how she knew what his smooth, firm lips felt like against her skin. And how under his clothes the contours of his bare chest did strange things to her when they were in her room by the fireside. Did he have any idea how difficult it was to sit next to him and not touch him, even in the slightest way? What had he been doing since she last saw him? Had he gone to see Lady Helmford, or had he found another lady to occupy his nights?

'He's here.'

His deep voice broke into her depressing musings and she jerked her head towards the pavilion. A thin, tall man wearing a hat and long brown coat with dull boots bent down and took out the empty box wrapped in black cloth. Sarah jumped up to follow him and Hart was immediately at her side.

'I just want to see where he goes,' she whispered. 'That is all.'

They followed his unhurried gait as he turned and walked back down the path he came from.

'What is he threatening you with? What will he do when he discovers he doesn't have the diamond?'

'There's a letter that he will make public when he realises he doesn't have the diamond. I can't let that happen.'

'Then we will find a way to stop him.'

He didn't ask her what was damaging in the letter. He simply said they would stop him. His confident manner boosted her belief that she still had a way to protect her family.

They walked a few more feet when something about the man struck a familiar cord with her. She watched him carefully. The way he swung one arm. The way his shoulders moved forward and back when he walked.

It wasn't possible!

She ran ahead, dodging around an elderly couple to reach the man, leaving Hart behind. When she was less than a foot behind him, she jerked his right shoulder back and spun him around.

Large brown eyes that resembled the pair she saw in the mirror every day grew wider as he looked back at her.

'Sarah?' Her name was barely audible over the soft sound of the birds.

How was it possible she was staring into the eyes of her brother?

'This can't be! You're dead! We received word

that you died when your ship was attacked in the harbour.'

Hart ran up to her side and looked between the two.

Alexander didn't speak, but he raised his hand as if to stop her from stepping closer to him.

'Why did you not contact us, Alex? Do you have any idea what we've been through?'

'Do you have any idea what I've been going through?'

She slapped him. Her hand stung through her glove and she reddened his cheek. The elderly couple that had been behind them hurried by.

'Why did you not tell us you were alive? Why didn't you contact us? We waited to hear word your body had washed ashore, but we never did. Now I know why.'

The brother she adored was alive. Her heart wanted to embrace him and not let him go. But her head was screaming that he had let them believe he died.

Then her eyes dropped to the box in his hands, and her gloved hand flew to her mouth as she recalled why he was in the square. 'It was you? *You* were blackmailing our father?'

She went to slap him again, but this time he grabbed her wrist and squeezed it tightly.

'And this is why I said you could never pass for a man. A man would do this.' She had completely forgotten Hart was at her side until he raised his fist and punched her brother in the gut hard enough that Alexander's body rose with the motion and he let go of her hand.

'Ruffians,' a man shouted from near the fountain. 'Off with you! Take your quarrel somewhere else!'

Alexander began to straighten up as Hart stood in front of him so they were toe to toe. 'I believe you and your sister have much to discuss. We are going to walk to my residence from here. I will walk behind you and she will guide you. Know that I have a knife in my pocket that I will use in your back with no question should you decide to deviate from my plan. Do you understand?'

In all the time she had known Hart, she had never heard him speak with such a deadly calm.

It didn't take long to get to Hart's residence and thankfully they had no problem being admitted by the porter. His set was vacant when they entered.

She assumed he had staff. Perhaps they were in another part of the building.

Under normal circumstances she would have wanted to explore the drawing room they were standing in. She had tried to picture his home many times. But this wasn't a normal circumstance.

Today she stood in Hart's drawing room, staring into her brother's eyes.

'I will leave the interrogating to you,' Hart said to Sarah before turning to her brother. 'Know that I will be across the room. Should you do anything to physically harm her, I have deadly aim with this knife.'

Alexander wiped sweat from his brow before giving a quick nod.

She watched Hart stroll to the window, picking up a book on the way. When he sat down in a wingback chair, she turned back to Alex.

'Is he your husband?'

The notion that Alex would think her husband would allow her to traipse about London dressed in men's attire to capture a blackmailer was ludicrous. The idea almost made her laugh.

'Heavens, no. Now, tell me how it is you are alive.'

He was sweating and would not look at her.

'It is over, Alex. Tell me. We thought you were on your ship in the harbour during the battle. Were you?'

'It is not as easy as that. I was on my ship. But when we got word the British Navy was heading towards Baltimore harbour, I began to panic. I wanted it over. The war. All of it. They had burned Washington. We were losing to them. I was tired of fighting. I just wanted it over. So in the middle of the night, I climbed down into the water and swam to shore. I wanted to run. I didn't think of you or our parents. I thought of me and I ran and I didn't look back. I knew Papa would never understand my desertion. He is too much a patriot. I worked my way up to New York and managed to get work on a merchant vessel that travelled back and forth between Liverpool and New York. Eventually I decided to remain in England. It was easier that way.'

'Easier for you maybe! None of this was easy for us. You could have sent word. You could have told us.'

'No, Sarah, I couldn't. I thought there would be no chance of me seeing you here. Imagine my shock when I read in the papers that our father was the newly appointed American Minster.' He licked his lips nervously. 'I started to make friends. Some of them were the wrong sort of friends. And I started to gamble.'

Sarah pushed against his chest. 'Your note said there was a letter proving you had supplied American intelligence to the British. But that was a lie, wasn't it, and now you're telling me you did all this because you have gambling debts? You blackmailed our own father over gambling debts?'

'They are rather large. I overheard two gentlemen whispering one night in a tavern. They were saying this yellow diamond from France was hidden somewhere in London and it was worth a fortune. That the key to finding it was in some English aristocrat's bracelet. I listened carefully to the details and wrote them down. Papa was the only one I knew who would be able to get to the bracelet. I couldn't do it myself. I didn't know how to find her.'

'So you thought he could steal it for you?' She pushed him harder.

'I'm not proud of what I did. I'm desperate. I thought it would be easy for him. He was always smart. He could always work out problems. Why are you here with the diamond and not him?

Why would he send you to deliver it dressed like a man?'

'Because he doesn't know, you fool. He doesn't know about the letter you sent. I saw it first and thought to save him the pain of finding out that you were a traitor. How is it I did not recognise your handwriting?'

'I wrote it with my left hand.'

'So you were smart enough to do that, but not to find the diamond on your own.' She pounded his chest with her fist, trying to hurt him as much as he hurt her. Hart charged across the room and pulled her off Alex.

'Easy, darling,' he said, stepping between them.

Alex looked down at the box. 'But don't you see? You got it. There is no harm done.'

'I didn't get it,' she said through her teeth. 'There is no diamond in that box.'

Confusion crossed Alex's brow before he opened the box and saw it was empty. Then panic set in. 'But…but…'

'Someone had reached it before I did. There is no diamond to settle your debts. Just like there is no letter proving your traitorous act, is there?'

'How large is this debt of yours?' Hart asked from beside her.

'Eleven thousand pounds.'

It was an exorbitant sum.

'I can settle it.'

She looked at Hart aghast. She could never ask that of him and furthermore she didn't want to. 'No. I won't let you help him. Not after what he did. Leave, Alex. Go back to whatever hole you crawled out of in Liverpool or wherever you live.'

'Are you going to tell them?'

She shook her head. 'I haven't decided.'

Her brother stood there staring at her for a few moments more before he nodded and trudged out of Hart's set. The sound of the door closing did nothing to move her thoughts from memories of spending time with her brother when they were young.

'What will you do now?'

It was Hart's warm voice that called her back to the present. She looked up into those blue eyes and took a steadying breath.

She took a step back, even though she didn't want to. 'I wish I could just pretend that he was still dead. I know that is a horrible thing to say, but then I wouldn't have to decide if I should tell my parents any of this. They were devastated by his death. To think he would allow them to suffer like that because he was afraid to have a conversation with my father...' She rubbed her brow and shook her head.

He stood very still, watching her, giving her the time she needed to finish thinking out loud.

'What do you think of him?' she asked.

He gave a slight shrug. 'There is no honour in what he did. However, I cannot pretend to know what battle is like. Therefore I don't feel it is right for me to judge his desertion. Fear is a strong emotion and can make a man do things he is not proud of. In any case, I find his actions to blackmail your father deplorable.' He took a step closer to her, then stopped and placed his hands behind his back.

Her blood was running cold and she rubbed her arms. 'I think they need to know. He sent the letter to my father, but I saw it first. I did all of this to save them the pain of hearing he was a traitor and removing the only thing that helped them accept his death. If they had learned his death had served no noble purpose, it would have destroyed them. I was afraid my father's heart would not be strong enough and my mother would hide herself away from the world. But he is alive. They need to know that. My father can decide what he wants to do about Alexander's debts. I'll tell them tonight.'

She picked up her hat from the chair by the door. He followed her, but kept his distance. She wanted to run into his arms and feel his strong embrace. In his arms she knew she would have found comfort from the hurt and feelings of betrayal brought on by Alexander's actions. For a few moments at least, all would have been right in the world.

But she couldn't. Hart didn't want marriage, which meant he didn't want her. And she needed to be with her family when her father's diplomatic mission here was over—and she didn't know how they would react when they found out the truth about Alex. She and Hart had no future together. If she turned to him for comfort now, his absence would only be more painful later. She needed to be strong without him.

The room she was standing in was lovely, with soft, comfortable furnishings, paintings of horses and the smell of almond oil, presumably from freshly polished tables and doors. 'I like this room,' she managed to say through a lump in her throat.

He went to take a step closer, but hesitated. Instead he just nodded. 'I like it, too.' His conscious distance between them said it all.

This was goodbye.

Placing her hand on the door handle, she prayed she would make it out of the room without breaking down in sobs.

'Sarah?'

This was probably the last time he would call her by her Christian name. His voice was low and deep, and she would remember the sound of it for as long as she lived.

She couldn't turn around. If she did, he would see the tears rimming her eyes. 'Yes?'

'Do try not to sway your hips so much when you walk. Men generally clomp about the street.'

She almost laughed, but it was hard to do that when she had to walk out on the man she loved.

Chapter Nineteen

Hart had spent the night staring up at the curtains covering his tester bed, thinking about Sarah. In a few hours he would be making the journey to the coast to board a ship bound for Italy. He thought he was trying to escape Prinny and Blackwood and the pain of not knowing who he was. However, after hours of remembering every kiss, every conversation they'd ever had, he had come to the realisation he was really leaving because of her.

Being around Sarah without being able to be with her would be too painful. He missed her already. He missed the sound of her voice. He missed the anticipation of never knowing what she would say next. He longed to hear the slight hiccup sound she made when she laughed too hard and that look that she would get in her eyes when she gave him her undivided attention. She was the only one who had ever lifted his spirits with just a smile. And he longed to be inside her—the one place he felt like he truly belonged.

Ever since he was a child, he'd known it wasn't wise to grow attached to people. The people you cared about the most would always leave you. His mother had left him when she fell from that cliff. His grandmother had left him when her heart gave out when he was ten. And he had been coming to care for Caroline, but she had left him for his father. After Caroline's death, he had sealed his heart away, refusing to get close to anyone else, except somehow Sarah had found a way through.

Needing her in his life while knowing she didn't want him was worse than any hurt Blackwood or Prinny had inflicted upon him. When her brother had asked if they were married, she'd practically laughed at the notion. He should have expected that. She had already told him she did not want to marry him.

The only thing he could do was go to Italy and attempt to forget her. He would stay as long as it took. And if he didn't return until after her father's diplomatic mission in London was over, then so be it.

But as the morning light slowly crept along his

floor and up the side of his bed to land on his bare chest, the thought of never seeing her again was leaving his heart in tatters. When Chomersley came in to notify him that he would have to rise soon if they were to have any chance of reaching the coast in time to board the ship he had booked passage on, it made him want to vomit. Hart rolled over and wondered if he could do it. Could he leave and never see her again? Could he do it without letting her know how he felt?

He was a man who did what he wanted, when he wanted. And what he wanted was Sarah and he'd be damned if he left England without letting her know that!

Throughout the short ride to her home, he sat in his well-appointed carriage, trying to find the right words to express how he felt about her. But each time he would try to explain it, words would escape him. How was he supposed to get her to understand how important she was to him, if he couldn't explain it to himself?

When his carriage rolled to a stop on the cobblestones outside the Forresters' town house, he looked up at the nondescript brick building and knew that when he re-entered his carriage his life would be changed in some dramatic fashion. He adjusted his hat, took a breath and stepped onto the pavement.

After presenting his card to her butler, he was shown into a bright yellow drawing room while the man went to enquire if she was receiving. Here in England it would be customary for her mother to join them since Sarah was an unmarried woman, but since Sarah was unpredictable, he had no idea what would happen.

He found he couldn't sit still and walked around the sunlit room, picking up odd pieces of porcelain and looking out the window. He was rubbing his lucky coin, which had been in his waistcoat pocket, when he heard her enter the room.

When he turned around, it was difficult not to smile at the sight of her wearing a yellow silk bandeau in her long, wavy hair and a demure yellow-and-pale-blue-striped dress with a white gauzy fichu tucked into the neckline of her gown. This was how she looked when she was at home and not expecting callers. He had not been able to wait for proper calling hours and now he was glad he hadn't. She looked beautiful in a freshly scrubbed sort of way and he was glad she hadn't arranged her hair to come in to see him.

Her eyes narrowed on him. 'You cut your hair.'

He didn't know how she would receive him after what they had been through together. He wasn't expecting that, though.

'I did,' he said, running his hand through his shortened locks that Chomersley had asked him a dozen times if he was sure he wanted cut.

Sarah approached him slowly, her eyes focused on his forehead. She stopped less than a foot away from him and took her hand and combed it through the short hair on the top of his head. 'Why did you cut it?'

'You told me you hated it.'

'You cut it for me?'

'You said that lock of hair that fell into my eyes was annoying.'

'I said *you* were annoying. I loved that lock of hair.'

Now she said she loved it—now, after he had cut it off just for her! Would she ever be predictable?

'It will grow back,' he said, watching her eyes following the progress of her fingers as she continued to comb them through his hair. She smelled faintly of lilacs and he took in his favourite scent.

'It feels strange when it is this short.' As if she

just realised she had been touching him, she lowered her hand suddenly.

He was sorry she had stopped. 'Strange good or strange bad?'

'Strange different.'

'Did you speak with your parents about the person you saw yesterday?'

She looked down at her blue silk slipper with tiny rosebuds as she pushed the sole of her foot against the rug. 'I did. My mother cried for hours. Most of it, I believe, in relief that Alex is still alive. My father was silent for a very long time, but exhibited no signs of cardiac distress. He intends to hire a man to find him. He says there are things he needs to speak with him about in person. I'm glad I told them. They have a right to know.' She looked back up at him. 'What are you doing here?' she asked, clasping her hands together in front of her.

'I needed to see you before I left.'

'Left? Are you heading to the country?'

He shook his head slowly. 'I'm going to Italy.'

Her forehead wrinkled and she didn't look at all happy. 'Italy? For how long?'

'For as long as it takes.'

'Takes for what?'

'To forget you. Although I believe it will be a lifetime before that happens.'

Her hand went to her stomach and she studied him. 'Why do you want to forget me?'

'Because knowing I'll be living without you in my life has left me in pieces. I want to see you every day. I want to laugh with you and see your nose wrinkle up when you taste something you find distasteful. I want to know what it's like to wake up to the sound of your voice. And see what your eyes look like when you're heavy with sleep. I want to walk with you while I hold your hand in the sunshine. And I want to shield you from the rain and kiss you again in the moonlight. I want to have that sense of anticipation I get in waiting to hear whatever unexpected thing you'll say next. And I want to hold and protect you through any hardships. I want to do all of that and it is tearing me up inside that I can't. So I need to leave and try to forget you are everything I have ever wanted.'

A tear slid down her cheek and he searched her expression for some sense of what she was feeling.

'Why can't you do those things?'

'Because you won't have me and even if you would, some day you'll leave.' He tried to swallow but it was difficult. 'Sarah, I'm just a man.

Not a very good one. But you are everything to me. I needed to say these things to you. I needed you to know what you mean to me before there is an ocean between us.'

'I think you are perfect.'

Now his eyes were watering up, which was impossible because he never cried. But there were teardrops clinging to his damn lashes. He scrubbed them away and waited.

They stared at one another, looking deeply into each other's eyes. He tried to determine what to say next, but the words would not come.

'What do you think it all means?' she asked. 'The way you feel about me?'

'It means I'm bloody miserable when I'm not with you.'

A hint of a smile played on those soft pink lips. 'I'm miserable without you, too.'

'You are?'

She nodded. 'I have been for some time now.'

He took her hand in his. 'Why didn't you tell me?'

'Because you are a man who doesn't just want to be with one woman. You're a man who doesn't want a wife.'

'That's not true. Well, it was, but it isn't true

now. I have always felt there was something missing in my life. When I'm with you, I no longer feel that way. There is no one else I have wanted since that night I saved you from dying in the rain. There hasn't been anyone since that night. And I know deep inside I never will want anyone else.'

'But what about Lady Helmford? I saw you with her at the Everills' musicale.'

'Theodosia and I are friends. She is a lovely woman. It doesn't mean I still want her. In fact, that night, I told her I was planning on a life of abstinence for a while.'

The smile on her face was reaching her eyes. 'Why?'

'Because I can't have you and you are all I want. My desires in life have changed in a profound way. I know what I will always want is a life with you. I know you want to marry an American man and I'm as British as they come.'

She swallowed hard. Her voice was breaking. 'It's important that I do not live my life an ocean away from my family. They need me and I need them.'

His eyes scanned her pained expression and his brows wrinkled. 'I would not ask you to leave your parents. I have enough funds that we could have homes on both shores. We could travel back and forth whenever you would like. You have mentioned a time or two that I might enjoy the American experience.'

Tears were in her eyes. 'You would do that for me?'

'Darling, I would do anything for you. I love you.'

Her hand flew to her mouth and there was hiccup mixed with a small sob. 'You do?'

'That's what I came here to tell you. I love you. I couldn't leave for Italy without letting you know that. But I don't know what to do. The depth of the feelings I have for you terrifies me. It terrifies me that I feel this way about you and in the end I will be all alone.'

She stepped closer to him. 'You are all I want in this world. You and your too-long hair. You never try to alter me. There is no attempt to change my impulsive behaviour. No desire to restrict my adventurous nature. It feels as if you see me for who I am and you like that person.'

'I love that person.'

'And I love you, too.'

He hadn't heard those words since he was a child and they almost brought him to his knees.

'Hart, I cannot stand here and promise you that I will not die before you. What I can promise you is that every day we spend together I will love you with every part of my being.'

Could he do it? Could he risk having his life collapse around him if something happened to her? Could he live without her, knowing her light was shining somewhere else in the world? He couldn't. It wouldn't be living.

He kissed her hand. 'Those pretty words of yours are what one says in bed, darling. I thought I would mention it, for the next time we are there.'

'But you're leaving for Italy. There won't be a next time.'

'I'm not going anywhere without you, Sarah.'

'Are you trying to ask me something?'

'I suppose I am.'

She raised her brows expectantly.

'Should I get down on my knee?'

'Do whatever feels right.'

They were the very words he had said to her as they rolled around her rug that night. He had vowed to himself he never would do this.

He got down on his knee.

And the kiss she gave him after saying yes was his favourite kiss of all.

'So now I'll be Lady Hartwick. That sounds quite lofty. It will take some getting used to. Perhaps when we are home in America, I could just be Mrs Sarah Attwood.'

'Now *that* sounds odd. Perhaps I'll let you try to persuade me.' He gave her his most charming smile. 'And since you are going to be my wife, there is something you should probably know about my surname...'

After agreeing they would be married in just two weeks' time, he left Sarah in the Yellow Drawing Room and went to her father to ask for her hand. It was a little late for the man's consent, but Hart wanted to begin that relationship with an honourable act and hopefully have a cordial relationship with his future father-in-law. He had never felt nervous conversing with another man but he did today.

During their somewhat brief conversation, in which Hart had to confirm that, yes, he did indeed want to marry the man's daughter even though he had never courted her and they had supposedly spent little time together, it was a jolt the first time Mr Forrester called him son. The word used as a term of endearment had never been uttered by anyone to Hart. His mother and grandmother had both referred to him by his Christian name. Hearing it used by Sarah's father brought a lump to his throat.

Experiencing what his life was going to be like with Sarah's mother was another unusual experience for him. One he wasn't prepared for. They had invited him to dine with them that night and she had asked Sarah to find out what his favourite foods were. Each and every one of them were on the table. The woman even found a bottle of an 1811 Croizet B. Léon cognac to serve that night. It was his favourite cognac and not easy to come by. She also hugged him. Twice.

Chapter Twenty

Three weeks later

Sarah stood next to her husband on the terrace of Lyonsdale House in her favourite blue silk gown, wearing her favourite new pale blue silk shoes with tiny keys embroidered in gold on them. The sun was shining. The clouds were drifting by in a lazy fashion. All around her was the buzzing conversations of the people she cared the most about.

She tilted her head up to the sky, soaking in the warmth of the sun. The baby in her arms snuggled deeper into her neck. Augusta really was a sweet child. And she had been so good throughout her baptismal service in St James's Church earlier in the day. She'd slept through the entire ceremony. It was a perfect day.

'When does your ship depart?' Lord Andrew

Pearce asked while taking a sip of champagne, standing to Hart's right.

'In five days,' Hart replied, glancing over at Augusta snuggled up with Sarah.

'London won't be the same without you.'

'I'm sure you will do fine without me.'

There was a look that passed between the two men and she got the sense that it was more than a casual comment made by Hart's friend.

'Look at him,' Hart said. 'The icy Winter has been melted by that little boy.'

The three of them looked to where the Duke of Winterbourne stood talking with Lyonsdale while he held his infant son against his shoulder. Sarah had spoken to the Duke a few times since her wedding breakfast. She still found him to be a man with a commanding presence, but she had to admire the way he was always immaculately turned out. He was a great friend of the Prince Regent. Hart still hadn't spoken to the Regent since he left Carlton House the day he learned he was the man's son, but he agreed that after spending four months in America he would call on him when they returned.

'Nicolas seems to enjoy his baby brother,' Sarah said to Lord Andrew, taking note of how Olivia and Winterbourne's young son was tilting his head from side to side to get his little brother to laugh.

Andrew watched his nephew and smiled like a proud uncle. 'He does. No one can get William to laugh the way Nicolas can.'

Augusta wiggled in her arms and she adjusted her hold on her goddaughter. She looked across at Katrina, who gave her an encouraging smile. Wiggly children left her out of her element and she started to rock her the way she had seen Katrina do when the baby fussed.

'What will you be doing while I'm gone?' Hart asked, tugging the soft white blanket up over Augusta's shoulder.

'I actually have plans to spend some time in the country for a while,' Lord Andrew said. 'One of Julian's estates has been having issues and, now that William has been born, I volunteered to go in his place.'

'That's very kind of you,' Sarah interjected.

Hart leaned into her shoulder. 'He's not being kind. He's running from Skeffington's widow before she catches him.'

'Hart, that's a terrible thing to say.'

Lord Andrew tried to hide his smile, but his

hazel eyes gave him away. A soft breeze blew through the terrace and lifted a few locks of his brown hair. She remembered when the wind would lift that charming lock of Hart's hair.

Lord Andrew looked down at Sarah from his impressive height. 'No. It's true. I am not proud to admit it, but it's true. That woman finds me everywhere.'

Augusta continued to squirm and Sarah shifted her a bit higher in her arms. The squirming continued until she looked up at Sarah and suddenly went very still. Oh, no. No. No. No. She knew that look. Augusta was not going to ruin her new blue satin gown. It was bad enough Katrina had ruined her favourite pink slippers with breast milk. This baby was not getting her gown.

She shoved Augusta into Hart's arms and he took her awkwardly. Had he even held a baby before? Well, now was as good a time as any to learn how.

'Why did you—' He looked down at where Augusta's small bottom was resting on his sleeve and his eyes widened in shock.

From personal experience, Sarah knew the warm wetness was spreading through his sleeve right about now.

A quizzical expression passed over Lord Andrew's face before a look of comprehension had him laughing. 'It happens to the best of us,' he said, shaking his head.

'But not to me,' Hart cried. 'Why would you do that? How did you know?'

Sarah gave an apologetic shrug. 'This is my new gown. I had it made especially for the baptism. I didn't want it ruined.'

'Well, this is my new coat. And now it's ruined.'

'Pity,' she said, 'you really do look quite dashing in that shade of blue.'

He narrowed his eyes on her.

'I am simply stating my opinion. You can go inside and borrow a shirt and coat from Lyonsdale. I do not fit into Katrina's gowns. She is taller than I am and...' She gave Hart a pointed looked at her breasts. She was not about to announce that she was more well endowed than Katrina. The last thing she wanted was Lord Andrew visually comparing their breast sizes.

The Duke's brother might not have noticed, since he had turned his head towards Winterbourne and Lyonsdale. The sudden sound of a belly laugh from baby William made it hard for Sarah to contain her own smile.

Suddenly Lord Andrew let out a loud bark of laughter.

Sarah and Hart turned to look at what he found so amusing.

Hart's eyes widened. 'Dear God, do things come out of every orifice they have?'

Sarah looked to find that Winterbourne's youngest son had spit up down the back of the Duke's expertly cut, deep brown tailcoat. Winterbourne stood frozen with his eyes scrunched closed as if he were in pain. Lord Andrew excused himself and sauntered towards his brother with a smile.

'I think we might need to borrow one of your coats, Lyonsdale,' Olivia said through the laughter she was trying to suppress from behind her hand. 'Although I fear it may not fit.'

'We'll need one, as well,' Sarah said, glancing at Olivia, who was now looking at Hart.

Katrina came running over, apologising profusely to Hart, and took Augusta inside to change her into dry clothes.

Her husband shook out his sleeve and leaned close to Sarah's ear. 'I can wait for children. I don't think there is a need to have them right away.'

She let out a relieved breath. 'We are in complete agreement.'

Their eyes met and there was a mischievous glint in his. 'I do, however, believe one needs extensive practice if one is going to get things right.'

'Without a doubt.'

'And I do need to go inside and change out of these wet clothes...'

* * * * *

*If you enjoyed this story,
you won't want to miss these other
great reads from Laurie Benson*

*AN UNSUITABLE DUCHESS
AN UNCOMMON DUKE*